ENDLESS

A STARCROSSED NOVEL

JOSEPHINE ANGELINI

SUNGRAZER
PUBLISHING
LOS ANGELES

For my faithful Starcrossed readers.
This one's for you.

CHAPTER 1

The bass pounding out of the speakers was so loud that the little hairs on Helen's forearms stood on end and pulsed in time. Helen watched them, fascinated for a moment, until she shivered suddenly from the unnerving sensation of feeling sound on her skin.

Her mind rabbited around the fact that if she were mortal, she'd be going deaf right now, and she reached for her drink to derail what she knew would be a downward spiral of thoughts that inevitably led to the conclusion that if Helen were mortal, her father would still be alive.

"Do-You-Want-Another!" Helen yelled at Hector.

He stared at her mouth, perplexed. She raised her glass and shook the half-melted cubes around to show that they were, sadly, no longer surrounded by vodka. She watched his mouth move, apparently soundlessly, as he failed to shout down the speakers. He finally gave up on verbal communication and shook his head. Helen didn't see the cocktail server anywhere.

She stood up from their VIP both and swam upstream against the current of partygoers who were trying to navigate away from the bar with hands full of sloshing drinks, and brains slippery with alcohol. Everyone in the nightclub was wasted, but that's exactly why she and Hector were there in Los Angeles on a Tuesday night at one a.m. To be just two more mammals in an undulating, anonymous herd, preferably a herd that had been so jaded by constant celebrity sightings that they looked right past any faces or bodies that were too perfect to be normal.

Helen made it to the bar by squeezing in sideways between two dude's backs, and smiled hopefully at one of the all-female bartenders wearing black halter tops that said, *Pour Girl* stenciled on the front. The bartenders were far from identical, but they seemed like sisters. Their body types and coloring varied. Skinny, curvy, short, tall, light, dark, whatever you were looking for, there was a Pour Girl representing, but even with all these differences they had one thing in common. They were scary hot. Scary because they sort of resembled vampires with their inky eyeliner and oddly sharp teeth, and hot because they oozed sex appeal with their cynical yet flirty half-smiles, cocked hips, and scantily clad bodies. One of the bartenders narrowed her eyes and tipped her chin up at Helen in invitation, but before Helen could shout her order, a man behind the bar came up to the Pour Girl and said something in her ear. The guy looked like a young, hip Santa. He was wearing a t-shirt that said, *Party God*. Helen recognized him instantly. She recognized the bartenders, too.

"Dionysus!" she shouted, pointing a finger at him. She hadn't seen him since the wedding.

The bartender-maenad gave Helen a sympathetic look.

"Sorry about your dad!," she shouted above the din, and then gestured past Helen to engage some other customer.

Helen stared at Dionysus, not sure what she wanted to say, but certain that they should speak. She felt like he owed her something. Maybe it was an apology, though she knew that wouldn't help. Maybe it was an explanation, though she already knew his reasons for doing what he had done.

Sighing, Dionysus gestured for Helen to meet him at the end of the bar. She fought against the crowd until she got to the place where the bar swung upward on hinges. Dionysus brought her behind the bar and into the liquor storage room where bar backs were shouldering bags of ice from the walk-in cooler, and changing out the lines on kegs of beers. It was quieter in there. Helen's heels sunk into the holes in the squishy, honeycomb floor mats, and she nearly tipped over as she rounded on Dionysus. By then she'd figured out what she wanted to say.

"Where's Hera?" she demanded, throwing off his attempt to steady her.

He held up his hands, backing off. "Gone. Back on Olympus."

Helen could hear that he wasn't lying. She didn't have to look at his heart to know how much he pitied her. Even while it was happening, Helen had known that he and his maenads had wanted no part in her father's death four months ago, but the Olympians were too powerful. Hera had forced them into doing it. Helen had never been able to stay angry at anyone before, but that had changed. Hating Hera was easy. In fact, hating people had become easy, period. The hard part was shutting it off before she did something irreversible. She balled up her hands and smothered the sparks shimmering just under her skin.

"If you see Hera, tell her I'm coming for her," she said, trying to move past him and leave.

"Does it matter?" he asked.

"Yes!" she shouted back.

"No, it doesn't. Your father's death was a parting shot from the Olympians. They're holed up on Olympus, and it doesn't look like they're coming back," he said.

"How do you know they're not coming back?"

Dionysus huffed with frustration, caught. "Because none of them are strong enough to defeat you, and Olympus is a damn sight better than Tartarus." He looked at her sympathetically. "Revenge isn't you, Helen. That's how *they* did things. You're different. You know I'm right."

It annoyed Helen to no end knowing that Hera had gotten away with it. But Dionysus was right. Hera didn't matter. Helen was using her as something to focus on, anything but what was really bothering her. She tried to push past Dionysus and leave the room.

"What are you doing, Helen?" Dionysus asked, sounding dismayed as he stepped in front of her, keeping her there.

"What does it look like?"

She knew what he meant. She just didn't want to get into it. More sparks. Her hands shook with the effort it took to hold them back. She shifted anxiously on the bad pairing of her shoes and the floor mats while Dionysus watched her struggle for control. In the low light he could see the electric glow under her skin. He knew what she could do with it, but he wasn't scared. Probably because he was used to being ceremoniously ripped into pieces by his maenads only to be reborn every year.

"You can't drink the pain away," he said, his intimate relationship with both partying and pain apparent in his tone.

"Isn't that the whole point of you?" Helen said. "To drink and dance until you forget about your problems?"

He smiled, shaking his head, like he was so accustomed to being misunderstood he knew better than to try to explain himself. "The question you should be asking is whether or not this is the point of *you*."

Helen opened her mouth, but realized she had no comeback. She stormed past Dionysus. He turned with her, making a frustrated sound.

"You're a leader, Helen," he said, raising his voice as she got farther away. "The small gods are waiting to see what you'll do. Stop wasting time the world doesn't have!"

Her throat tight and her fists clenched, Helen dove back into the sea of people on the other side of the bar. Threading through flailing arms and gyrating pelvises, she was quickly disoriented. Helen stopped in the middle of the room, trying to get her bearings, and deflated when she heard the sound of angry bellows over the deafening music. Even amidst the frantic dancing, the off-rhythm motions of a brawl were unmistakable.

"Dammit," she mumbled to herself.

When she got back to the VIP booth area, she saw that Hector was letting some meathead beat on him. He just stood there for a bit, taking the abuse, before he pretty much threw the drunk idiot off of him and into someone else. This only spurred the havoc on, reeling in more drunk idiots who were spoiling for a fight.

"Seriously?" Helen asked Hector as a new guy stepped up to him.

Hector shrugged, happier than Helen had seen him in a while, and pretended to throw a few jabs, all of which he pulled. Hector wasn't trying to hurt the guy, he just wanted to get him angrier before sending him into the general mayhem that Helen was sure he had created. Helen noticed the black-clad bouncers with earpieces and walkie-talkies making their way toward them.

"Time to go!" she said, grabbing Hector. She searched for a shadowy place to hide them while she portaled them away, but there were too many people around them. All the shadows were taken.

Cursing Hector while dodging flying fists, Helen dragged him toward the door. She had to influence a few hearts along the way to get him out of there, convincing the bouncers that they were innocent bystanders even though Hector was still pushing people into each other, trying to make more trouble.

"I can't take you anywhere. Why must you always start something?" she snapped when they were out the door and half a block away.

"It's too early to go home," Hector said, still amped up, grinning. He grabbed Helen's waist and pulled her against him while they walked. "Let's go to Vegas."

"Not again," she said, trying to push him away, although he had suddenly seemed to have sprouted ten hands and all of them were trying to tickle her, or lift her up, or just pester her in general. There was a gust of wind that pushed her against Hector even as she tried to veer away. The Santa Ana winds were blowing, hot and dry.

"Yes, again," Hector said as he picked her up and carried her. "Come on. It'll be fun."

"For you," Helen said.

"Vegas," he insisted, holding her tight to his chest and burying his face in her neck. He kept chanting the word until she was squirming and squealing. She finally gave in.

"Okay!" she said. She pointed to a dark doorway. "Bring me over there."

As soon as they were in shadows, Helen portaled them to Everyland first.

Hector groaned when he saw that they were in the house Helen had created for herself in her world. "Not the Vegas *here*. I always win here. There's no point."

"You need a change," Helen said, jumping out his arms. "Your shirt's ripped and I'm pretty certain that's someone else's blood," she said, pointing to a red stain on the thigh of his pants. "I could change you on the way there, but..."

"Too freaky," Hector agreed, already walking away from her toward his room while he stripped off his shirt.

He hated it when Helen changed him while going through a portal. There was no physical bathing or handling occurring, it was just a wish-like thought that was instantly granted by Helen's ability as a Worldbuilder, but the experience was alarming. Lucas had done it to Helen once and she knew how strange it felt.

"But we're not staying all night," she called out, shoving the thought of Lucas back down into whatever hole in her soul it had crawled out of.

She went into her enormous closet and looked at all the clothes hung or shelved in there. She could think herself into anything—gowns, jewels, jeans, t-shirts. She could even portal herself back in a Ferrari or a yacht if she wanted, as long as she'd seen it somewhere in the real world first. Helen had a good imagination, but that didn't mean everything she imagined would work in the physics of the real world. For instance, she could imagine a jet that looked like a teddy bear, but that didn't mean it could fly.

Technically, she didn't need a closet or garage to store anything either, because the shift could be made in transit between Everyland and Earth, but sometimes she wanted to go through the process of selection. Deciding on clothes, makeup, cars, and shoes helped keep her from dwelling on anything emotionally damaging, which was why she had created this house and its closets to begin with. Distraction.

Her glance landed on a dress she'd seen in a magazine, and had filed away in her collection a few weeks ago, but her gaze slid off the elegant garment as the exchange she'd had with Dionysus came back to her.

"You okay?" Hector asked behind her.

Helen spun around, feeling caught, like she was breaking their unspoken rule to keep it light when they went out together. She smiled at him as he approached her.

"Are you going to put that on?" she asked instead of answering, pointing at the fresh shirt he held in his hand.

He kept coming toward her, his expression neutral while he tried to read hers. "Don't," he said, taking a guess as to what she was thinking about and deciding it was Lucas.

"I won't," she replied, looking up at him.

He was practically pressing up against her and she

wondered if he would kiss her this time. She wondered if she'd let him.

Over the past four months since they'd been betrayed by the people who'd claimed to love them, Helen and Hector had nearly kissed several times. They were aways touching each other, standing too close, hands straying, but nothing definitive had happened between them yet. It was as if their body language was telling everyone else that they were a couple, but when they were alone neither of them were willing to be the first one to step over that line.

"Let's go," he said, moving back to put his shirt on.

She grabbed the dress and portaled them to Vegas with plenty of cash in their pockets.

Helen knew she was technically counterfeiting, but she'd cleared her conscience of that long ago. A few thousand dollars here and there was not about to upset the world economy, and Hector needed a physical limit to his gambling. Ones and zeros in a bank account meant nothing to him, but if he had actual cash or chips that he was playing with he'd stop when he got to the end of them.

His father had already cut him off. Left to his own devices Hector would get himself into serious trouble. He was looking for it, too. Hoping to anger the kind of the people who broke kneecaps just to give himself an excuse to get into a real fight, but Helen wasn't going to let that happen. He'd never forgive himself if he went too far and killed a mortal. It was another line neither of them was willing to cross. There weren't many of those left for them.

Normally, it cooled down considerably in the high desert at

night, but when Helen portaled she and Hector to a quiet spot just off the strip in Las Vegas, it was hot and windy. Though there was no sun in the sky the atmosphere still radiated heat like there was. In the half a block it took them to get into the casino, Helen felt sweat jump to her skin, only to be sucked away by the thirsty air. It had been dry everywhere, though. It was spring, and usually it would rain nearly every day in Massachusetts, but there had been nothing.

Going into the climate-controlled lobby of the casino was no less shocking than entering another world. They immediately sought the most action, doing a lap around the casino, past flashing lights and bleeps and bloops that seemed more geared toward children who wanted to play video games than grown-ups. Helen hated Las Vegas. It was like one, big, joyless carnival where avarice and disappointment collided, and like the gaudy wall-to-wall carpeting, it was only brightly colored to cover up the stains. At the moment, gaudy joylessness suited Helen's temperament just fine.

They roamed from one room to another, hardly noticing when the décor of the never-ending labyrinth changed minutely. She never knew what would catch Hector's fancy. Sometimes he played blackjack, sometimes roulette or poker. He didn't have a favorite.

They followed the sound of raucous cheering to a craps table. A group of men in tuxedos were clustered around one end of it, goading on the roller. Their energy was teetering between excitement and violence. That was the real reason Hector wanted to come here, Helen realized. He was still looking for a fight. He joined the action and placed a bet. Helen had no idea how craps even worked. She knew there were dice involved and that was about it.

A quick glance around told her that there were no women standing with this group of men, which was odd. For some reason Helen couldn't fathom, Vegas adhered to strictly misogynistic rules that were stuck in the Rat Pack era. High rollers always collected arm charms, but there wasn't a short skirt in sight at this table, apart from Helen's. Usually, Hector and Helen had to block any incoming suitors for each other, and by this point Helen would be busy letting all the starry-eyed females know that Hector already had a date. Given the circumstances, Helen decided it was okay for her to sit down.

"Not the gambling type?" asked a male voice.

Helen turned her head and found that one of the tuxedoed men was taking a seat beside her. His bow tie was undone, his hair was mussed, and he draped himself with inebriated ease over the chair and the edge of the table. Though he was loose-limbed after what appeared to be a long night, his gaze was clear and steady, like he'd drunk himself sober. In one hand he was shuffling a pair of coins, weaving them over and under each other in a smooth and constant motion. He wasn't the most handsome man Helen had ever seen, but he had nice hands.

"I've never seen the appeal," she said, answering his question.

"Then why are you here?"

She gestured toward Hector. "I'm his muscle."

Tux laughed and nodded, appreciating the banter. He took one of his coins, put the edge of it on the table and gave it a twirl, sending it spinning.

"It's all fixed, anyway," Helen continued, watching the coin blur into a sphere as it skimmed across the tabletop. "The house always wins."

"Eventually, yeah," Tux agreed. He pressed his hand flat over the coin, stopping it. "Heads or tails?" he asked.

"I told you. I don't gamble."

He kept his hand over the coin. Helen saw a preternatural gleam in his eyes. "This isn't gambling. It's chance."

"What's the difference?"

"The odds are evened. Fifty-fifty. We both risk an equal amount. There is no 'house' and no one is in control. Just—" He waved his free hand, as if to indicate something ineffable.

But Helen wanted an answer. "Fate?" she guessed.

He frowned. "The opposite, actually. Uncertainty."

A breath of a laugh escaped her. "What's your name?"

"Plutus."

"Interesting name." He was obviously Greek, but if he was one of the lesser gods, Helen had never heard of him.

"You're stalling. Take a guess," he coaxed.

"Why?"

His expression softened with a whimsical thought. "To see if you're lucky."

"Heads," she replied immediately, though not sure why.

Before Plutus could lift his hand and reveal the outcome, all hell broke loose over at the craps table. An influx of gamblers had joined Hector and the tuxedoed men, and for whatever reason the newcomers had been stupid or drunk enough to get into it with Hector. One of them was flying through the air toward Helen table. She jumped up before he landed and ran to intervene.

Starting a fight at a dark night club was one thing, but Vegas didn't mess around. Casinos were too well lit and there were cameras everywhere. There was no way for them to hide their abilities, and they couldn't just run or portal away to avoid getting arrested. Helen was not going to jail. It was a school night. She clamped onto Hector's forearm and dragged him out of the casino, her eyes seeking out cameras along the way.

"What is *wrong* with you?" she growled at him. A pair of security guards stepped in front of them, motioning for them to stop. "It's okay," Helen said to them, smiling brightly until confusion clouded their faces and she could push past.

"This time it wasn't my fault, I swear," Hector argued as Helen pulled him outside. "I was having a conversation with one of the servants of Tyche, and this jackass..."

"*What?*" Helen marched Hector around a corner.

"Tux guys. Servants of Tyche." He pulled back on his arm, forcing Helen to spin around and come back to him.

"Who's Tyche?" Helen asked, looking up at him. He had blood on his face. Helen kind of hoped it was his.

"Lady Luck. Goddess of Chance." Hector grinned. "If *she* were on my side I'd never lose."

Helen scoffed. "The last thing you need is to go on a winning streak and draw even more attention to yourself," she said. And, deciding the night was over, she portaled them back to the Delos brownstone in New York City.

"I've seen them before," Hector said as they started climbing the stairs from the ground floor.

"Where?" Helen asked. She certainly hadn't seen a bunch of tuxedoed servants of Tyche hanging around before that night.

"Atlantic City," Hector said, his pace slowing as he reached the top of the stairs and pass the entrance to the nap room. When Helen got alongside him, she saw why. Pallas, Hector's father, was sitting on one of the comfortable couches in the nap room, waiting for them.

"Is that where you were tonight? Atlantic City?" Pallas asked.

"What are you doing here, Dad?" Hector did not choose to join his father in the nap room, so neither did Helen. They stood in the doorway, half in and half out of Pallas' ambush.

"Don't you have classes tomorrow morning?" Pallas sounded calm, but underneath he was obviously simmering.

Hector sighed. "What is this? An intervention?"

"If it were an intervention the whole family would be here. I came to talk to you."

This confrontation had been coming for a while, and Helen was actually glad it was coming from Pallas. Of all the adults in their lives, he was the least likely to make Helen feel guilty for partying too much. And if he *did* try to wag a finger, Helen wasn't about to buy it. She'd heard stories about him in his twenties—she'd even seen him back then, looking like a suave, New York City party boy—and she knew he didn't have a leg to stand on.

"Look, I know you're upset about Andy," Pallas began. Helen cringed. Leading with Andy was a terrible idea.

The details about what had happened to Andy while she'd been doing research in the Arctic had come out in bits and pieces over the past four months. Her professor on the research boat had actually been Hera, and once Andy had been separated from Hector for a few months, Hera had fed the small spark of jealousy in Andy until she had allowed herself to be a vessel for one of the vengeful spirits that Hera had convinced to side with the Olympians.

When all was said and done, not only had Andy ghosted Hector, but she'd also turned against the Scions, and was even willing to help Hera capture and kill Helen. Hector had felt more betrayed by this than Helen had. To Hector, family was everything, and in the attempt on Helen's life Andy had attacked Ariadne. While Ariadne was still mortal, no less. Ariadne was strong enough to handle Andy a dozen times over —even before Helen had gotten Everyland back and made her immortal—but she was still Hector's little sister. Attacking his family was the worst thing anyone could do to him, regardless of what vengeful spirit was to blame.

When she snapped out of Hera's delusions, Andy had been devastated by what she'd done. Still, she couldn't deny that she had allowed herself to become a vessel for an evil spirit. She'd tried to apologize a thousand times, but Hector wouldn't hear it. He was too hurt. She hadn't trusted him, so he no longer trusted her. He'd been betrayed, just as Helen had been betrayed by Lucas.

"Upset doesn't begin to describe it, Dad," Hector said. He looked at Helen. "Can we get out of here?"

"Wait," Pallas said, grabbing Helen's arm before she could portal them away. "Kate lost him, too..."

"Oh, hell no," Helen muttered, trying to disentangle herself from his grasp. She couldn't talk about her dad.

"You think you can't screw up your life," Pallas continued, still holding her there. "That you have a solution to everything. And sure, you can party all night and make it to school the next day, and phone it in, and what it's going to do to your future? Probably nothing you can't fix with a quick trip to Everyland. But I'm not here to lecture you about how you're messing up your future. I'm here to tell you that you're messing up *right now*. You're hurting the people who love you *right now*, and that's something you can't take back no matter how powerful you are." Pallas let go of Helen's arm.

Helen felt a surge of anger. She hadn't been the one to screw up her life. That had been done for her, *to* her, just hours after he'd promised to love her forever.

The words came flying out of Helen, thoughtlessly. "Why don't you ask Lucas to give back Aileen?"

Helen's question hit Pallas like a physical thing. He froze, staring at her, unable to answer. She felt Hector put a hand on her waist.

"Let's go," he said quietly in her ear and she portaled them to Everyland.

They stood in the middle of the living room area. White furniture and walls of glass that looked out over a sparkling cityscape surrounded them. The huge room felt dark and lonely in the night.

"I'm sorry. I shouldn't have brought up your mother," Helen said.

Hector shook his head. "It's okay. And he hasn't, by the way. Asked for her back."

Helen wondered how he knew that. She supposed they all must have seen Lucas plenty of times over the past few months, though no one had spoken to her about it.

"Have you?"

"I miss her, but I don't know if it's right to bring her back." He shrugged and gestured around in a vague way. "She's been gone for twelve years. And she's in a better place."

"How do you know that?"

He looked reluctant to say it, but he finally did. "Lucas had a long talk with me, Jason, and Ari about her. He said she drank from the river of Joy. She's at peace."

Helen knew she should let this go, but she couldn't. "He talks to you?"

"He comes home every day. He has until the end of summer before he... you know."

Before he descends into Hades and never comes back, Helen finished in her mind silently. She'd never say that out loud to Hector, though. He still felt it was his fault that Lucas had traded himself for Hades in a bargain to bring Hector back from the dead. That guilt was part of the reason he was hiding here in Everyland with Helen, though she knew Lucas' vow was not Hector's fault. If anyone was to blame, outside of the Fates who had engineered the entire situation, it was Lucas. In her experience, he made a lot of choices that involved the lives and deaths of others without ever asking anyone what they wanted first.

"And you never asked to see her, or talk to her? Not even just one more time?"

"No, but not for me. For her."

She turned away from him, feeling ashamed of her own self-ishness. "I don't get that."

"I know," he said. "But you might someday."

CHAPTER 2

They slept only a few hours before Helen's alarm went off. She heard Hector protesting the obnoxious sound from his bed in the next room.

"You're a sadist!" he yelled.

Helen went to the fridge. It was stocked with some special foods and drinks that she had designed. Her versions of ambrosia. On the door was a beverage she and Hector had been drinking more and more lately—an instant cure for hangovers. She grabbed two of the glass bottles and brought them into Hector's room. He was sprawled across the bed, the sheets and covers thrown about him wildly. He took his drink and sat up.

"Why do you even *have* hangovers in Everyland?" he asked, not at all happy with the amount of sunlight streaming through his window.

"Because that's what happens when you drink a bucket of vodka." She clinked her bottle to his. "Bottom's up. You'll feel better."

"But you could just take all the alcohol out of our systems with a thought. Why make a drink to do it?"

Helen thought about that for a moment. Why did she have skyscrapers and furniture and food and clothes in Everyland? What was the point of any this stuff, or of consequences that followed certain actions if she could so easily erase those consequences? Helen couldn't articulate exactly what she felt about it, but after witnessing how the Olympians played fast and loose with mortal's lives, she'd realized that if nothing mattered, then nothing mattered. She didn't want to live in a world without consequences because she feared that if she did, over time she'd become as bored and selfish as the Olympians. Everyland was far from finished, and there were a lot of details left to be hammered out, but one of its founding principles was that it had some built-in checks and balances.

"How can you enjoy a refreshing drink if you never get thirsty? I'm just keeping it real," she replied.

He downed his hangover cure in a series of rhythmic gulps. Helen watched his throat working, amused. Everything Hector did, he did completely.

"We've got to hurry or we'll both be late," she said, standing.

"That's another thing," he said as he got out of his stadium-sized bed. Helen averted her eyes. He was only wearing a tiny pair of boxer-briefs and he was just too much beefcake to look at this early in the morning. "Can't you stop time? Not forever, but occasionally. Like, *now*, for instance."

"No!" she snapped, leaving the room.

He'd complained about this before, usually when he had to get up for an 8 a.m. class, and Helen had no interest in getting into her motives as to why she had made certain Worldbuilding choices yet again. Her trips through the Underworld had taught her how nightmarish being stuck in a moment could be. As a result, Helen had opted not to mess with time in her world. It was one of the first rules she'd laid down for Everyland, back when she'd originally created it to heal Lucas.

"Jeeze, Hector, you're already immortal," she said, muscling past yet another unbidden memory of *him*. "The last thing you need is another fifteen minutes to put on some pants."

"It's just that Everyland and Earth are so similar, sometimes I can't tell the difference between them."

Helen stood in her closet, deciding on a basic pair of jeans and a comfy t-shit. "I got it right, then," she said, smiling to herself.

When they were dressed and fed, Helen portaled Hector back to the Delos brownstone on Washington Square Park. Orion was in the kitchen, eating a bowl of cereal. He paused mid-spoonful and was about to call out to her, but Helen just waved to him with an apologetic smile and portaled away before he could actually speak to her. She didn't have the energy to get into it with him right then. Orion was like an emotional dentist and Helen had a painful cavity deep inside. He wanted to help her get it out, but she couldn't bear to open up and let him near it.

She portaled to an empty bathroom in her high school on Nantucket. It was the best place for her to magically appear out of thin air because no one ever used it. Most of the year it stank of formaldehyde due to its unfortunate proximity to the biology labs. It was the perfect place for her to portal to and from school, and she barely noticed the stench anymore.

The first bell rang just as she exited the bathroom. She didn't need to stop by her locker. She had appeared with her books and her completed homework. Not that she had much homework to do anymore. Most teachers had stopped giving seniors any real assignments, as there were only a few weeks left until graduation, and all of Helen's classmates had either been accepted into universities or had made other plans. She'd gotten into NYU, but she wasn't sure if she was going to go yet. It seemed rather pointless now.

After staring sightlessly through her first few classes while words like *climate* and *water shortage* flew over her head, Helen debated whether she should just skip the rest of the day. Her teachers had quietly agreed that none of them expected her to have perfect attendance after her father had died so tragically. She could pretty much come and go as she pleased, but where was she going to go?

The thought of having a coffee in Rome flitted across her mind. Helen was tempted, but the last time she was in Rome she couldn't get rid of this rather nice young man who had become smitten with her when she'd laughed at his joke. Helen didn't like going to public places without Hector or Orion for that reason. Wherever she went, unsuspecting mortals chatted her up and there was no way she was going to get involved with one of them, and drag them into her insane life. Also, she tried not to skip school as a rule because it made her feel too guilty. Her dad would be disappointed.

But staying at school meant that she would have to brave the cafeteria for lunch. Jason and Ariadne would be there at their usual table, and Helen's relationship with the twins had become strained over the last four months. They felt Helen should forgive Lucas. He must have had a good reason for keeping her father in Hades, they'd said. Lucas would never hurt her on purpose, they'd said. Helen should be more understanding, they'd said.

What Helen understood was that her father was dead, and Lucas could bring him back to her and to Kate, and he wouldn't—not couldn't. Wouldn't. Helen couldn't forgive that —not wouldn't. *Couldn't.* The twins just didn't get it.

Claire had stayed out of it completely, remaining uncharacteristically silent about the whole thing. Helen hardly talked to Claire anymore, but it wasn't an argument that had driven the best friends apart. It was memory. Sometimes when they were together it was so much like the old days that Helen would forget anything had changed. Then, when she remembered again, as she inevitably did, it came back a hundred times more painfully. She avoided Claire now. And not just because Claire was usually with Jason, who disapproved of just about everything Helen did nowadays, but because sometimes it hurt to even look at her.

Helen arrived at the cafeteria before she had made a conscious choice about it one way or the other, and found herself in the awkward situation of having to choose to go to Jason, Ariadne, and Claire, or cause a scene by sitting alone. Either way she was causing a scene, Helen realized, as every eye in the room flew between her and Claire while she stood there, hesitating.

It had not escaped the attention of the entire student body that after Helen's father had died, she and Lucas must have ended things in the ugliest way possible. The few times he had returned to school since then, he and Helen hadn't even looked at one another. Though he had been given special permission to end the year online, most assumed he had dropped out of school because of her.

Their catastrophic break-up was all anyone under the age of fifty on the island was talking about. The gossip bomb had gone nuclear when whispers that Helen was dating Hector had begun. Helen had no doubt who had started that rumor. Though free of her Olympian passenger, and none the wiser about it—as were all the other Nantucket hosts of the ancient Greek spirits—Gretchen was still just as spiteful as ever. She didn't need to be possessed by Hera to want to wound Helen. She came by that impulse with no supernatural influence necessary.

Helen had come to understand that some people were just jerks and there was nothing she could do about it except stop caring what everyone thought about her. In that way, Gretchen had done her a favor. Not everyone was going to like her, and that was fine. Besides, they were all graduating, and none of this high school stuff was going to matter soon anyway. Helen just wished she'd understood this in the fifth grade and not as a senior.

Claire, however, would always matter. She locked eyes with Helen from across the cafeteria, looking like she was about to cry. And when Claire cried, Helen cried. It was hardwired into both of them, purely Pavlovian, and Helen had no intention of bursting into tears in front of half the school. She went and sat next to Claire just to end the tension.

Ariadne opened her mouth to say something, but Helen cut her off. "Have you guys ever heard of Tyche before?" she asked, derailing whatever plans they had to interrogate her.

"Goddess of Chance?" Ariadne guessed, looking at Jason for confirmation.

He nodded, then asked Helen, "Why?"

"I met a few of Tyche's minions last night. What I can't figure out is what they want from me," she said.

"Who says they want anything?" Jason asked.

Helen gave him a look. "Nothing happens accidentally. Not to me. I also ran into Dionysus. He said the small gods were watching me, waiting to see what I was going to do."

"Tyche *and* Dionysus? You had a busy night," Jason commented in a snarky way.

Ariadne put a restraining hand on her twin's forearm. "The small gods are watching to see what you're going to do about what?" she asked.

"I don't know, but I'm pretty sure it's not this," Helen replied, gesturing vaguely to the high school life going on around them. "Is there a prophecy I missed? Maybe something about Tyche or the small gods?"

Helen hadn't seen Cassandra in months, either. She'd stopped coming to school, and Helen and Orion never spoke about her, though Helen knew that he spent time with her. Helen didn't even know if they were dating or not, now that Cassandra was maturing naturally due to Helen's intervention, and she didn't want to know.

Jason, Claire, and Ariadne shook their heads in response and then lapsed into silence while they finished their lunches. For the remainder of the meal Helen felt Claire shooting her nervous glances and saw Ariadne curtailing several attempts Jason made to speak. It was the most awkward meal they'd ever shared, and when the bell rang Helen couldn't stand up to part ways with them fast enough. She heard Claire start to say her name as she walked away, but she had gotten far enough that she could pretend like she hadn't.

She went to her next class, feeling anxious and frustrated. Helen had been hoping more than she cared to admit that they'd have an answer for her. Even if Jason yelled at her, she'd gladly suffer one of his lectures about enabling Hector's self-destructive tendencies in exchange for knowing what all these small gods were waiting for her to do. It'd be nice to know what her purpose was. Helen was beginning to fear she didn't have one.

After school Helen went to the News Store to start her shift. She peeked through a dime-sized portal into the storage room to make sure Luis or one of the new people Kate had hired wasn't back there. When she saw that the coast was clear she widened her portal and stepped all the way through it.

Helen went out front, donning a Kate's Cakes apron in case she was needed on the bakery side of the conjoined shops. She preferred working in the bakery to the News Store nowadays. There were too many ghosts on her father's side of the store. Quick walking as she worked, Kate passed Helen and stopped short when she saw her.

"You came in," Kate said.

Helen stopped tying her apron with her arms awkwardly reaching behind her. "Yeah," she said, her eyes shifting around and then back to Kate's surprised face. "Wasn't I on the schedule?"

"You were, but I haven't seen you in days," Kate said. She

passed a used cup and saucer between her hands and turned to throw some balled-up napkins into the waste bin. "I asked Luis to come in."

Helen didn't know how to respond to that. She didn't know how to respond to most things where Kate was concerned. Kate wasn't her parent and Helen was over eighteen. Legally, she was an adult. They lived in the same house and worked at conjoined shops because Helen owned the house and the News Store now.

She had no intention of ever asking Kate to leave either place. In fact, if Kate had asked, Helen would've signed the whole thing over to her in a moment. She didn't need it. Her dad had left her a ton of money in an insanely large life insurance policy that Helen suspected Daphne had augmented. Maybe she'd use it to go to college, or invest it, or buy a giant house in the south of France. She hadn't made any decisions.

Kate and Helen were like roommates in a way, and not in another. Helen could tell that Kate felt she should try to parent her, but was at a loss as to how to go about that. The situation between them would have been strange even if Helen hadn't been an immortal goddess who had created her own world, but the fact that she *was* all of those things made long, awkward pauses in their conversations inevitable.

"Does Luis want the shift or..." Helen trailed off. "I could stay or go. You tell me what you want."

Kate shrugged helplessly. "I can't send him home now."

"Fine." Helen took off her apron.

Kate took a step closer. "Are you going to be around for dinner later?"

Helen met her gaze. Kate looked a little scared, and a lot sad.

It was just so much *work*. Every conversation. Every situation. Helen was tired, and not just because she'd gotten only three hours of sleep the night before, but because all of her relationships had turned into minefields. It was exhausting to have to dance around everyone, not knowing how to act or what to say. Before, Helen had always known who she was—even way back when she had no idea *what* she was—but not anymore. She was bone tired of it all.

They stared at each other for a little while longer. Helen finally rallied, knowing she needed to be the one to make the effort.

"I could make lasagna," Helen offered.

Kate smiled with relief. "I'd like that."

Helen went home and stood on the threshold of her empty house for longer than she needed to. It didn't smell like her dad in there anymore, even if they hadn't changed much since he'd died. She went to the kitchen and started cooking. She pulled the ingredients from Everyland to ensure that they were perfect, but she made and cooked the lasagna by hand rather than creating it with a thought. Going through the motions of stirring, draining, and layering soothed her. She'd learned how to make lasagna from scratch when she was fourteen and she'd been making it regularly ever since. The familiar scents and repetitive motions brought a little bit of herself back. She could almost pretend she still was who she'd been.

Helen put the baking dish in the oven and started cleaning. She could sense someone coming toward her house and looked up from her sink full of sudsy water. A familiar shape passed through the dim light of dusk, and Helen's breath caught with something like terror, something like excitement. Then she noticed the silver in his black hair and let the breath go. She went to the door and opened it for her surprise visitor.

"Daedelus," Helen said, opening her door wide.

He stood on her doorstep with his hands shoved into his jacket pockets, his lips pursed and his eyes guarded. Daedelus always looked like he was bracing himself for some kind of disaster. It was the thing that distinguished him the most from Lucas, apart from his age. He always looked like he was waiting for the sky to fall on him.

"May I come in?" he asked.

Helen gave him a funny look. She was already holding the door open. But Daedelus was raised differently. He had odd customs—old ones—and Helen knew that she had to formally invite him in.

"Please come in," she said and he finally stepped over the threshold.

He didn't relax, though. He stood halfway between her living room and her kitchen with his hands stuffed in his pockets. It still amazed her that this prickly, uncommunicative man was Orion's father. They couldn't be more different. Helen could hear a clock ticking somewhere in the house, maybe it was one of her dad's old watches, while she waited for Daedelus to start speaking.

"Can I get you something to..." she began when the silence proved intolerable.

"I guess I'll just get right to it. You know my son is an Earthshaker, right?" Daedelus said, plowing forward into what would usually come in the middle of a conversation, not the start of it. "And that in the House of Athens we're bound by oath to leave Earthshakers exposed at birth?"

Helen nodded. "But you didn't."

"Yes, I did," he said, looking down. "Your mom rescued Orion after I left him. I didn't—" his voice broke.

"Oh." Helen shifted from foot to foot. She had no idea what to do with that confession.

"There's a reason I abandoned him," he continued, meeting her eyes. His were so blue. Just like Lucas'.

"They're dangerous." Helen guessed. She didn't know why she was still trying to be understanding. He'd just admitted to having tried to kill someone she loved dearly, and any good feelings she might have had toward to Daedelus should have evaporated, but they didn't.

"Have you ever heard of Stoicism?" He waited for Helen to nod before continuing, though the more he talked the less she understood. "It's not just about being tough and un-emotional in difficult situations. It's an ancient Greek philosophy with its own conceptualization of the universe. The House of Athens have always been Stoics. It's our religion."

Helen was so stunned to hear Orion's tough-guy father using a multisyllabic word that she laughed and blurted out, "Nah, you? A Stoic? Who'd have guessed."

Daedelus' mouth lifted in a half smile and she saw something sparkle in him. Again, she had to adjust her understanding of him. He didn't openly laugh at jokes, but he seemed to appreciate sarcasm, like there was a wiseass buried deep down in him somewhere.

"The Stoics believe that the world will end in one of two ways. A cataclysm, or ecpyrosis. The cataclysm is a world-wide wave that is supposed to drown human civilization. It's a tsunami, started by an earthquake." He paused before continuing. "Even as a newborn Orion was such a powerful Earthshaker."

Finally seeing some threads of this conversation weaving themselves together, Helen nodded so he wouldn't have to continue. She couldn't fully hate Daedelus. He'd really believed his son would end civilization and he'd felt obligated to stop it. Helen wondered what she would do if she had been given that choice.

She could tell it still haunted Daedelus. One glance at his heart told her that choosing to leave his infant son on a mountainside had broken something in him. He'd forever be ashamed of what he had done, and on guard about what the Fates might demand he do next. Especially around his son. Maybe that's why he kept Orion at arm's length.

"Orion would never start a cataclysm. You know that, right?" Helen asked.

He nodded in an offhand way. "Orion's not why I'm here."

"Oh," Helen said, thrown.

She gave up. He was the single most cryptic person she'd ever met in her entire life. His emotions went one way and his words and facial expressions went another. He was the only person Orion couldn't understand, and Helen could finally see why. The guy was a cypher.

"Cataclysms aren't the worst that can happen. A cataclysm would just be the end of human civilization for a while until we picked ourselves back up again. It's like the wash part of the cycle—an ending that leads to a fresh beginning. Ecpyrosis isn't," he said.

"What's ecpyrosis?"

"Total destruction of the cosmos by fire," he said, pinning

Helen with a meaningful look. She froze. "Fire started by *lightning bolts*," he continued. "The Stoics believe it's supposed to be Zeus' final obligation before 'lights out' on the whole thing. The true end."

Helen suddenly remembered something Zeus had said to her before she'd banished him to Olympus. Something about how she wouldn't like the job. Daedelus stared at her pointedly with those piercing blue eyes.

"Since Zeus is really gone this time with no clause in the contract that lets him get out of jail like last time, we think you're going to be the one to do it now."

Plutus and Palamedes walked out of the big, white, brick building of the Tokyo Stock Exchange with the sounds of calamity issuing behind them.

"Bad day," Palamedes said.

Plutus nodded in reply, smiling secretly to himself.

"Did you have to devastate their entire economy?" Palamedes regarded his companion as they walked around the block to the subway station.

"I had nothing to do with it," Plutus said, flipping the gold coin he carried into the air with his thumb and catching it again with a snug slap against his palm. He kept his hand closed over it. "You know that."

Palamedes reached into his pocket and worried about the pair of dice he kept there. To this day he held the secret belief that the Greeks would have left Troy's shores after only six months if he hadn't invented them. Boredom had curtailed more than one siege, and there's not much to do on a beach in a foreign country but throw dice.

They took the subway to Haneda Airport. As the god of wealth, Plutus could have afforded a car, or a fleet of cars if he wanted to make a show of it, but he rarely traveled that way, and as such, Palamedes had grown used to public transportation. Plutus liked to be among the people as much as possible. So did Tyche, though she had been harder to find lately, even for her devoted servants.

Luck had worn thin.

They went to their gate and stood in line. Next stop, Russia. They'd devastated the European and New York economies days ago, sucking the wealth out of the world like the water had been sucked out of the air by Aeolus. Russia ran on slightly different rules than America and Europe, but they were not immune. No one was, not anymore. It used to be that entire civilizations could rise and fall in a bubble, unbeknownst to all others, but those days of the Rapa Nui and the Etruscans were long gone. The world rose and fell as one now. Push over one domino, and the rest would topple.

Palamedes gave the man at the gate his ticket and shuffled onto the plane with a resigned sigh. They always sat at the back of the plane. But Palamedes hated the back of the plane.

"People are starting to panick," Palamedes said as he stuffed himself in his too narrow seat with too little leg room and buckled his seatbelt. Honestly, how was a Greek warrior-prince turned small god supposed to fit in one of these things?

"Uh-huh." Plutus grinned as he flicked his coin in the air again and caught it before taking his seat. He always sat in the middle, even if the aisle or the window was empty. Always right down the center of the row.

Palamedes was getting annoyed with his husband. "What can you possibly be so blithe about?"

Plutus opened his hand and looked at the coin lying there. He thought about the feeling he'd had. It was a gut feeling. Something indescribable, but something that he knew guided humans and gods alike.

"She picked *heads*," Plutus replied.

"And she wasn't supposed to," Palamedes reminded him.

"Exactly," Plutus said, excited and intrigued. "This one doesn't do what she's supposed to."

"If she doesn't do what she's supposed to do, then Everyland will fall, just as Atlantis did, and she will die."

"That's correct," Plutus agreed, saddened. There were only two outcomes. Heads or tails. "But then this world will be spared again, as it was in ages past."

Palamedes harrumphed. "As if the Fates would allow that to happen twice."

Plutus nodded, his expression falling. He, more than anyone, knew the odds were against them. He looked past Palamedes and out the window wistfully as the plane took off.

"It *is* different this time," he admitted sadly.

CHAPTER 3

Helen would have laughed if she thought there was the slightest chance that Daedelus was joking, but he wasn't.

"I'm not going to burn down the universe," she said, feeling her cheeks get hot. Even the thought was ridiculous.

"Maybe not intentionally," Daedelus replied. He made a frustrated sound and ran a hand through his hair. It made him look so much like Lucas Helen couldn't stand it. She walked past him into the kitchen. "Look, you of all people should know that the Fates maneuver us into doing stuff we never thought we'd do," he continued, following her. "Pretty much my entire life is me saying *I'd never do that,* and two months—no, two days later—and I'm doing it. You can't tell me you're not the same way."

Kate walked in at the moment, looking startled. "Oh, sorry!" she said, suddenly smiling with relief at Daedelus. "For a moment—the way you two were arguing—I thought you were someone else."

Daedelus gave Helen a sympathetic look. "Yeah. Sorry about that by the way. Believe me, I know how much it sucks."

Him and Helen shared a rueful smile. After a few quick reintroductions and polite words, Kate invited Daedelus to stay for dinner, but he declined.

"I was actually hoping Helen would come with me. There's someone who wants to speak with her about—" he glanced at Kate and back at Helen, "—what we were just talking about." he added.

Helen turned to Kate apologetically, knowing this would ruin their dinner plans.

"Go," Kate said. "More lasagna for me."

Helen gave Kate and hug, promised that they'd have a real dinner together soon, and then left the house with Daedelus.

"Where to?" Helen said as they headed toward the beach.

"We have to swim there. Is that okay with you?" Daedelus asked. "I remember your mom used to hate the water."

Helen had never liked the water. Not so much now that she didn't sink like a rock, but it still wasn't her favorite. "I can portal us, you know. No swimming required."

"But you've never been there. Don't you have to know where you're going to portal there?"

Helen eyed him. The mechanics of portaling weren't common knowledge. "How do you know that?"

"Lucas."

"Okay. What's going on?" she asked, stopping at the water's edge.

"It'd be so much better to have *her* explain." Daedalus said.

"Who is *her*?"

He gestured out to the water. "Do you need me to breathe for you?" he asked, ignoring her question.

"No," Helen replied immediately. Orion had done that for her once. It required that he cover her mouth with his, very much like kissing.

"Good," Daedelus said, sounding relieved. He strode out into the water and then glanced back at her. "Are you waiting for me to hold your hand?"

"You're hilarious."

She joined him in the water and steeled herself as she went under. It may have been early spring, but the Atlantic was still freezing. She kicked out and followed Daedelus down through the deepening dark of the ocean.

Soon she couldn't see much of anything, but she noticed that her eyes adjusted just enough that she could keep Daedelus in sight if she didn't let him get more than a length in front of her. She didn't begrudge the darkness. If there was something toothy and slimy lurking out there, she didn't want to know about it.

Helen couldn't gauge how long they were swimming underwater or how far they'd gone, but she figured they had crossed the Atlantic and were now somewhere off the coast of England or Ireland. When they broke the surface, it was in a rocky cavern not dissimilar to the subterranean subway station that Ladon had inhabited in New York City when she and Lucas had been there in 1993, though there was no tile-decorated platform or trains nearby. It was rough and natural, but it still reminded her so strongly of Ladon's former cave that she was not at all surprised to see him standing at the water's edge, waiting for them to come ashore to his elegant living room sitting smack dab in the middle of a limestone cave. She was surprised, however, to see the woman standing next to him.

"Antigone?" Helen said, staggering out of the water and toward the slight, dark-haired woman. "But... you're supposed to be dead," she continued, too shocked to be tactful.

"Good to see you too," Antigone replied, smiling. She looked older. Somehow, she had managed to escape the Fates and the curse of never attaining womanhood that comes with being their vessel.

"Didn't you know? Faking your death was big in the nineties," Daedelus said, striding past Helen with a smirk as he banished the water from his clothes and hair. "All the best people were doing it."

"Who *are* you? Does Orion know what a joker you are?" Helen said, following him from the water's edge to the living room that seemed to float like a bubble of civilization in the middle of some spelunker's dream. Stalactites and stalagmites rimmed tunnels that probably led to other rooms. Crystals as large as a person grew out of the walls and glimmered in the flickering lamp light. It was beautiful. Like a dragon horde, Helen thought with a smile at Ladon's shimmering scales.

Once the shock had worn off, Helen was happy to see Antigone again and learn about how Antigone and Ladon had hidden all these years, him shielding her from the Fates so she could age naturally and they could have something of a normal life together.

Daedelus explained how Antigone had faked her death. How he and Ladon had retrieved Antigone's body from the Delos crypt and revived her. How that had freed Daedelus and

Leda from the Furies toward the House of Thebes, and how they then went on to hide dozens of other Scions from Tantalus.

They were careful when they spoke about the Delos brothers, always making sure to lay the blame on Tantalus, but Helen could tell that Castor and Pallas must have played a big part in the bloodshed, and that Antigone would rather Helen didn't tell anyone that she was still alive. Antigone hadn't decided if she wanted to rejoin the Delos family yet.

"It was war. We were all at our worst," Daedelus said when he saw Helen struggling with this information. "I know you were raised by your mortal father, and that a lot of this stuff won't make sense to you, but honor means something different to Scions. It's family first for us, House first, and Castor and Pallas are both honorable men. They did what the Head of their House told them to do."

"Honorable?" Helen remarked disbelievingly.

"The definition of right and wrong are different for us. Castor and Pallas were doing what they had been raised to believe was right. Your mother helped so many of the youngest Scions to safety, but in doing so she was betraying her House. She was doing the right thing, but in our world, that made her an Outcast," Antigone said. "It's your mother I wanted to discuss. She's the one who came up with the plan."

"What plan?" Helen asked.

"To defeat the Fates. Once and for all," Ladon said.

Months ago, Hecate had said something about Daphne being the architect of a great plan to defeat the Fates, but in the events that followed Helen had taken that to mean retrieving the Omphalos and freeing Atlas in order to defeat Zeus.

"There's no way to defeat fate forever," Helen said, shaking her head. "I mean, we managed to use Orion as a Shield and work around them, but that was just a one-time thing. A trick so we could beat the Olympians."

Ladon, Antigone, and Daedelus shared a look around her that Helen couldn't understand.

"What?" she snapped when no one was forth coming.

"We don't have much of a choice, Helen," Ladon said. "We have to figure it out."

"Why?"

Daedelus leaned forward, putting his elbows on his knees. "Remember the ecpyrosis thing we were talking about earlier?"

Helen was torn between yelling in disbelief and laughing. Destroying the entire earth with lightning bolts was unthinkable, and not just in the moral sense. She couldn't even imagine doing it physically. The earth was enormous and covered in oceans—like the one she'd just swum through. Oceans didn't burn. And where would one even *stand* in order to destroy the cosmos?

"Is this all based on something Daphne told you?" Helen asked. "My mom saved a lot of people's lives, and that does change the way I think about her, but you guys know she was probably the biggest liar I've ever met, right? I am *not* going to light the world on fire."

Antigone shook her head, like Helen wasn't understanding them. "I saw it."

"You saw wrong." She couldn't believe they were even having this conversation. Helen was insulted. After everything she'd done, everything she'd sacrificed, and they still believed that she was going to turn into some vengeful goddess who would smite the whole world. She stood up, done with this conversation.

"Helen, don't go," said a familiar voice from the darkness, just outside their bubble of light.

Lucas appeared, stepping forward from the clinging shadows that blended seamlessly with his black clothes. Helen turned and faced him, rigid with anger that she had been ambushed like this.

She looked at Daedelus. "I can't believe you'd do this," she said.

"It's not his fault," Lucas said, taking a step closer. Helen took a step away from him. He stopped trying to come any closer. "I was just supposed to listen, but we don't have time for this."

He looked pale. His eyes were wrong. Too bright. And they didn't look *at* her anymore, but through her. She wondered how long it had been for him—how many years had he been in Hades since she'd last seen him. The sight of him made a familiar ache start at the back of her throat, a clenched feeling that was like a tearless sob. It was everything she wanted to scream at him but couldn't.

"The List of the Dead is full," he continued, sounding detached. "Every single name in the world is on it."

Helen felt the cold squirm of fear in her stomach. "What does that mean?"

Antigone stood and went to her, placing her hand on Helen's arm as if to comfort her. "It means everyone is going to die in three days, Helen. Everyone."

· · ·

They had called out to her, tried to get her to stay and discuss it rationally, but Helen couldn't sit there and listen to them—listen to *Lucas*—tell her that in three days she was going to freak out and burn down the world. She'd portaled back to Nantucket.

She paced around her bedroom, not sure what to do with the nervous energy she felt. Kate had to be up at dawn to start baking and she was already fast asleep in her room. Helen laughed at herself, thinking that if she'd swum back and then walked across the island rather than portaling, she'd have had the time to think things through. It was something Claire would appreciate—the fact that everything in Helen's life was both too easy and too hard at the same time.

Helen suddenly missed Claire more than she feared the emotional upheaval of being with her. Leaving her house silently, she walked the short distance to Claire's house. She could see a light on in Claire's bedroom. She was still awake. Helen floated up to her window and tapped on the glass. Claire practically jumped out of her skin, making Helen smile. They'd done this before.

"Lennie, what the hell?" Claire put her phone down and came to the window.

"Sorry," Helen said when Claire opened her window. "Can I come in?"

Claire let her in and they stood there, looking around awkwardly at everything but each other.

"Do you want to go first, or...?" Claire asked. Helen shrugged, struggling for words.

Then Claire said, "I think you're allowed to be a mess right now." At the same time Helen said, "I've been such a jackass to you."

When they both started laughing, they knew that their friendship was going to survive this.

"Thank god that's over," Claire said, sighing heavily as she led Helen back to her bed so they could sit. "You really had me worried."

"Me too," Helen admitted. "I don't know what I'm doing, Gig."

"I don't think you're supposed to know right now."

"I'm sorry I shut you out." Tears started leaking out of Helen eyes, and she swiped at them angrily. "It's like I'm stuck. Like I'm absolutely powerless. I have no control over anything that really matters to me. I'm immortal, but I can't even save my dad? How messed up is that?"

"Totally messed up. I'd go on a rager if I were you. I'd turn a whole section of Everyland into one giant obstacle course with targets and old cars and I'd run through it with a bazooka, just blowing shit up."

Helen guffawed and sniffled at the same time. Claire handed her a tissue from the box on her bedside table.

Helen wiped her eyes. "Speaking of blowing shit up—Lucas thinks I'm going to destroy the whole world."

Claire stared at her blankly. "Back up. Start over."

Helen brought Claire up to speed, ending with a rant about how she couldn't even imagine being capable of ecpyrosis. "Just think about it in a purely functional sense," Helen said logically, "how could I make the earth catch fire, even with my lightning? It's mostly water."

Claire's eyes were wide. "Except for the fact that there's a worldwide drought going on right now?" she said. "It hasn't rained anywhere in weeks."

Helen stared at her, stupefied.

"Len, you gotta watch the news."

Claire picked up her phone and opened a browser. She showed Helen the headlines. Helen had known that it hadn't rained in a while, but this was different. The drought was already causing devastation and food insecurity across the world, and meteorologists were stumped. There weren't even clouds in the sky. Anywhere.

"That's impossible," Helen whispered. "There are always clouds over the mountains or somewhere over the ocean."

"Not anymore. It's only been a couple of days since they've put it together. Everyone just thought it was a fluke at first but now..." Claire trailed off. "What if it never rains again?"

"I won't let it happen," Helen said. "I can make it rain, you know. Zeus is the Greek god of weather and I'm a Cloud Gatherer, like him."

Claire looked at her fearfully. "Weather is a tricky thing. If you mess with it, you never know what could happen. Didn't someone say once that *a butterfly flaps its wings here and there's a typhoon in Japan* or something like that?"

"The Butterfly Effect," Helen said, nodding. "Is that a real thing?"

"I don't know. It's not like catastrophic weather disturbances were on the SAT's. How am I supposed to know any of this crap?"

"Well, help me figure it out!"

"I will!" Claire stopped to think, looking hassled. "We're

going to have to ask other people for help, you know. Other people probably related to Lucas."

"I know." Helen sighed. She felt overwhelmed. "It's like I can't get away from him."

"I'm sorry." Claire took Helen's hand. "For all of it."

Helen nodded. She knew what she had to do. She rolled her eyes in agony at the thought of having to go to Lucas' father for help. "I wish Matt were here. He'd know what book I'd need so I wouldn't have to ask Castor and Pallas."

"Yeah, but the book would probably be *at* Castor and Pallas'." Claire thought of something and looked surprised. "You know, Matt believed you were going to start the end of the world. That's why he fought you."

Helen nodded. "He said I was going to become the Tyrant and destroy everything. But that was about me having too much power and losing control over it. I don't think that's the same thing as ecpyrosis. Do you?"

"Ari might know more about it," she replied.

Helen stood. "Let's go get her."

CHAPTER 4

H elen portaled she and Claire into Ari's bedroom.
After a hurried apology for waking her and scaring her half to death, she portaled all three of them to Everyland so they could talk without bringing the whole Delos clan into it. Helen wasn't ready for that yet.

"I don't remember Matt saying anything about you *burning* down the world, specifically. Just that your powers would start coming out of you and you wouldn't be able to control them," Ariadne said after they were situated in Helen's living room in Everyland. "He said you wouldn't mean to do it, but it would still happen. He compared you to Pandora and the box put together."

"But it's not like Matt was an Oracle or anything," Claire said, playing devil's advocate.

Ariadne tilted her head in partial concession. "It was an old prophecy, and you know how vague those are. But Matt

45

believed it enough to challenge Helen, even though he hated himself for it."

He'd believed in it so much he'd died for it, Helen thought, but she didn't need to say that out loud. She stopped pacing. "I don't feel out of control," she said.

Ariadne and Claire shared a look.

"What?" Helen asked defensively.

"You haven't been yourself, Len," Claire said in her typical, bald-faced style. "You've been a little nuts lately."

"I know that!" Helen huffed back.

"Well," Claire said, gesturing with a hand. "Weather's nuts. You're nuts. You're a weather goddess. I'm just putting stuff together here."

Helen slumped down onto an edge of her huge sectional sofa. "What do I do?"

"Think damp thoughts?" Ariadne suggested.

"But not here," Claire added hastily. "Let's go back first."

Helen portaled all three of them into her bedroom on Nantucket. She went to her window and opened it. "Okay," she said, taking a deep breath and closing her eyes. "Thinking damp thoughts."

Helen imagined the soft touch of moisture on her cheek and the sound of gentle spring rains at night. She recalled the pressure of the air when it got heavy with mist and the feeling of thunder in the distance as it rolled over the ocean, like a growl building behind her sternum. And nothing happened. She tried again, this time picturing a drenching rain that splashed down cold and thick and hit the ground so hard it bounced back up and churned in a haze of white around her feet. Still, nothing happened. She could feel Ariadne and Claire growing restless as she tried and failed repeatedly to summon the rain the earth so desperately needed.

Finally, Helen opened her eyes and turned to Ariadne and Claire. "I've done it before on accident. I know I can do this on purpose," she insisted.

"Maybe it takes a couple days to warm up?" Claire guessed.

"It's the Earth, not a toaster oven," Ariadne said. She turned to Helen. "Try summoning some lighting and maybe the clouds will follow."

Helen thought about the logistics of that, and portaled the three of them to the beach where she could be relatively certain she wouldn't destroy anyone's property. She went down the beach so she wouldn't electrocute Claire and Ariadne, and then summoned lightning bolts to strike the sand. She did it multiple times, waiting a few minutes after each strike to see if the clouds would come.

"Now what?" she yelled to Claire and Ariadne. They came down the beach and joined her.

"It's not going to work," Claire said, digging around the spot where one of the lightning strikes had scorched the sand.

"Why not?" Ariadne asked.

"She's summoned lightning tons of times without summoning rain," Claire said, still digging.

"Why didn't you say that to begin with?" Helen asked.

"Just to make sure. And I wanted one of these," Claire replied, pulling what looked like a glass tree out of the sand. "Fulgurite. So beautiful."

Helen started pacing around in a circle in frustration. She went to the water's edge and tried to not scream. Every time she thought she had a handle on her life it spun out of control. She threaded her fingers through her hair and fought for calm.

"It's not your fault you can't control the rains," said a dulcet voice. "They do not answer to the mind. Only the heart."

Helen looked down at the sea foam gathering around her feet. A face appeared, became skin, and rose up from the waves. Aphrodite stood before Helen as glorious as a summer's day. She reached out to take Helen's hands in her own.

"This is not something you can decide to do," Aphrodite said, stepping out of the water. "The rain will only come when the drought ends in your heart."

Helen shook her head disbelievingly. "That can't be how it works."

"The weather is controlled by your feelings, not your mind, Helen. It was the same for Zeus. When he was angry the winds would blow whether he wanted them to or not. When he was joyful the sun would shine. You're holding on," Aphrodite said, squeezing Helen's hands. "The clouds won't let go until you do."

Claire and Ariadne came up behind Helen. "Let it go, Lennie." Claire said.

Aphrodite looked past Helen and smiled at Claire. "If only it were so easy."

Helen dropped her head, feeling like she was choking. "That's... just... *bullshit*," she growled under her breath. She looked back up at Aphrodite. "Help me. Help me get rid of this feeling. Take it away."

One of Aphrodite's shoulders went up and down helplessly. "I could take it away for a moment, but it would only come back. *You* are holding on. *You* have to let go. No one can do it for you."

"You're saying the world literally depends on me getting over my dad?"

"And Lucas. Let them both go and it will rain again."

Helen felt trapped. She could say in her head that she was letting go, but to really do it was something else entirely—something she didn't know how to do any more than she knew how to speak Mandarin. No, she decided, this was harder. At least Mandarin was something she could learn. Helen didn't even know where to start with letting go of her dad.

"How?"

Aphrodite released Helen's hands and stepped back, returning to the water's edge. As the waves lapped at her, she sank into the water.

"Forgive," she said. "Goodbye, sister."

Aphrodite turned back into sea foam and disappeared.

Claire and Ariadne were kind enough to sit patiently on the sand while Helen stomped around swearing for the next fifteen minutes.

"So all of this is on me? It's my fault people are dying!?" she shouted, kicking the sand up in gritty arcs.

"I don't think anyone blames you—" Ariadne began.

"I've tried to switch it off. I'm sick to death of feeling this way!"

"No one's asking you to—" Claire began.

"I didn't ask for any of this!" Helen raged at the ocean.

It obliged her by raging back, but that angered Helen more.

She was now aware of the fact that she was making the wind kick up and the waves get higher, and she knew that if she kept going damage would be done. She couldn't even feel her feelings without potentially destroying the world.

"I don't want this. I wish I could…" She stopped suddenly as a thought occurred to her and spun around to face Claire and Ariadne. "That's it! I'll give my powers back. I'll go to Everyland and take away my powers."

Claire jumped to her feet. "Don't!" she yelled, grabbing Helen by the arm to keep her from portaling away without listening to her first.

"What if you give your powers back and it still doesn't rain?"

Helen took a breath to argue. She *wanted* it to be the answer. It would be so easy for her to do. It wouldn't involve an epic battle and the potential loss of someone she loved. Secretly, the thought of being normal again was enticing. Like freedom.

"Sounds like something the Fates would love—you becoming truly powerless just when you needed your powers the most," Ariadne said, agreeing with Claire.

Claire nodded. "It would be *ironic*. And you know how they love that. Sorry, but you're not meant to take the easy way out, Lennie."

Helen plunked down onto the sand, exhausted now that her anger was spent. "You're right." She laughed bitterly and gestured to the frothing waves that were pounding into the sand. She took a breath and watched the waves as they seemed to breathe with her and relax. "I can't even get angry without there being consequences."

"None of us can. Say I get angry at my brother because he's

acting like a dumb frat boy on Spring Break, that has conse-quences," Ariadne said. Then she smiled at Helen wryly. "Though most people don't have to worry about making tidal waves when they want to yell at someone."

Helen searched for censure in what Ariadne was saying and found none. "About Hector," she began.

"He told us nothing was happening between you two, and that you were the only thing keeping him from doing anything permanently stupid, so we should probably all thank you," Ariadne said, cutting her off. "And it's none of our business anyway, except for one thing."

Helen raised an eyebrow, curious as to what Ariadne considered her family's business where Helen's love life was concerned.

"Hector already blames himself for what's happening to Lucas. If you and he got together he'd flat out hate himself. He'd never be the same, and I'm not sure the person he'd turn into would do the world any favors."

Helen thought about the fights Hector had been starting lately. He'd always been a brawler, but before it had always been to measure his strength and skill against another, and because he enjoyed the athleticism of a clean fight. Lately, his desire to fight had taken a darker turn. He seemed to revel in mayhem. Helen had no idea why.

Helen nodded. "He doesn't even fight anymore, not really," she commented. "But he starts fights and then stands back and watches."

Claire trailed her fingers in the sand around the base of her fulgurite sculpture. "Like Ares did on Halloween," she mumbled. She looked up at Helen and Ariadne. "You've noticed we're all replacing the Olympians, right? Lucas is Hades, you're Zeus, Hector is Ares. Orion might be replacing Aphrodite."

"Orion is definitely replacing Aphrodite. That guy is pure *fire*," Ariadne said. Helen chuckled and nodded in agreement.

"And you're becoming Apollo," Helen said to Claire, catching on.

Claire made a non-committal noise, still absentmindedly arranging the sand with her fingertips as if they couldn't stop making art. "I think I'm an aspect of Apollo. He had way too many jobs. I think Jason and I are meant to share them."

Ariadne nodded thoughtfully. "I guess I'm Athena. Or Artemis."

"Both," Helen agreed immediately. "They're kind of interchangeable, when you think about it."

The three young goddesses sat on the sand, staring at the sea, thinking about what these new responsibilities could mean. Helen already knew what hers was supposed to be. Zeus had told her she wasn't going to like the job. He was right, and she refused to do it.

"So, what do we do?" Helen asked. She was not surprised when no one answered.

Of all the markets in the world, the Moscow Exchange proved itself so used to closing, reopening, and all other forms of volatility that its collapse was met with less hysteria than in other sectors of the world. That does not mean it was met without great sadness and crippling anxiety, however.

"Don't you find this depressing?" Palamedes asked his companion.

"It's the end of the world," Plutus replied, flipping his coin over his fingers in sequence, so it flashed heads-tails-heads-tails as it seemed to walk over his knuckles before disappearing in his palm and reappearing on the other side. "It was always going to be awful."

"Then why don't we *do* something about it? You don't have to ruin them." Palamedes knew he was being ridiculous. He'd been granted immortality by Tyche thousands of years ago after he fought in the Trojan War, and he had since inured himself to the many different forms of human suffering that came and went with that ineffable thing known as luck, but this was beyond the pale for him.

Plutus stopped flipping his coin. "So they can all die rich?"

"Yes! Rich and happy and not like this," he said, gesturing to the despondent expressions of the people around them. The hotel bar they were in around the corner from the trading floor was nearly silent with the pall of worry cast over it.

"Drink your vodka," Plutus snapped.

Palamedes did not reach for his chilled glass. "I can tell it's bothering you too, you know."

Plutus sighed. "What am I supposed to do? I serve Tyche."

"And who does she serve?"

Plutus looked at his partner sharply. "Do not speak her name."

They stared at each other. In all the thousands of years they'd been married, they had never argued like this, not for days on end as they had been since New York. They'd always been in it together, and Lady Luck was not an easy goddess to serve because there were always those who suffered more. There were people who lost everything and were wrongfully hated and abused their whole lives long, and Plutus and Palamedes had overseen aspects of their never-ending streak of bad luck right up to their death beds. It was hard for both of them to watch, but before there had been hope in it.

The unluckiest people usually suffered so much because out of that suffering came some miraculous boon to all of society, whether it be an invention, a great work of art, or a change in a law or long-standing societal injustice. Sometimes, it was the offspring of the unluckiest who had the most positive impact on the world, inspired by the suffering of their ancestor. Humans were scrappy. Give them hardship and some of them would rise up and succeed out of sheer spite for the bad hand they had been dealt. Not that luck, good or bad, was planned in any way. As far as Palamedes could tell, the Lady they served had no rhyme or reason.

Luck was a fickle, unknowable thing—a coin toss, Plutus insisted, though he knew little more about how it worked than Palamedes did. Yet, Palamedes had always been able to see the eventual benefit in the bad luck as well as in the good before, and he had comforted himself with the knowledge that one person's misfortune would usually lead to something good. That was not so now, and he did not see how that would be any different in two days' time when the world ended.

Neither did Plutus, though he was being stubborn about it. He had always been a god, a child of Demeter some said, a child of Zeus said others. He did not question the justness of his actions, though Palamedes loved him in spite of his annoying habit of believing in his own infallibility. Now they were at an impasse. Palamedes could not continue on as if this were just another mission.

"Nemesis," Palamedes whispered defiantly.

Plutus' eyes flared with a spike of fear. "I told you—"

"Is this seat taken?"

A veiled woman in a long, grey dress stood behind the empty chair at their table. The small gods stood and bowed to her. They had never been in her presence before. She was one of the Great Ladies who worked behind the veil, shaping the lives of all.

"My Lady," Plutus said reverently before shooting Palamedes a dirty look. "Forgive us. We did not mean to disturb you."

"It is not you alone who have summoned me." As she sat, she swept an arm draped in the finest linen out to include the mortals huddled wretchedly over their drinks. If the other patrons at the hotel bar found the woman's flowing chiton and veil oddly arcane, they did not show it. "There are many here who call on Righteous Anger and would like to see the balance re-struck. Too much misfortune has befallen the world. Would you be those who speak against it?"

"We would," Palamedes said eagerly, taking his seat.

Plutus put a restraining hand on his husband's arm. "Though we know that we must bend ourselves always to the will of the Great Ladies."

Nemesis made no sound of movement behind her veil. Her body was straight and unyielding. "Good and evil cannot exist without free will. In order for free will to exist there must be those brave enough to choose," she said cryptically.

Plutus looked to his companion. He knew what Palamedes

wanted. "We would choose a fate other than this, if we could," he said.

"Can we?" Palamedes pleaded. "Is it so simple?"

Nemesis did not answer right away. "Free will is anything but simple."

Palamedes knew that the gods never gave answers. Only riddles that they insisted you answer for them. In this they must make a leap of faith—another thing the gods both demanded of mortal and did not do themselves.

"How may we help avert this fate?" Palamedes asked.

"Go to the north. Find the Arimaspi. Tell them that their ancient foes will be released upon the world again and they are needed in the fight. If they so choose, they will come with you. If not..." Nemesis let her words trail off. She was unreadable behind her veil.

"We'll do it," Palamedes said too quickly.

"We're supposed to be in South America next. We have orders," Plutus said, shaking his head at his partner.

"We'll do it," Palamedes insisted and Plutus nodded. In end, he could not deny Palamedes anything.

Nemesis stood. "Remember, free will is often mistaken for disobedience. I wish you *luck*, servants of Tyche."

And she disappeared.

Helen sat up in a panic at the crack of dawn, waking her friends. She fumbled for the watch on Ariadne's wrist to see how many hours she'd wasted of the precious three days the world had left.

"I can't believe I fell asleep." Helen couldn't help but think of Hector's repeated assertions that she'd regret not being able to stop time. She could kick herself, because it finally dawned on her that that's where the answer lied. There was only one place that Helen knew of where time would stand still long enough for her to figure out what to do next.

"I have to go to Hades," she announced.

She stood before either Claire of Ariadne could stop her, but neither of them tried to. They understood why she was doing it. Helen dusted herself off, rolled her eyes, and opened a portal to the last place in any universe she wanted to go.

It only occurred to her after she was standing in Lucas' throne room that he hadn't barred the way for her. She was still allowed to come and go in Hades, which surprised her. But as she realized this, she also considered that Lucas could technically go to Everyland if he chose. She'd never specifically denied him entrance. He had never gone to Everyland without her, though. Not once. Helen would've known.

She didn't have to wait long for Lucas to materialize out of the shadows of his throne room and come striding toward her. He was pale. Lucas used to have honey-tan skin even in winter, but not anymore. His black hair and black clothes framed the translucent white of his face like the night sky around the moon. He'd always been a good dresser. He liked nice things, fancy watches, and expensive sneakers, but his style before had always been relaxed and suited to a teenager. Now he dressed formally, like someone much older than he was. The jeans and sneakers were gone, and he wore long, elegantly tailored jackets that enveloped him in crisp layers.

The warm jackets made sense in Hades, though. Helen had

forgotten how cold it was here. She shivered partly from the cold, and partly from the creeping sensation inspired by his Shadowmaster talent. Slips of shadows, like darker creases in the gloom, were always alive around him now, and the shadows sighed and whispered as he passed through them on his way across the marble floor to her. Lucas stopped a respectable distance away from her and waited for Helen to speak first.

"This ecpyrosis thing," she said, looking down at her hands rather than at him. She realized she was twisting her fingers anxiously and stopped.

"I never said you would be—"

"Yes, you did," she said, cutting him off indignantly.

"I never said you would be the one to cause it," he repeated, speaking over her. "That was Daedelus, and his fear is based on an ancient Stoic belief that I'm not certain I agree with." He took a moment to shift away from the confrontational tone they had jumped into and started again. "All I'm certain of is that the List of the Dead is full. I never said you were going to be the one to fill it."

"It was implied, but whatever," she said, trying not to sound bitter. "But if I don't do it, do you have any ideas as to how the whole world is going to die, then?"

"I might," he said.

She waited, but he just stood there, watching her. "Well?" she huffed when he didn't continue.

"What aren't you telling me?"

He always did this to her. Turned things around on her. Asked more than she wanted to tell, looked deeper, demanded more. But he didn't have the right to question her anymore, especially not when she was the one who deserved answers.

"Why did I even come here?" she asked, anger clenching in her chest like a fist.

"Helen, wait."

"Why would you help me anyway?" she asked scathingly. "If everyone's dead then you're free, right?"

Incomprehension clouded his gaze for a moment, and then sudden, piercing clarity brought it into focus. He recoiled from her.

"You really think I'd do that?"

"I notice you're avoiding using declarative sentences," she said. "I wonder if that's so I won't hear your lie."

Helen didn't stop to think about anything she was saying long enough to consider whether she truly believed it or not. All she knew was that it hurt him, and that's what she wanted. Until she saw the lost expression on his face, like he didn't understand anything anymore, and she very much didn't want that.

"Lucas, I—" He stepped away from her as she stepped toward him in apology.

"Right, because I'm the Hand of Darkness. Why wouldn't I want everyone dead? Then I'd rule the world from here," he said, gesturing widely to his cold kingdom.

"I'm sorry," she snapped, angry now because he was angry. He didn't have the right—she was the one who had the right to be angry. Not him. She sighed. "This isn't going to work, is it?"

"No."

Helen appeared in her bedroom. Lucas had kicked her out and sent her to her room like a sulky brat. Which, she had to admit, was how she'd been behaving. Hiding in her room, listening to angry music was not an option, though. She didn't even know if three days meant a full 72 hours from the moment Lucas told her about the List of the Dead being full, or if it was less than that.

Helen portaled herself to the Delos brownstone in New York City.

No one was in the kitchen, which was odd. That was where Helen usually found one or both of them.

"Orion?" she called.

"Up here," he called from his room on the third floor.

Helen climbed the stairs and knocked on his door like a normal human. She'd learned the embarrassing way not to appear in either Orion's or Hector's bedrooms even if they knew she was coming. Everyone needed a moment to collect themselves before they were ready to go from private to public. Except for Lucas. But he wasn't really a human anymore. Out of all of them, he was the only one who had seemed to change entirely into the god he was meant to replace.

Orion came to the door and opened it, still pulling a shirt over his head. "You okay?" he asked.

Helen gave him a wan smile. "No."

She told him everything while he went around his bedroom —which, fun fact, used to belong to Tantalus—gathering his things for class. When she finished he put his bag down and sat down heavily on the edge of his platform bed.

"Less than three days?" he repeated back to her, his expression blank.

Helen nodded, staring off into nothing. She shook herself and regrouped. "I kind of told your dad to kiss my ass after he told me about the whole ecpyrosis thing, but I need to get in touch with him. We've got to tell everyone. Puts some heads together. Come up with a way out of this."

Orion slid his phone out of his bag and sent a quick text, his eyes never fully focusing on the screen. He was still in shock.

"Lucas said he had an idea?" he asked, tiptoeing around Helen's churning emotions.

Helen swiped a hand across her face in frustration and resisted the urge to start screaming. "Yes, but I can't deal with him right now, okay? Let's just find your dad first."

"Okay." He checked his phone but there was no reply yet. "Look, I'm not trying to tell you how to grieve..."

"Don't."

"... But Lucas usually figures shit out first."

Helen stood and he jumped up with her, grabbing her arm so she couldn't portal away without him.

"You don't have to forgive him, but you are going to have to work with him. We're talking about the death... of everyone, Helen."

She gave him her best glare, but the word *forgive* was echoing in her head. She recalled Aphrodite's admonishment, but she just couldn't. Even thinking about Lucas made her so angry she couldn't breathe. How could she forgive him? Lucas may not have killed Jerry, but he was the reason her father was dead.

"Come here," Orion said, gathering her against his chest for a hug.

The door opened wider revealing Hector, who looked between them with an eyebrow raised in question.

"What's this?" Hector asked, not convinced that he'd walked in on a platonic exchange.

Orion launched into a quick explanation before Helen could stop him. If Hector was the god of war, Helen didn't know if involving him was the best idea, but it was too late. Hector was skipping right over the shock a normal person would feel upon hearing that everyone in the world was going to die, and he was heading straight into being excited about who or what he'd have to fight in the process of avoiding that fate.

"You're not going to slaughter the entire planet," Hector said, like the thought was ridiculous. "It's gotta be something else that's going to do it. Or try to." He grinned in an unsettling way. "I hope it's something huge. Like *Typhon* huge."

"You're enjoying this too much," Orion said to Hector before turning to Helen. "Since we have zero time to waste, what's your plan until my dad gets back to me?"

Helen opened her mouth, hoping something great would fall out of it, but the only thing that came out was, "I don't know, maybe we should go find Cassandra? Ask if she's seen a Typhon climbing out of Tartarus?"

"Oh, man—" Hector said, rubbing his hands together in excitement.

"You really shouldn't be enjoying this," Orion scolded.

Helen had put it off for four months, but there was no way out of it now. She'd have to go face Lucas' parents and sister. Helen portaled all three of them outside the Delos' house on Nantucket. It was still early morning and she could hear the family moving around inside, getting ready for school and work.

"Why are we in the driveway?" Hector asked.

"I can't materialize in the living room," Helen said, rolling her eyes.

"Why not?"

"Because maybe I'm not welcome?"

Hector growled something profane and led the way, calling out to whomever was home as soon as he was inside. Ariadne had already filled in the Delos family about the situation and her exploits with Helen and Claire the previous night, and no one seemed particularly surprised that Helen was there looking for help, but it wasn't a comfortable reunion. Helen didn't belong, despite Hector's constant assurance that she was still part of his family. She wasn't.

She knew Claire, Orion, Hector, Ariadne, and Kate were her people, and they would do anything for her if she asked, but she wasn't part of the greater pack anymore. When Jerry had died and Lucas had betrayed her, Helen had lost the last of her family. She was an orphan, and nothing made that clearer to her than being in that house again, on the outside looking in.

As Pallas' girlfriend, Niobe, gathered in the kitchen, Helen found herself changing position awkwardly, hovering here and then there without ever finding a spot while everyone else got coffee and arranged themselves throughout the spacious kitchen. This morning gathering was something she had witnessed countless times, and in the past she had always known where to go. She used to have a spot at the table, next to Lucas. She did not get herself anything to eat or drink and she did not sit at the empty place at the table.

Cassandra was the last to join them. Her gaze first sought out Orion, who was talking quietly with Niobe, his Heir to the

House of Rome. Helen caught herself feeling frustrated that the concept of Houses and Heirs still existed. None of that mattered anymore. Cassandra noticed Helen second, and she looked taken aback to see her. Helen gave Cassandra a chilly smile and looked away.

They hadn't exactly fought after the wedding, but they weren't on speaking terms either. Helen felt like Lucas' whole family blamed Helen for something. She didn't actually know what. Maybe they blamed her because of the part she was playing in Hector's debauchery, or maybe they blamed her for being angry with Lucas, which she considered outrageous. What right did they have to blame her when he was the one who had hurt her? Anger kept peaking in her and she folded her arms, tucking her hands beneath them to hide the shimmer of sparks that had started pulsing in her fingertips. She shifted to another spot as if changing position could change what she was feeling. It didn't.

Orion looked up from his conversation with Niobe and over at Helen, alert to her unraveling emotions. He seemed to ask her silently if she was going to be alright, but she waved him off, frustrated. She was so tired of it all. Tired of being overwhelmed with emotion one second, only to be left exhausted and drained of all feeling the next. Tired of needing to lean on him and Hector and only feeling less able to stand on her own because of it. Everything and everyone in her life was a crutch now, not support, because support was supposed to be temporary. It only held you up until you got better, but nothing got better anymore, only worse, and she just wanted to get this part of her never-ending downward spiral over with.

She let Hector, Orion, and Ariadne do all the explaining.

One of the things she didn't miss about being part of such a big family was the constant re-hashing that was required when absolutely anything happened. If someone got so much as a bad haircut, there'd be about twelve different conversations about it, and even still, months later, there'd be one person who looked around in confusion during a family gathering, asking what the heck was going on if everyone else laughed like crazy when so-and-so said the word *mullet*.

"Something funny?" Niobe asked Helen, interrupting Hector's overly eager musings on which monster was going to destroy the world.

Helen had been laughing at her personal thoughts about the Delos family. Niobe was a little too keen for Helen's comfort. She decided she needed to deflect.

"Hector's right in assuming it has to be something pretty big and ugly if it's going to destroy the whole world," she said.

"Or blonde and beautiful," Niobe murmured.

Helen ignored her comment. "I need to talk to Daedelus and Ladon again, see if there's anything Kraken-sized still floating around down at the bottom of the ocean," she said, pressing on, "but if not, I could go to Tartarus and see if anything has escaped."

That shut the whole room up.

"You can do that?" Pallas asked. "Just walk into Tartarus and walk out?"

Helen switched her focus to him and tried to think of the least alarming way to explain the extent of her power, but before she could answer she sensed a shadow in the corner of the room detaching from the wall and swung around to face it. She wasn't going to let him sneak up on her again.

"Something did slip out of the Underworld," Lucas said, addressing everyone as he synthesized out of shadows and took a place in the group far from Helen. "The Cimmerians told me of a burning wind that arose from Tartarus. It blew through their land and across Ocean, toward the dawn."

She knew Lucas wasn't following her, but she couldn't help feeling like everywhere she went he magically turned up, like he was watching her somehow.

"The Cimmerians?" Ariadne asked. "Who are they?"

Helen knew this one. "The people who live in the perpetual mist and darkness on the border of Hades," she answered, never taking her eyes off of Lucas. "And *dawn* means this world. Does this dry wind have anything to do with the drought?" The last she directed at Lucas, as if daring him to look her in the eye.

"I don't think it's the cause, though it is making things worse," he replied. "The drought isn't the real problem. A drought doesn't explain how everyone on earth could die within the same hour of the same day."

His calm demeanor only made her angrier. "So you're saying I may not be the only thing causing the drought, but I'm still going to be the one to blame when everyone dies?" she snapped.

"No one blames you, Helen. And I can't help that I've *seen* you at the center of a huge lightning storm," Cassandra said, sounding strangled, like she was forcing herself to say it.

Helen rounded on her. "And this vision has nothing to do with the fact that you all can't stand me now?" she asked accusingly. She turned away, scoffing. "This is bullshit."

She felt hands on her shoulders and Lucas was instantly before her, holding onto her so she couldn't portal away. The shock of having him so close was like a slap. He hadn't touched her since they had danced at her father's wedding.

"Don't run away," he said, his face inches from hers. "You're isolated, angry, and acting on instinct. Instincts the Moirae control. They're telling you to burn the world down, and you're buying into it. And don't bother trying to lie to me. I see the lightning in you." He let one of his hands slide down her arm and lift up a hand that glittered with energy just beneath the skin. "*Think* Helen. Think about how you've been manipulated for the past four months. Think about what you need to do differently, because you're already on the path that leads to the end of the world. Only *you* can get off of it."

She stared up at him, mentally fighting every word he said and still knowing he was right. She wanted to scream, or cry, or hit him. Anything to get away from the intolerable feeling of being so close to him.

"How?" she said, wriggling out of his grasp. "If I can't trust my instincts, how am I supposed to make any decisions? And don't you dare say that I should trust you."

"I wouldn't dream of it," he said, his expression darkening as he moved away from her.

She suddenly became acutely aware of their audience. Everyone was silent and staring at Lucas. They were scared of him and the way he moved now, appearing out of the shadows like a nightmare. Something tugged inside of Helen, and she swept it away with an exasperated gesture before it had a chance to grow into pity.

"You need to stay with Orion to shield you from the Fates, and you need to make a plan with both Oracles," Lucas continued. "Antigone has been shielded by Ladon for decades now

JOSEPHINE ANGELINI

and she's seen very different things from Cassandra. If you'd stuck around when I had you brought to her..."

"Wait, what," Castor said, interrupting. He and Pallas still didn't know, and the devastated looks on their faces were too much for Helen.

"This family's such a mess," she said under her breath, but still loud enough to be overheard by those closest to her. She gave Lucas a challenging look. "You tell them. I'm done doing damage control."

Niobe made an exasperated sound. "Could you two stop tearing each apart for five minutes so we can talk this out?" she asked, like she couldn't bear to watch anymore.

Lucas and Helen broke to opposite sides of the kitchen. Orion explained what had occurred between Ladon and Antigone to the Delos family. While they weren't exactly shocked—they already knew that many Scions had faked their deaths with Daphne's help—it still hurt them to know that they had been deceived by their cousin and that she had continued the deception even after Tantalus' death. Antigone hadn't wanted to reunite with the Delos family, and she was only doing it now because it was being forced on her.

Helen fidgeted with the edge of a dish towel. Lucas paced in tight circles, his jaw set. Helen was impatient to get moving, to do something rather than stand in Noel's kitchen, watching her look at her son like he was drowning, unable to save him. Helen thought about how trapped they all were. Trapped by the Fates. Helen was still a pawn, driven from one decision to another by emotions she couldn't control. Emotions she must learn to control, or the lightning that she saw in her fingertips would shake loose eventually. It was the Fates controlling her, and if

68

she didn't want to lose her mind, she had to get control over her heart.

When Orion was done speaking, and everyone had made their comments and asked their questions, she took a deep breath and faced Lucas. "Do the Fates live in the Underworld?" she asked him.

"I don't know if anyone knows where they live," he replied. His gaze wandered in thought. "I can't see them in Hades, but that doesn't mean they aren't close by." A small smile tugged at his mouth. It was just a ghost of the mischievousness that used to come so easily to him, but it was still there. "If we could find them..."

Helen nodded. "We could bring the fight to them."

She looked away from him before she allowed herself to feel camaraderie. They were both in this, but they weren't in it together.

"I'm coming," Hector said immediately, as if he feared being left out.

"Me too," Orion added, though as their shield from the Fates, he obviously had to. "Let's go to Ladon's first, though. My dad could be with him. Cassandra?"

There was friction between them, Helen noticed, something different in the way Orion said her name. A quick glance at his heart told Helen that he had such a strangle hold on his emotions he wasn't allowing whatever it was that might grow between them any room inside him to breathe. But there was something beginning there, whether he liked it or not.

Cassandra nodded in answer to his question. "Yeah. I'm going." She laughed nervously. "I've never met another Oracle."

The twins stood together, Jason angling himself behind

Lucas, and Ariadne moving more in Helen's direction as if they were subtly taking sides. Helen appreciated Ariadne's silent vote of confidence, but it wasn't necessary.

Noel made her way across the room to Helen while everyone started milling around, preparing to go. "May I speak to you?" Noel asked.

Helen nodded and allowed herself to be pulled into the other room, though it was one of the last things she wanted to do. She braced herself for any number of attacks or accusations. Instead, Noel started with a small chuckle and an eye-roll at something she thought in her head.

"Awkward, right?" she said.

Helen nodded in agreement. She was still on guard, though. Noel had a way of sneaking up on her.

"I never told you this, but my dad was the only family I had, too. My mom was an alcoholic. She left us when I was a little girl. It was just my dad and me, really. He died shortly after I met Castor. He was killed by a Scion. I was nineteen."

"I-I'm sorry," Helen stammered, shaken. She'd had no idea.

"I blamed Castor. Even though he didn't do it, it was because of him and his stupid war that my poor father—who never had one lucky break in his entire, shitty life..." she stopped herself from going off on that tangent and took a deep breath. "I hated Castor."

"What happened? How did you—?"

"Forgive him?" Noel considered. "That's a long story. But I did, eventually."

There's that word again, Helen thought. *Forgive*. As it ran around in her head, breaking into the syllables *for* and *give*, she started to lose the meaning of it. Was she supposed to *give* something *for* someone else? That didn't even make any sense.

"I was an angry person when I was younger," Noel continued. "I wasted so much time."

It would have been impossible for Helen to have imagined Noel as an angry young woman unless she'd seen it for herself. Helen recalled the spite in Noel's voice in 1993 when she'd overheard Noel and Castor fighting on the street. Helen wondered if that's how she sounded now.

"We all love you, Helen, and if anyone in the world can understand what you're going through, it's me. But I had all the time in the world to forgive the man I love. You don't."

Everything inside of Helen felt tight and hot. "I don't know how," she whispered, scared she might start crying. "I wish I did, but I don't."

"Just let go."

Helen grimaced. "Of my anger? Okay," she quipped, like that was easier said than done.

Noel shook her head, looking perplexed. "Of your dad."

Helen was so surprised she just stood there, speechless. It was unthinkable. Never. She'd never *ever* let go of her father.

"Mom."

Lucas stood in the doorway looking between the two of them, like he was wondering how worried he should be.

Noel turned to face Lucas. "We're all set," she said, going back into the kitchen.

Helen and Lucas were left alone. Or at least to Helen it felt like they were alone, even though a crowd stood just twenty feet away. Lucas had way of filling up every inch of her horizon. They'd done this so many times before. Meeting in quiet hallways when they shouldn't have. Spending long, heavy minutes just looking at each other. It had always been complicated between them, but now it was insufferable.

An image from the single night they'd slept together flashed through her mind, full of skin and whispers, galvanizing her whole body. She had to move, or go, or do something to get away, but Lucas' tall frame loomed in the doorway, his broad shoulders partially blocking the exit. He saw her shift on her feet and wavered, seeming torn as to whether he wanted to say something or let her pass.

"Did she..." he began. Broke off. Started over. "What did my mother say to you?"

Lucas hated not knowing things. It drove him crazy, and Helen knew it. She kept her lips pointedly pressed together as she brushed past him to rejoin the rest of the family in the kitchen. Behind her, she heard him let out a rough breath that was part frustration, part disbelief, and part amusement all in one. It was gratifying to know that at least she was as insufferable to him as he was to her.

"Okay. Everyone going to Ladon's cave get over here," Helen said in a rousing tone, gesturing them into a circle around her. She glanced at Lucas as he joined the circle. "Do you want to go yourself, or should I...?" It was such a strange question to ask, *should I portal you?*

A smile twitched at his mouth, and Helen knew what he was thinking.

"Don't," she said.

"You can drive," he said.

She hated that they had history together for seemingly everything—even for portaling, a rarified ability only a handful of beings in the universe had. She did not smile at him as she opened a portal. Not to be cruel, but because it hurt too much to be reminded that no matter how hard she had tried to destroy everything that connected her to him, she had already given him too much of herself to survive it.

CHAPTER 5

W hen they arrived at Ladon's new cave a moment later it was obvious that something terrible had happened.

The plush living room furniture was overturned and shredded. There were scorch marks on the walls, and the water sloshing against the beach was churning with counter-current waves that had been created by some sort of huge disturbance in the water—or some kind of huge creature.

"Uncle Ladon! Dad!" Orion called out frantically, already running for one of the stalactite-studded tunnels to search for them.

Lucas disappeared and then seem to blink in and out of the room like he was lit by a strobe, finally appearing at the mouth of the dark tunnel before Orion could enter it.

"They're not here and they're not dead," Lucas assured him.

Orion startled away from Lucas, surprised by how quickly

he had appeared, and took a second to let what Lucas said sink in.

"That's... good to know," Orion said, disgruntled. He was still revved up on adrenaline, and unsure what to do now that Lucas had skipped a few steps for him.

Hector spotted something among the churning waves, plowed into the water, and dove down beneath the surface without saying a word. A moment later, he reappeared with a girl in his arms. She was bleeding badly and her hair was covering her face, but Helen recognized her.

"Andy," Ariadne gasped, running to the water's edge with Jason by her side.

"This is bad," Jason mumbled, unheeding of the effect his words would have on his brother, as he and Ariadne took Andy from him. Hector's expression was stiff, but Helen could see his heart twisting in his chest.

They laid her out on the sand, their hands already glowing with healing light. Andy's arm was nearly severed from her body.

"Too much damage," Ariadne muttered to Jason, and he nodded in reply. Andy couldn't die, Helen had made her immortal, but she could lose a limb.

"Give her to me," Helen said. They moved back, and Helen portaled Andy to Everyland, then portaled back with her, completely healed.

Andy bolted into a sitting position, eyes wide, staring, and dragged in a shuddering breath, very much like she was waking from the dead. Helen crouched down next to her, taking one of Andy's hands as she looked around wildly without seeing anything. Hector, who was on his hands and knees next to her dropped his head with a relieved exhale, his back and shoulders shaking.

"It's okay," Helen said. "Look at me. Andy? Look at me."

Andy struggled to focus her eyes. When she finally joined them in mind as well as body, she looked as if she couldn't make what she was seeing mesh with her reality.

Lucas crouched down next to Helen. "What happened?" he asked her in that newly adopted calm tone he had. It was like a wild, horse-tamer voice, Helen thought, and he seemed practiced in using it. Helen considered that there were probably lots of traumatized souls who couldn't process that they were dead. Though to be honest, she had no idea what his job in the Underworld entailed.

"They just started pouring out of the ground," Andy said, still ashen with shock.

"What came out of the ground?" Hector said, struggling. Helen could see him barely keeping himself still long enough to get an answer. He needed to beat something up. Andy looked at him, and away again like it stung. She wanted to reach out to him but didn't dare.

"I don't know what they were," Andy replied. "They were like... lions... or eagles... or something... and they breathed fire. There was a swarm of them. I tried to get here, to Ladon for help. I didn't think I was going to make it."

Helen didn't know Andy and Ladon were acquainted, but it made sense. Andy was half siren, a sea creature, and so was Ladon.

"Where were you when they attacked?" Lucas asked.

"Iceland. On the beach. I barely made it into the water," She looked around. "Did they attack here, too?"

Lucas looked around, nodding vaguely. There were claw marks on the furniture, and there were blackened scorch marks dotted randomly about.

He turned to Orion quickly, a new thought overtaking him. "Where would your father and uncle go if they were under attack?" he asked.

"My dad would go to my mom first to check on her," Orion replied.

"Your mom? She's alive?" Cassandra asked.

Lucas was too focused on this new thought of his to have patience for little things, like other people's feelings. "But he wouldn't stay in Newfoundland with her, would he? He'd move her?"

"How did you know where—" Orion began, and then stopped. "Where are you going with this?"

"Griffins. That's what responsible for the attacks," Lucas said.

"Griffins?" Hector repeated, grimacing, as if that answer didn't satisfy his aspirations. He was still hoping for Typhon.

"Also known as the *Hounds of Zeus*." Lucas looked at Helen. "Maybe Zeus can't leave Olympus, but that doesn't mean other things that he controls can't come and go from there."

"But what's the point of sending anything after us?" she persisted. "Even if he somehow manages to kill us, which he can't, he'll still never leave Olympus. He's stuck there *forever*, regardless of whether or not the Scions are alive."

"Forever here. In this universe, where Zeus made his vow," Lucas said. "But *this* forever ends when you end it, Helen."

She slumped down onto the least destroyed piece of furniture, covering her face with her hands. "Which I'm supposed to do in two and a half days," she said. "And Zeus gets to start over."

Helen knew how the Fates loved cycles. An ending always led to a new beginning. She had no doubt that Zeus was counting on the same thing. As soon as this world was destroyed, the Fates would create another one that he could come back to from Olympus. A brand-new playground at the naive dawn of its existence, just the way he liked it.

"Hang on," Lucas said. He blinked away and back again several times so fast it hurt to look at. "Our families are okay, but we should get back to them. Guard the ones who aren't immortal."

"Wait, what's the point of all this, though?" Jason asked. "How are these attacks going to make Helen destroy the world?"

"I don't know yet," Lucas said. He stared at Helen, half seeing her, half using her as an anchor for his eyes as his mind spun. "Hector and Cass, I'm bringing you to our house on Nantucket to guard our parents. And you're taking Andy with you." Lucas walked over, portaled them away, and returned again in a puff of airborne ice crystals. "Ari, you've got Kate." He disappeared with her and returned alone. "Jason, you're going to Claire's. Bring her back to our house." Lucas disappeared with Jason.

"Hold on a sec," Orion said when Lucas reappeared and approached him.

"I know you have to stay with Helen. You can look for your dad together," Lucas said, as if anticipating what Orion was going to say next.

"I need you to *wait*," Orion said. "You can't portal people places without getting their consent first, you know."

Lucas faltered, noticing the affronted look on Orion's face. "Fine. Helen can take you to find your family when you're *ready*." he said, and then he disappeared through a portal.

Orion let out a long sigh. "I didn't mean to make him feel..."

"Strange? Scary? Controlling?"

"All of them," he said, sounding regretful. "He's really changed."

"He's always been controlling," she said, refusing to feel bad for Lucas. She stood and went to Orion, putting her hands on his shoulders. "Do I have your consent?"

"Shut the hell up," Orion said, chuckling sheepishly, and she portaled them to Newfoundland.

The house that Daedelus and Leda lived in was just as Helen remembered it. The small but sturdy-looking building was isolated on a rocky outcropping, surrounded by high surf, far from any neighbors. As it needed to be.

Leda's psyche was fragile and she occasionally had loud, even violent outbursts. Driven to a mental break-down by the Furies, she'd never recovered from having to kill her brother, Adonis, to protect Orion. Helen paused outside the house as her own memories of Adonis overtook her.

Helen hadn't spent much time with him during her brief visit to 1993, but she'd liked him immediately. He'd risked a lot to help save Antigone's life when Ladon had accidentally injured her, proving himself to be both brave and compassionate. He'd also had an open, impish way to him that Helen gravitated to, and the fact that he'd been the spitting image of Orion, someone Helen already adored, had made her feel an instant kinship with him.

One glance at Orion, who had made no move toward the house, told her how he was feeling about being back here. The nature of his mother's mental illness had made Orion's childhood in this house traumatic. Helen knew he was going to need help with this. She took his hand and led the way.

There weren't any lights on, but that didn't mean no one was there. Helen peered through one of the windows to find the furniture upright and unscorched.

"It doesn't look like it's been attacked," she said.

Orion took out his house keys and let them inside. As soon as they crossed the threshold, Helen sensed movement to her right and portaled them to the opposite side of the room.

"Holy shit!" Daedelus exclaimed from his hiding place behind the front door.

"Dad, it's us!" Orion called out from across the room, in case his father charged them.

Daedelus stepped in the disk of ice left on the ground from Helen's portal, his footstep crunching, and sidled away from it. "Are you both okay?" he asked them when he'd gathered himself.

As they exchanged stories about the griffin attacks, Antigone crept up the cellar stairs and joined them, followed by Leda. Orion tensed when he saw his mother, who frowned uncertainly when she saw him. She didn't know who she was looking at—her brother or her son. Antigone whispered something to her, and Leda relaxed a little, but Orion kept his distance just in case.

If Leda decided he was Adonis and not Orion, she would probably attack him. Driven by an oath he'd taken to keep the Houses separate, Adonis had tried to kill Orion. Leda had been forced to kill her little brother, which eventually drove her mad. Now that Orion was a man and looked exactly like Adonis, his mother mistook him for her little brother and usually attacked him. Helen took Orion's hand again in support. It was so unfair he had to deal with this.

"They started coming out of the walls and floors. I think they were doing what you did," Daedelus said, gesturing to the melting disk of frost.

"More likely it was being done for them," Helen said. She doubted that griffins were Worldbuilders with the ability to make portals. She quickly explained Lucas' theory, how Zeus was behind all this to Daedelus.

"By attacking the Scions in your periphery, especially those who aren't immortal, he's forcing you into a fight," Daedelus said, nodding. It was annoying to her that everyone always agreed with Lucas.

"There's a way around that," Helen said.

"Not everyone wants to be immortal."

Helen nodded in acceptance. Daedelus' life seemed exhausting, always torn between his wife and his son, but maybe it didn't have to be. She stared at Leda, wondering if she could do something for her. There were a few examples in Greek mythology of gods cursing mortals with madness. Could a goddess take it away? Helen didn't know if mental illness was physical or emotional or some combination of the two. She suspected it had a physical component, but she didn't know enough about it to be sure.

If she were being honest with herself, she'd admit that she didn't know enough about any of the forces she wielded to consider herself worthy of them. Even some of the concepts behind the gifts she threw around were beyond her. Like the immortality that Daedelus had just scorned. She didn't even know what immortality meant. She hoped it didn't mean forever, not *really*.

Infinity as a concept was too strange for her to get her head around, and she didn't think any of the gods she'd encountered had the metal breadth to truly understand it either. Maybe Cronos. But definitely not Hera or Zeus, and yet they were immortal. Helen had once tried to break *forever* down into a manageable idea. Standing on the beach outside of the Delos compound she'd looked at the mounds and mounds of pale, fine sand, and tried to imagine every grain of it as a year, and even then, a voice in her head said that what she was imagining was just a drop in the bucket of *forever*. The thought experiment had freaked her out so much she'd stopped doing it, gone inside, and asked Noel if she could make French toast because that was about all her brain could handle after trying to stare down infinity.

"Daphne?" Leda said, thinking Helen was her mother.

Helen realized that she'd been staring at her while she'd been lost in thought. "Would you like to come somewhere with me?"

"Where?" Leda asked, looking wary, but intrigued.

"A place I think might be able to help you think more clearly."

"Wait," Orion said. "What are you going to do?"

"I'm going to try to help you mother," Helen replied.

"Are you sure that's a good idea?"

"No, I'm not," Helen replied honestly.

"Is that possible? Can you... cure her?" Daedelus asked, looking equal parts terrified and hopeful.

Helen shrugged. "I don't know what's going to happen, but I'd like to try." She turned to Leda. "Only if *you* want me to, of course."

"Yes," Leda replied immediately.

Helen felt like she should add some caveats. "I can't change the past or take what's happened away."

"I want to try," Leda said, barely allowing Helen to finish speaking. "I've felt like I've been in a fog for so long now."

Helen gestured for everyone to gather around her, though it occurred to her that she didn't know if she needed to be actually touching someone to portal them, or if they needed to be a certain distance from her or not. She didn't even know how large she could make a portal, or if there was a maximum size or weight to what she could put through one. She hadn't tested the limits of that ability yet, and now that it was brought to her attention, she knew it was something she was going to have to look into soon.

"Please, let this work," Orion murmured to himself as he took Helen's hand and she portaled them all to Everyland.

Hector paced from the hallway, to the kitchen, to the great room, and back again to the hallway with the smell of blood caught in the back of his throat.

He looked down at his hands. They were still covered in it. In Andy's blood. It was different from fully human blood. Her half-siren blood was saltier, thicker, more metallic. It was gorgeous. He had to stop himself from lifting his fingers to his face for another whiff of it.

He hadn't told anyone this, but he could smell the difference in everyone's blood. Taste it, too. It wasn't something he had always been able to do, but lately he could. He could also look at a body and know instantly where the arteries were, how deeply they lay under skin, muscle, and fat. It was a little different for everyone. A tiny puncture, the smallest slice, and that person would bleed out in minutes. He dreamed about blood now. Oceans of it, running out of people and over him.

He turned on his heel as he turned away from his own thoughts, hating them and himself. He needed a distraction. Something to stop his shaking hands, the sounds of screams in his head, and the smoky smell of battle that he imagined over the smell of Andy's blood. His arms ached to swing a sword. Of even better? A war hammer. His grandfather, Paris, had used the war hammer instead of the sword. Not many in the House of Thebes had the brute strength for that, but Hector did. He could see that beautiful weapon in his mind's eye and hear the crunch of bone as he swung it.

"Where are you going?" Pallas asked.

Hector stopped and turned to face his father. He realized he was at the front door, his hand on the knob. He was still covered in Andy's blood. He couldn't go outside like that.

"I don't know," Hector answered.

"She's *okay*," Pallas said, raising a hand to take his son by the shoulder, but Hector put him off, moving past his father and back into the house.

"I know," he said, frustrated, about to jump out of his skin. How could he explain this? "I just. I can't. I don't know how to..." After three attempts at speaking, he gave up and started pacing again.

"Go shower. Throw out those clothes and put on some fresh ones," his father ordered gently. "And when you're done with that... make up with Andy."

Hector was grateful to have someone to tell him what to do right now because he couldn't trust his instincts. They were telling him to go kill something.

Pallas thought of something and smiled. "Your mom and I, we must have broken up about a dozen times. She used to get so jealous. Or I'd do something stupid and she'd start screaming at me. In Spanish, no less." He paused, waiting for the memories fade. "Hera took advantage of Andy while she was away from you. It says nothing about Andy's character, except that she's human. Ariadne's fine. You gotta let it go, son."

Pallas left and Hector stared after him, wanting to scream something, but not sure what he would say if he did. It would probably be grunts and howls, as inarticulate as the animal he felt he was becoming. Instead, he climbed the stairs and went to his room to shower. Animals didn't shower, and in this small way he could prove to himself that he hadn't completely devolved.

He was opening the door to his room when Ariadne's door opened and Andy came out. She startled and stopped, staring up at him. Hector proceeded to go into his room.

"Will you please talk to me?" she begged, her voice barely above a whisper.

Speech abandoned him again and he stood there staring back at her, wordless and aching, like a dumb brute.

Andy went to him, grabbed his hand, pulled him into his room, and shut the door behind them.

"You shouldn't..." He wanted to tell her that she shouldn't be alone with him. That he wasn't sure what he'd do. That there was a wild thing inside him and he had the thinnest of control over it. However, none of those thoughts made their way, fully formed, from his mind to his mouth.

"I'm sorry about what happened. It was all my fault. I got caught up in my research, and I neglected you, and when I realized that, I got scared. I thought, you and Helen... but it wasn't you I was doubting, or Helen. It was me. I gave in to the worst and weakest part of myself." She reached out for him and he moved to get away from her.

"Please, you have to go," he said, trying to hide his shaking hands.

She was crying now, literally backing him into a corner. "You have every right to hate me." He was thinking of doing all kinds of things to her, and she knew it, too. She wanted it, but he didn't trust himself not to hurt her if he did. She reached out to him again, her face turning up to his and her lips parting.

"Hector...," she sighed.

It was hearing his name that brought him back to reality.

"Stop it!" he yelled, making her jump. "Just... go over there." He pointed to the other side of the room. "Go," he repeated when she just stood there looking devastated. "I... I have to shower."

She rubbed her wet cheeks and looked him up and down, noticing the blood. "Right. Sorry. It's gross."

"It isn't," he groaned.

Andy looked at him blankly, until confusion gave way to understanding. "You *like* it?" she said, a corner of her mouth lifting knowingly.

Convinced she was smirking at him in disgust, Hector fumbled for the bathroom door. "Please get out of my room," he said, keeping his voice low so it didn't shake.

He slammed the door shut behind him, ripped off his clothes, and jumped under the spray before the water even had a chance to heat up. He watched the red run off his body in streams that got paler until the water ran clear. He shut his eyes and soaped himself all over, finally obliterating the smell.

It had been thousands of years since Palamedes had last worn armor. He didn't relish putting it back on, but these were desperate times. Proof of that was the fact that he and Plutus were in the foothills of the Carpathian Mountains, once part of ancient Scythia, half freezing to death.

Spring had yet to come to this rocky land, and the winds were still quite punishing. As a gust snatched at his nearly useless cape, Palamedes tried to nestle closer to the horse under him. He hated the cold. He hated armor. He didn't even like horses very much, but this was important. The Arimaspi valued horses above all things, except possibly warfare. Or maybe gold. That being the case, he and Plutus had to present themselves accordingly. Meaning they had to show themselves to be warriors, astride the mythical horses of the north, and bearing much gold. The cask of treasure swaying between two attendant riders behind them clanked and tinkled with a fair portion of Plutus' solid gold coins. Not that he didn't have infinitely many more.

They came to a giant cave in the mountainside and halted. The mouth of the cave seemed to breathe as gusts of brumous wind stirred the hanging vegetation around it. Then, figures began to appear, just a few at first, but soon hundreds were streaming out of the yawning chasms.

"Is that really them?" Palamedes asked his companion.

Plutus gave him a lopsided smile. "What were you expecting? One-eyed giants?"

"Er—yes."

"That's just a myth. As you can clearly see, they have two eyes," Plutus replied. He shifted in his saddle as the Arimaspi came closer and closer and kept getting bigger and bigger. Too big. "The giant part, however, is quite true."

They weren't *giant* giants by Palamedes' estimation, but whether male or female the warriors were exceptionally tall. Seven, maybe eight feet in height, the Arimaspi had mops of shaggy hair on their heads and their armor was made of studded leather rather than bronze. They carried the long spear that is usually paired with a hoplite shield, but none of them had lugged their heavy shields out to meet a minor god and a few minions. In fact, half of the Arimaspi weren't even carrying spears, but Palamedes decided he shouldn't get offended by that. They were extremely outnumbered, and this was supposed to be a peaceful meeting after all.

Their leader bore a sword at his hip rather than a spear and was flanked by two female warrior attendants. Plutus dismounted to greet them.

"O, great Geryon—" Plutus began.

"I know why you're here," Geryon, the leader of the Arimaspi said, taking all the wind out of his sails. "It's already too late."

Plutus was not to be put off, however. "Nemesis says otherwise."

Geryon shook his shaggy head. "She alone cannot fight the Weaving Three."

"She is not alone," Palamedes said, stepping forward. "We are the servants of Tyche."

"And does Lady Luck favor the Scions?" one of Geryon's female attendants asked.

"Yes," Palamedes said hastily, holding onto Plutus' forearm to keep him from speaking. Lady Luck had not said anything to them one way or the other. Palamedes looked at his partner pleadingly, sensing the Plutus was losing his faith in this mission. "The girl, she picked heads," he said in a low voice, reminding Plutus.

Plutus narrowed his eyes in thought and a gold coin appeared between his fingers. He flipped it over his knuckles, pitched it end over end into the air and caught it. "She picked heads," he said. "And heads it was. Thus, she is lucky."

Plutus gestured for the cask to be brought forward. It was laid at Geryon's feet and flipped open. The luster of solid gold exuded from the pile within, eliciting a low hum of excitement from the Arimaspi.

"This gold is yours. We ask only that you defend it from your ancient foe, the griffins," Plutus announced.

This seemed to be well received by Geryon's warriors. Many of them seemed ready to leave the shadows of their hidden caverns and come out into the light to fight once more, but their leader did not agree as hastily as his warriors. He looked troubled.

"There are more than just griffins in this fight. We have seen all manner of beast ascending," Geryon said. "Even centaurs."

Plutus and Palamedes shared a regretful look. Centaurs could not be bought with gold. "They may ascend to fight for us," Palamedes suggested with a shrug.

"What are the chances of that?" Geryon asked.

"Fifty-fifty," Plutus said, still keeping his coin sealed tight in his palm.

The female warrior at Geryon's side restrained his forearm in much the same was Palamedes had done with Plutus. "The Scions have never been lucky," she said in her leader's ear. "They have always been pawns of the Fates."

"This time it's different," Plutus said, his brow furrowed in thought. "Luck is on our side, Geryon of the Arimaspi. Ride out with us and we will be victorious."

Palamedes noticed that though Plutus' voice rang with sincerity, he did not check his coin to see if it was heads or tails. He had no idea whose side luck was on. *What was this,* Palamedes wondered. *Faith?*

Chapter 6

By now, Helen was used to new visitors to Everyland commenting on how it seemed as if they were not in another world, but in a city on earth. Granted, it was a gorgeous city with clean air and no garbage, but still familiar.

"It's like Bruges married New York and had a burrow or two made out of Kyoto," Daedelus said when he looked out the wrap-around windows in her living room.

Leda stood next to him. She pointed at the part of the city that was built on a river delta which flowed into a calm sea. "Venice," she said, smiling.

Helen didn't know what people were expecting. Cotton candy trees? Crystal butterflies? The great cities of the world basked in their own special beauty. Nature was glorious, and so full of variation and splendor Helen couldn't think of anything more exotic or complicated that she imagined could be better. There wasn't a need. Earth was a paradise already. All Helen had done was cleaned it up and remixed it.

She stood next to them and stared. "It's Everyland," she said simply. She reached over and took Leda's hand. "Ready?" she asked, nervous now, wondering if she could pull it off. Healing the mind was not like healing a broken arm. If she failed, she could make things spectacularly worse.

"Yes," Leda replied, looking at Daedelus.

He looked like he was expecting the sky to fall on him again, but he didn't object. He was letting Leda make this choice on her own, and Helen respected him for that. Lucas had tried to make all kinds of decisions for Helen. That's why it was over between them, and Daedelus and Leda were still together, she supposed.

"This is going to work," Helen said, and she knew it to be true. Leda had said it felt like she was in a fog. Holding onto Leda's hand, Helen pictured that fog parting. She pictured locked doors opening, and dim lights being turned up brighter. She couldn't remove the fog, but she could make a tunnel through it so Leda could see.

Leda's eyes widened. "Oh my gods," she whispered, her face blanching.

"I'm sorry. It's about all I can do."

"You don't understand," Leda whispered. "It's like the seas had parted."

Whatever it was that had acted as madness in Leda's mind, had been placed there by something or someone else. Physically, Leda's mind was unharmed. The confusion that had caused Leda so much anxiety that she occasionally became violent, was an artificial obstruction placed there by some other entity. Figuring out why some other entity had put it there was another issue.

"Mom?" Orion said uncertainly from halfway across the room. He was braced and ready to bolt in case she turned again.

"Hi, Baby," she said to him, her expression soft now. Orion made his way over, and she took him in her arms.

Helen stood back while Leda took a private moment with her family to reconnect after all the years they'd lost. Though they were sorely pressed for time, they needed this, and Helen was grateful for the chance to think.

Leda finally made her way back to Helen and took her by the hand. "Thank you."

"I'm glad I was able to help. Orion... he's very special to me."

"Something your mother said years ago, before—" she passed a hand over her forehead, "right before I lost it... just came to me. It was something she needed me to tell you."

"What?" Helen asked cautiously. Leda's gaze was unmistakably lucid, but Helen didn't know if she wanted to hear what her mother had to say.

"She'd said that Nemesis had told her that the only way you were going to be able to save earth, was to give it all up. It was the only way to win."

"I don't understand."

"This world you created," Leda gestured with an arm to encompass the entirety of Everyland. "It's another Trojan Horse."

First of all, Helen didn't know if she could trust anything Daphne had wanted to tell her, and secondly, she didn't know if she could trust a message that had been locked away inside a woman's magically befuddled mind for over a decade. While Helen knew that her mother didn't have the power to make anyone insane—as far as Helen knew no Scion had the power of mind control—she didn't put it past her mother to use Leda's insanity to her own ends. Daphne was working with Nemesis, and there were several goddesses who had the ability to inflict madness on their followers. Helen had no idea what Nemesis could do in order to achieve her ends.

That brought up another problem for Helen. If Nemesis had wanted to tell her something, why not just tell her? Why this convoluted route of going through Daphne and hiding a message in a clouded mind? And what was up with the Trojan Horse thing? Helen had already used Everyland as a Trojan Horse to trick Zeus. She'd given him Everyland like a gift, but inside that gift was his downfall because she hadn't given Zeus the borders of her land. At the time she'd seen it as a reverse Trojan Horse. Instead of Greek soldiers pouring out of it, nothing could get out. Not even Zeus.

Leda had specifically said *another* Trojan Horse, so somehow Helen was supposed to do it again. The Greeks loved nothing more than repeating patterns, but Helen didn't see how a Trojan Horse scenario was possible in this instance. The Moirae were Helen's enemy in this current world-ending scenario, and they hadn't asked her to hand over Everyland as Zeus had. Helen didn't even know how to go about giving Everyland to them. With Zeus, Helen had looked him in the eye and said it aloud. She'd felt Everyland pass to him, like something taken from her hands and put into his. The Fates were like ghosts. Helen didn't know where to put Everyland in order to give it to them.

It occurred to Helen that their elusiveness was a part of their power. They touched every aspect of Helen's life, and yet she'd never encountered them. Never looked them in the eye. Never stood across from them and been in a position to give her world to them, which she would gladly do if it meant saving everyone on the planet. She didn't even know where the Moirae were. How was she supposed to pull a Trojan Horse level trick on them if she couldn't even find them?

Eventually, Orion came to Helen and hugged her, his face turned into her neck. "For years it was like she was worse than dead. Thank you for giving her back to us," he said.

Helen touched his silky hair, thinking for the thousandth time, *why couldn't I have met Orion first and fallen in love with him?*

"I'd bring a million people back from the dead for you. It's what any halfway decent person would do for someone they love," she replied.

Orion pulled away, catching Helen's dig at Lucas. He was about to say something to defend Lucas.

"Don't," she said, stopping him. She rolled her eyes and laughed. "Why couldn't an Oracle have told me how much I'd regret meeting him?" She was only joking. But it gave her an idea.

"What?" Orion asked looking worried.

"What if *I* told me?" she asked. Helen turned to Antigone. "Has an Oracle ever made a prophecy from the future that was given to her by someone other than the Fates?"

"It's scary how alike you are," Antigone muttered under her breath.

Helen sat down on the couch and Orion took the seat next

to her. What if she'd just gone with Daphne when she had tried to kidnap her from the back room of the News Store? Helen knew if she had, she'd be with Orion right now. And none of this would have happened. The gods wouldn't have returned because the Houses wouldn't have been joined. Helen would never have met anyone in the Delos family. She would've left Nantucket before she'd had the chance to. If only she could speak to her mother.

"Do prophecies work in reverse?" Helen asked musingly. "Meaning, if I were to say something to an Oracle now, could past-you see it as a prophecy and say it to my mother?"

"Why? What prophecy would you send to her?" Antigone asked, her eyes narrowed.

"Say to her: When I turn seventeen, do whatever you have to do to get me away from Lucas. The future depends on it, and if you fail at first, do everything you possibly can to keep us apart. Lie, cheat, steal. Just get me away from him."

Antigone froze. "This is it. This is the moment," she said quietly.

"What do you mean?"

"I delivered this message to Daphne decades ago," Antigone said louder. She looked as if she wanted to continue speaking, but didn't.

Daedelus sighed. "Haven't we already established that withholding information, no matter how well intentioned, never worked out in our favor?" he asked her.

"We have. And there *is* something I haven't told you all yet," Antigone finally admitted, looking around at everyone. "Helen is *supposed* to start the ecpyrosis. It's fated. But she doesn't kill everyone in the world. In fact, she doesn't kill anyone. The second message that I delivered to your mother all those years ago, is that Lucas is the one who kills everyone in the world. And he does it for Helen."

Helen guffawed. "I don't buy it. Lucas won't even give me my father. I highly doubt he'd murder the entire world for me."

"Helen," Orion began, turning to her.

"Look, first of all, I'm not going to be the cause of ecpyrosis," she said, being serious. "Second, all of this is going to be beside the point if we manage to stop the Fates. What did my mother have in mind? You said she had a plan. What was it?"

"She said that you would have to put the pieces together yourself, or the Fates would know what you were trying to do and stop you. All I know is that the piece I was to deliver was the last one. Use the world you created like a Trojan Horse to bring down the Fates," Leda said.

Helen threw up her hands. "If I see an opportunity, I'll be sure and do that," she grumbled. As usual, her mother's motives were beyond her.

Leda gave Helen a wry smile. "I like you," she said, glancing quickly at her son and then away again. "I don't think you're supposed to know what it means until you know what it means."

"Right now, I don't know anything. I don't even know where the Fates *are*."

"So maybe start there," Daedelus suggested with a shrug. "Go find the Moirae."

Orion gave her an apologetic look for what he was about to ask. "Would Lucas know where they are?"

Helen groaned and let her head drop back. Why did every step she took, no matter the direction, lead her back to him?

"Fine," she relented. "Let's go talk to him and get it over with."

It was decided that they should collect Ladon from his patrol in the shallows by the house in Newfoundland first, and then Helen would bring everyone to the Delos compound on Nantucket. If they were going to get attacked by griffins, it was better to have as many fighters on hand as possible. The reunion with her estranged family was going to be awkward for Antigone, and Castor and Pallas, but better awkward than dead. Helen hadn't seen the griffins yet, but from Daedelus' description they were a serious threat.

Helen was half hoping, half dreading that Lucas would be with his family, but he hadn't returned from wherever it was he had disappeared to, nor had he told anyone his plans. As usual. He somehow managed to show up when she didn't want him to, and be absent when she needed him.

"He'll know we're in Hades as soon as we appear. He'll come to us," Orion said, guessing what Helen was fuming about.

Grateful she didn't have the time to be present for the stilted reunion between Antigone, Castor, and Pallas, Helen took Orion's hand and portaled them to Hades.

They didn't appear inside Lucas' palace, as Helen had always done before. Instead, they appeared in a twilit land of gloom and fog. A flat, charcoal-gray body of water hunkered under a pewter sky, lapping phlegmatically at the shore. It was Ocean, the great Elemental that lay at the edge of all things.

Shadows gathered, and Orion spun to meet the shape coming out of them, angling Helen behind one of his shoulders as he did so.

The shape proved to be Lucas, but it took a moment for Orion to register him as a friend and not an enemy. Orion stayed tensed for a beat longer than he should, as if he had not decided yet if he could trust him. Lucas cleared away some of the black shadows clinging to him and stopped advancing. He waited that extra moment for Orion to relax, as if he was becoming accustomed to negotiating the disquieting effect he had on other people.

"We should get going," Lucas said in a subdued voice. "This is not Hades, but Cimmeria. Time passes here."

Lucas gestured with a hand and they started walking along the shore of Ocean toward a line of craggy cliffs that rose up like a black wall from the flat and sandy shore.

"Where are we going?" Orion asked.

"I've been thinking about how to find the Fates, like Helen suggested," Lucas said. "And there might be a way. We're going to the other side of those cliffs."

The cliffs looked like they were made of black volcanic rock, which would be sharp, unstable, and a nightmare to climb. The jagged peaks that seemed as if they were trying to bite the sky did not rise up very far, but Helen still didn't like the idea of having to climb them. In the Underworld, Scion abilities were vastly diminished.

"Why not portal us there?" she asked.

"I can't," Lucas replied, glancing past Orion to look at her.

"Cimmeria is part of the Underworld, and its borders are left open to all who are already down here, but it's not Hades. I don't control it and I've never been to where we're going."

Lucas retained his powers anywhere in the Underworld, just like both he and Helen had their powers on earth, but neither of them could portal to a place they had never been to if it was outside of their realms. They'd have to walk there.

As they continued along in silence, it nagged at Helen that Lucas hadn't received them in his palace, but in Cimmeria. It was as if he had known what Helen was going to ask of him. She used to accept that Lucas was always one step ahead of her, that he was good at figuring out what people were going to do, and that he was just smarter than everyone else. But now, rather than being impressed, and slightly annoyed that Lucas was mysterious and all-knowing as he always had been in the past, it unsettled her. He did not have a window into her or anyone else's thoughts, yet he still knew things he shouldn't.

"How did you know that Orion and I were coming here to find the Fates?" she finally asked.

Lucas didn't reply right away. "You had been talking about finding them," he replied, choosing his words carefully.

Helen stopped walking, forcing everyone to stop. "Lucas. How?"

"I pay attention," he replied, his expression closed.

It wasn't a lie, but Helen knew he wasn't being completely honest. "Can you hear us talking even if you're not there?"

"No."

Helen heard no lie. Lucas started walking again, leaving Helen to glare mistrustfully at his back. Orion touched her arm.

"It's highly suspicious," Orion said, validating what Helen was feeling.

"Everything he does lately is suspicious," Helen whispered when she figured Lucas was out of earshot. Orion nodded, his mouth set in a grim line, as they started after Lucas.

When they reached the base of the cliffs the rocks proved themselves to be just as treacherous as Helen had assumed. Helen tried to disengage gravity and fly, but she felt only a faint release that was not enough to untether her from the ground.

"Our powers are diminished here," Lucas told them. He looked around, annoyed. "This place is like a diluted version of the world."

That's exactly what it felt like here, like they were insubstantial and ghost-like. Helen felt tired and worn thin. They had only ascended a few feet before the rock beneath Helen's feet broke away and she had to put her hands down to stop herself from sliding. She gasped, knowing instantly that she had injured herself. The Cestus either did not work here, or its power was greatly diminished.

Orion steadied her. "Let me see," he said, inspecting her bloody palms. "This is hopeless. It's like trying to climb razor wire. Is there another way?" he asked Lucas.

Lucas looked uncertain. "There is," he finally admitted. "But you have to allow me to do something you might not like."

"What?" Helen asked.

Lucas came back down the slope until he was level with

them. "Shadow traveling. You've seen me do it. The experience would be unsettling for you."

"Can you do it, though?" Helen asked. "I can't even fly here."

Lucas nodded. "Wherever there are shadows, I can pass from one to another. Not even this place can stop me from doing it. Being a Shadowmaster is not a talent that I have. It's something that I am."

This was how Lucas had seemed to appear out of dark corners and cross rooms without moving. He could slip from shadow to shadow in an instant, essentially appearing anywhere there was an absence of light without having to make a portal.

"Better to be unsettled than cut to pieces," Orion decided. "I'm sure we'll manage."

Lucas looked sad as he came toward them—sad, but still menacing. The way he moved reminded Helen of all the old legends of night creatures, the ones that come swathed in darkness to steal your blood or your breath. Lucas swooped down and wrapped around them like a smothering black cloak. Helen couldn't see or breathe, and it felt like a thousand cold hands were brushing over her skin under her clothes. But in an actual blink of the eye, it was over. The three of them were standing in a shadowy nook at the base of the other side of the cliff. Orion looked like Helen felt. Spooked.

"I told you, you wouldn't like it," Lucas said, turning away from them.

"The hands—" Orion said, breaking off with a grimace. "What are they?"

Lucas' shoulders rose and fell with a sigh. He still had his back to them. "Me," he admitted. "I have to lift and carry you along with me. I am the shadows."

"You become *a* shadow, or *all* of them?" Helen asked, having her suspicions about which it was.

"All of them."

"So every shadow could have a bit of you in it?"

"Potentially," he said, glancing back at her. "But mentally I can't be everywhere at once."

She wondered if he could see her through the slender darkness created by the edges of things. Or if, tucked inside the night, he could wrap himself around her. She flushed at the thought, knowing somehow that he could. The darkness between her clothes and her skin was enough of a shadow for him to slip into if he wanted.

"Is that how you know things you shouldn't? Are you listening to all of us?" Helen asked, truly afraid of him for the first time.

Lucas faced them, frustrated. "I hear bits and pieces. It's too much to listen to everything all the time, and it's not like I want to. I don't have a choice." He gestured at the shadows that clung to him like smoky cobwebs. Helen had heard them whispering in the past. "I only hear conversations if I'm inside a shadow in the room when they're happening. I heard you at Ladon's cave and at my parent's house because I was there both times."

"Hidden," Helen said, not at all surprised. Lucas had always kept secrets from her. Now she was wondering where else Lucas had been hiding and watching.

He knew what she was thinking. "I'm not stalking you," he

said with a huff. "You think I'd want to watch what you've been doing lately?"

He wasn't lying. Helen didn't have to hear a lie to know that. She'd thought she'd wanted him to think the worst of her. It was his fault she was behaving the way she was and she wanted him to know how he'd damaged her. But the aversion she saw in his eyes, the pinched expression that bordered on disgust, was not at all what she wanted.

"We should keep moving," Orion said, brushing past Lucas.

"That way," Lucas directed, pointing across the sandy crescent-shaped cove to a cavern in the rock.

There was no moon by which to see, but a dim, wavering light permeated the atmosphere enough to make out some details. The arch of the obsidian entrance was too regular, too polished to be natural. Glinting sand that was level and hard-packed fanned out from the front of the cavern like a carpet. Ocean lay across from the cavern, as still and viscous as mercury.

"Who lives there?" Helen asked.

"The Graeae," Lucas replied as he started toward the cavern. "They know where everything is."

"Except for that one time they misplaced their eye," Orion said under his breath.

Even those with only a passing knowledge of Greek mythology knew the story of Perseus. At one point in his great quest, he and Hermes went to the Graeae to find the location of the nymphs of the north. Perseus stole the single eye the Graeae shared between the three of them in order to coerce them into telling him. If the Fates could be found, the Graeae were the only beings who might possibly know where they were.

"I don't think getting their eye away from them is going to be as easy as it was for Perseus," Helen said.

"We'll have to find another way to convince them to help us," Lucas agreed.

They arrived at the entrance to the cavern and Helen held out an arm, stopping Lucas and Orion. "Should we, like, *knock*, or should we have brought gifts? Or weapons?" she asked uncertainly. She had no idea what to expect.

"Or both. Flowers and a hand grenade," Orion said, smirking jokingly at Helen. She elbowed him in response.

"They know we're here," Lucas said. Helen and Orion shared an uneasy look and followed Lucas inside the gloom of the cave.

A fire crackled against the far side of the cavern and threw dancing shadows up the polished obsidian walls. The smoke was not thick, but it smelled acrid with resin and powerful herbs that made Helen's throat itch and her eyes burn. As they approached the fire, they saw curls of gray vapor rising from a brazier suspended over it. Three hunched shapes moved in the wavering light on the other side of the flames.

"Deino, the eye," hissed Enyo, the gray lump in the middle of the huddle behind the fire, thumping the sister to her right.

"I have it," squawked Deino, the one on the left in a high-pitched voice. She gasped. "Sisters! He is as handsome as Hades himself!"

"Give it here!" croaked Enyo.

There was a flash of feathers, and the shadow of an outstretched wing rose on the wall behind them, only to disappear again when the tussle between the sisters settled down.

"Round of lip and lissome of limb as his mother goddess.

Oh, how the Weaving Three hate him!" Deino said, collapsing into a fit of unpleasant laughter.

There was another flurry of movement. Strange, bird-like shadows were cast upon the wall behind them. When the feathers had settled, the middle sister had the eye. Though the air seemed to ripple and the flashes of light and dark were disorienting, Helen could see the eye clearly now that Enyo held it up to her forehead and trained it on her. It was as big as a grapefruit with a pale gray iris, large black pupil, and red veins forking through the yellowing white of the lidless sclera.

"And there *she* is," Enyo said, her voice hissing and winding around Helen spine. "Weep, sisters, at her beauty. It is the death of all things."

"Give me the eye!" shrieked the still unnamed one on the left.

"My turn!" insisted Deino on the right.

"It is not!"

Lucas stepped forward, and the shadows that flashed so starkly seemed to settle and lose some of their harsh edges, allowing them to fully see the three primordial hags. They were gray all over. Long, wiry strands of gray hair thatched their heads and tangled about their shoulders. Gray skin hung in craggy slabs on their faces, arms, and hands, and gray feathered wings hunkered over their withered shoulders like moth-eaten robes. Their lower halves were not human at all, but that of swans, with scaly legs and webbed feet.

"Daughters of Phorcys and Ceto," Lucas said, his tone polite yet commanding. "We come to ask a favor."

The Gray Women spoke rapidly, their phrases blending

together as if they were one person, and only distinguishable by the different tones of their voices.

"Then ask it," said Enyo in her voice like a hissing goose.

"We may grant it," said the unnamed one in a high-pitched screech like a raptor.

"Or not," cawed Deino like a crow.

"As we see fit," finished Enyo, making it clear that the chance of that was slim to none.

"We seek the Moirae," said Orion. "Can you please tell us where they are?"

"Such nice manners," said the unnamed one, cooing this time like a dove as she snatched the eye and placed it on her forehead. "I think we ought to eat him first."

Orion recoiled and turned widened eyes in Lucas' direction. Lucas put him off with a subtle gesture of his hand and continued.

"Sisters, we can offer you much in return for your help," he promised.

"Like what?" hissed Enyo.

"A palace next to yours in Hades?" tittered the unnamed one.

"I should want a large pool like his," peeped Deino.

"Yes, a pool in which to dip our feet," agreed the unnamed one in her tremulous voice that could, at any moment, tip into panic.

"But a pool is not worth the wrath of the Moirae," hissed Enyo.

"Pity. Well, at least we get to eat them."

The three of them spoke again as if with one breath, their

thoughts and voices seamless, all the while their hands, ever in conflict, snatched and scrabbled for possession the eye. It occurred to Helen that it would be easy to inch closer in the confusion of wings and elbows and take the eye away from them, but she decided against it. She pitied them. She did not want to steal their eye, even though they apparently planned to eat them.

"Where's the tooth?" said Deino, reaching now for her sister's mouths to find which of them had the one tooth that they shared between them.

"You said I was to be the death of all things," Helen said, interrupting another round of squabbling. "Does that include you?"

The Graeae paused in their heretofore ceaseless grabbing. The one in the middle, Enyo, had the eye pressed to her forehead and she peered at Helen through it.

"Do you know what they call me, girl?" she asked.

"I know your true names," Lucas replied. "Deino is Dread, Pemphredo is Alarm, and you, Enyo, are Horror. The Waster of Cities."

"Yet, even I am not so horrible as she," Enyo hissed. "We *all* will perish in her lightning. It is her fate."

Helen shook her head and tried not to cry. These three cannibals looked at her and saw something even worse than they were. Everyone, even the people who had known Helen her whole life, saw destruction in her. Matt believed she was the Tyrant, and Claire had agreed with him. Though Lucas didn't explicitly say he thought she'd be the cause of ecpyrosis, as soon as he saw his List of the Dead, he had Daedelus seek her out to explain what ecpyrosis was. She knew that deep down Lucas believed she was going to do it, even if he wouldn't admit it.

Cassandra had seen it in a vision. Antigone saw it, too. Helen's own mother believed Helen was going to be the end of all things, that's why she'd named her Helen. If all of these people, some of whom had known her since she was born, believed she was capable of ending *everything*, she had to entertain the notion that they were right. Even if she choked on the injustice of it.

She felt Orion take her hand and looked over at him, blinking back tears, nodding at him to communicate that she was okay. This wasn't about her feelings. She pulled herself together.

"And are you happy with that fate?" Helen asked, her voice sounding much steadier than she would have credited.

The three sisters stood motionless with surprise for a moment before they started in on their reaching and hand-slapping again.

"Happy?"

"What can you mean by this?"

"What is 'happy' to Fate?"

"Fate cares not for happy or sad. Fate cares only that it is fulfilled."

They spoke so quickly, hands and wings flashing wildly, that Helen could no longer tell which of them had said what.

"If you tell us where the Moirae dwell, I might be able to stop this," Helen said. "Help us and you might live. Don't, and you'll definitely die. It's up to you."

Enyo took up the eye and peered at Helen. "Not much of a bargain," she said in her whispering voice.

Helen shrugged. "Yeah, well... too bad. I'm not enjoying my options much, either."

Enyo's mouth lifted in the barest of smiles before the Graeae fell into a huddle. Three pairs of wings festooned with enormous gray feathers that stuck out at odd angles stretched above them, casting crooked shadows on the wall behind them.

"We will tell you a truth," said Deino.

"And from this truth you must discern the way," hissed Enyo.

"Everything shares a border with Hades," shrieked Pemphredo in her perpetually alarmed voice.

"For no one, not even the Moirae, are more than a shadow's width away from death," hissed Enyo. "This is the truth."

"But, where?" demanded Lucas. "There's no place—"

"It is not a *place* in which they live," said Deino.

"It is a state of being," tittered Pemphredo nervously.

"That which they exist to tame," hissed Enyo.

"Go now, Hand of Darkness. There's no more we can tell you without angering the Moirae," Deino finished.

Lucas tried to get more clues from them, but the Graeae only repeated the riddle several times before Pemphredo started whining to her sisters about how delicious Orion looked. Helen pulled Lucas away, still arguing with them, before somebody ended up in a pot.

Outside the cave, Lucas paced up and down the length of beach where Ocean met the lifeless sand. "I *know* all the borders to Hades," he said, frustrated.

"How many lands are there?" Orion asked. "Time stands still in Hades, right? Maybe with endless amounts of time we can check all of them."

Lucas calmed himself before answering. "There are thousands, and every time we crossed into one of those lands time will start flowing again in most of them."

Reminded that the clock was ticking, Lucas made a faint movement with one of his hands, and in a flash of cold they were all standing in his private rooms inside the palace of Hades.

"You have all the time you need to rest here," he said, and food and drinks appeared in front of them.

"Where are you going?" asked Helen.

"I have to go deal with a few things."

"What?" Helen asked, shocked. She stepped closer to him and put a hand on his forearm in case he tried to portal away. "What do you have to do that's more important than this?"

"My job. People are always dying, Helen," he replied. "And right now, an army is using one of the Roads of Erebus as a shortcut."

Helen removed her hand. She knew Erebus was where the dead gathered for Charon to ferry them across the river Styx. Many paths threaded through Erebus, and the dead were said to walk them from where they had died to the banks of the Styx. Although she'd never seen the Roads of Erebus for herself, she had encountered souls on their way there when she was wandering around Hades, descending night after night, sleepless and dreamless.

"Like, a *dead* army?" Helen tried not to cringe, but she'd seen too many zombie movies.

Lucas chuckled under his breath as if he couldn't stop himself. "No. They're alive. But I have to find out what they're doing and deal with it."

"As soon as you leave me, the Fates will be able to see you. They'll know the Graeae gave us a clue as to where they live, and they'll start to work against it," Orion reminded him. "Take us with you."

Lucas hesitated for a moment, then he flicked his fingertips and Helen felt the cold of a portal.

CHAPTER 7

Palamedes and Plutus watched the angry red and black line of fire eat its way across the savannah. There was nothing they could do to stop it.

The centaurs and the griffins had already left the battlefield. There was no adversary here to fight but nature.

"Do you think it will go out?" Palamedes asked, already knowing the answer.

"Not until it hits the river," Plutus answered. "And maybe not even then. The river is dry."

They rode down the rise from which they had observed the battle, which they hadn't quite lost but hadn't exactly won, to where the Arimaspi were massing. Once the wounded were tended, they would use the underground passageways that honeycombed the earth, known as the Roads of Erebus, to chase after their multiplying foes.

Geryon's lieutenant, Arne, the stern one who had initially

opposed them, was giving orders to her sergeants. She saw the servants of Tyche and met them with a grim set to her jaw.

"Geryon will need reinforcements if those that ran from this battle head north to face him," Arne said. "The Roads of Erebus speed us from place to place, but we still cannot travel as quickly as they do through Zeus' portals."

Nemesis had given them access to the Roads of Erebus along with guides so they would not become lost and join the dammed that wandered for eternity in that shadow land. Time stopped on the Roads of Erebus, but they still had to travel *to* those roads before they reached a destination that Zeus' portals brought their foes to immediately. Twice now the Arimaspi had arrived at the battle to find that the land was already burning.

"We go North, then, to aid Geryon?" Plutus asked.

Arne shook her head. "That battle will have come and gone by the time we get there. We must regroup with Geryon on the Roads of Erebus and decide then what to do."

Palamedes got the distinct impression that Arne suspected there was nothing left *to* do. The Arimaspi were legendary fighters, but they could only fight what they could catch. For now, their foes were staying one step ahead.

"What I don't understand is what they want," Arne said in frustration. "It's like they're taunting us. Trying to draw us into battle, but then running away when we come."

Plutus' mouth tightened into a line. "Maybe we are not the opponent they seek."

His coin appeared in his fingers. It flipped quickly in the air and landed solidly in his palm. Again, Plutus did not check to see if it was heads or tails.

. . .

Hector had spent the day prowling around the house, his eyes flicking from one window to the next. He could feel a fight happening somewhere. No, more than a fight. A war.

If he closed his eyes, he could see it. He could *go* there, somehow, like Helen and her portals. He knew that if he willed it, he could be wherever the war was. He would just appear in the middle of it, summoned by the smoke and blood and the battle cries of the combatants. The warriors called to him, each side praying that he joined them so that they could win the day. He could feel their prayers. Their fear and their adrenaline were their sacrifices to him, and soon some of them would give up their lives in his name.

His aunt tried to get him to eat. The twins tried to get him to talk. He could do neither. Castor, Pallas, and Daedelus watched him as he went from room to room in a perpetual loop of his territory, but they said nothing. They marked his paranoid prowling, and they knew better than to interfere.

He heard people speaking but he couldn't make out what they were saying. He heard Andy and Ariadne, knew their voices sounded tense, but actual words were eluding him again. They had no meaning anymore.

At sundown, Andy walked toward the front door with a backpack over her shoulder. His hand shot out and he grabbed her arm, stopping her.

"Go," he said, pointing back inside the house to stairs. "Back upstairs."

She tried to shake him off, and he couldn't allow it. One of *his* was trying to go outside where many of *them* were going to appear at any moment.

"Hector, let me go! I can't stay here," she said, struggling and pulling. She was like a hawk in his hand, yanking against her jesses. "I can't be around you anymore."

"You can't leave."

He heard others coming to bargain for her. They said what were probably reasonable words, none of which he could hear through the roaring in his ears. He saw his father trying to calm him. He saw Daedelus, a great warrior, trying to unwind his hand from Andy's arm, and he simply waited for them to stop. He was not letting Andy go.

"You're mine. Go back upstairs," he told her.

Andy stopped struggling, and really looked at him. As she studied his face her expression changed from desperation to curiosity. "What's going on with you?" she asked.

Hector looked for the words he knew he had in him somewhere. Someone tried to speak for him, but Andy silenced them. She framed his face with her cool hands and he took the first deep breath he'd had all day. She would be able to decipher anything he said. He just had to speak. The red tinge he had been looking through for hours faded and he saw the world clearly.

"They're coming," he said, all of his words restored. "Tonight. The moon will set after midnight. In the darkest hour, Zeus will send everything that belongs to him. Griffins, centaurs, giants. They're all coming."

Andy didn't need to question how he knew the things he did because she understood him. She had always understood him, even when she hadn't fully understood herself.

"Okay," she said and he knew he could release her. She wasn't going to try to leave him. She turned to face the others. "We need to prepare."

. . .

Helen had never felt so disoriented in her life.

Not only did the air seem to waver as if they were inside a mirage, but strange lights would also appear in the middle distance, like a house light turned on in the deepest fog, and then the light would drift and fade as they neared. If they had followed the lights or allowed their minds to drift for even a moment while looking at them, the lights would have drawn them off the path. The Roads of Erebus were treacherous. To lose the path is to be lost forever. Lucas said he knew where they were going, though he had never been this way before. He said he understood the Roads of Erebus, though that was little comfort to Helen and Orion.

"I think I read something like this in a fairy tale once," Orion said as they passed over a rise and saw the vague, shimmering outline of a castle in the distance.

"The Roads of Erebus have had many names. They were once thought to be the land of the Fey..." Lucas replied, trailing off as he saw something up the path. "There they are."

Helen had no idea what he was talking about, and then suddenly the fog parted and an entire army seemed to appear before them on the winding road. Orion startled and she felt a little better. At least she wasn't the only one who hadn't noticed thousands of warriors on horseback marching toward them. The four leaders at the front of the column seemed just as surprised as Helen and Orion. Their horses reared under them as they pulled up on their reins and shouted with alarm.

Lucas stepped forward to initiate introductions, but Helen recognized two of them right away and spoke first.

"We met in Las Vegas," she said. Lucas raised an eyebrow at her and she waved him away with a mumbled, "Hector," before addressing the guy with the coin again. "You're the Servants of Tyche. Are you the small gods Dionysus told me about?"

"Two of them," Plutus replied before introducing himself and his companions properly. "And though we still serve Tyche, we are here at the behest of another."

"Who gave you access?" Lucas asked. When they didn't immediately answer Lucas continued. "If I don't know why you use my roads, I will assume you use them against me."

"Nemesis," Palamedes admitted. "We serve Nemesis and she means to help you." He rolled his eyes in a thoroughly human way. "Though she has a roundabout way of doing things that I don't quite understand."

"Palamedes," Plutus said, sighing as if they'd been through this many times before. "Our choices must be of our free will, and so must theirs, or she would be meddling."

"If ever there was a time to meddle, I'd say it would be right about now, before the world ended, wouldn't you?" Palamedes said.

"That would make her no better than the Fates. Her whole point is—"

Helen smiled at their bickering, thinking that the two of them were like an old married couple, when they were interrupted.

"You're *her*," said the enormous warrior woman at the front of the column. "The one who's supposed to end it all."

"I am," Helen replied warily. "Who are you?"

The warrior woman introduced herself as Arne, and the big man next to her as Geryon, King of the Arimaspi.

There was something about the way Arne's hand hovered over the hilt of her sword that made Helen think she was considering drawing it. Though Helen had her own feelings about getting stabbed, she was rational enough to see the sense in such a choice for Arne. If Helen was dead, the end couldn't come. Lucas was also following Arne's line of thought and angled himself in front of Helen. The road seemed to shrink and the gloom that surrounded them darkened even more. Lucas' body stood out more sharply, like they were all just shadows and he was the only real thing left in the world.

"Arne!" Geryon scolded. "We are here to aid the Scions. Not make war with them."

Arne relaxed her posture at her king's command, but she looked chagrined about it. "She's the one Zeus wants," she said bitterly.

The oppressive darkness lessened and the shrinking feeling expanded back to normal again as Lucas relaxed.

"Explain," he said, and the Arimaspi king told them how for days now they had been playing a game of catch up with their foes.

"They see us take the field, set their fires, and then disappear," Geryon said. "At first, we flattered ourselves that it was out of fright, but when the centaurs joined them and outnumbered us by two to one, and still they ran, it became clear that we were not the combatants they sought."

"Why would they want to fight *you*, though?" Orion asked Helen, baffled. "You'd destroy them."

Helen had no answer. She looked questioningly to Lucas, who shook his head. "How do you know where to meet them in battle?" Lucas asked Plutus.

"We follow the guide given to us by Hecate." He half turned in his saddle and a ferret-like creature ran from his horse's hindquarters, up his back and over his shoulder to stand with forepaws braced against the pommel of his saddle.

"Gale!" Helen and Orion said at the same time.

Gale chirped and then jumped from the horse, ran past them, and into the arms of Hecate who had appeared behind Helen, Lucas, and Orion.

Lucas gave the Titan a wry smile. He'd never fully trusted her. "You use my roads without due payment," he said.

"Careful, Darkness. Hades rules here still," she replied, equal parts amused and annoyed by Lucas' assumed authority. "And he gave me leave to use *his* roads."

Hecate's tri-faced head flashed, prism-like, as she turned it to look at the gathered host. "Zeus sends his armies to attack your Scion family," she said, the forward face addressing Helen. "They appear on your island now. This army will not be enough."

Helen and Orion tensed, ready to move, but Lucas stilled them with a gesture, reminding them that as long as they were on the Roads of Erebus, no time passed.

"But if we go to find the Fates, who knows if time will start up again in that realm?" Helen said urgently, grabbing Lucas' wrist.

"No, we should go to our family before we try to find the Moirae," Lucas agreed. He looked down at the hand she'd placed on his forearm and, realizing she was still touching him, snatched it back. He then faced Geryon and Plutus. "I don't know how this became your fight, but if you know of any other small gods who happen to have an army, now's the time."

Lucas wasn't being entirely serious, but to his surprise, Palamedes spoke up.

"Actually, I might."

Helen portaled with Orion to the alley behind the nightclub in Los Angeles, where she had last seen Dionysus, and immediately pulled Orion into a jog. They came around to the side entrance, passed the bouncers lifting the red velvet ropes, and went inside the thumping nightclub.

"Wow. Is it always like this?" Orion shouted over the din.

It was a particularly wild night. The dance floor was packed so tightly that it seemed to swell and pulse as one mass. The ever-moving lights had to fight their way through the chemically created smoke, making clouds of color from which faces, slick with sweat, would appear as if from nowhere. Bare skin was abundant. There was always someone who took their shirt off on the dance floor, but to Helen it looked like nearly everyone was in various stages of undress. A face flashed in front of her and she realized that the revelers had their eyes closed. Nearly everyone on the dance floor did. It was odd for everyone to look so uniformly rapturous. Usually, there was at least one of two sober people.

"Something's going on," Helen said, turning to search the bar.

The maenads were on top of it, a whirlwind of pumping fists and flinging hair. They weren't even pouring anymore, just whipping the crowd up into a frenzy. Their clothes were torn and a dark, thick liquid stained their hands and washed down their chins from their mouths. There was no way to tell what color the liquid was in the changing lights, but Helen had a feeling it might be red.

Helen noticed there was a banner behind the bar. One section of it had been torn down, but the rest was hanging on. It said *End of the World Par—*.

She spotted Dionysus behind the turntables opposite the bar and, grabbing Orion by the hand, portaled to him. Dionysus jumped at their appearance and pulled the headphones off his ears.

"We need your help!," Helen shouted over the frantic music. She portaled all three of them to the liquor room behind the bar. Dionysus was startled to find himself transported, but he adjusted as Helen quickly explained the situation.

"Look, I realize you need an army," Dionysus replied when she was done, turning his palms up in a helpless gesture. "But the maenads aren't soldiers. They're pure chaos, and just as likely to attack your side as Zeus'."

"Let me worry about that. How many maenads are there?" Helen asked.

"About six hundred. I have to keep them separate because together they'd wreck a city."

"Or an army," Orion said. "We don't have a lot of time."

Dionysus shook his head, chuffing. "It's either brilliant or the dumbest thing ever." He grinned suddenly at Helen. "But what the hell, right? It is the end of the world."

Orion shot her a slightly worried look, as if to ask if Helen was sure about this, but what choice did they have?

"I can get us anywhere in an instant," Helen said to Dionysus, "Do you know how to find all the maenads, and fast? We're running out of time."

"Then let's go," he said, shrugging a shoulder like they were talking about going to an afterparty and not a battle. Helen figured he'd been torn limb from limb every winter solstice for a couple for thousands of years. To him war probably looked exactly like Christmas.

"Where to?" Helen asked.

"New York," Dionysus replied, flicking through the browser on his phone. He pulled up a map and showed her the exact location.

Helen portaled them to the top of the bar knowing everyone in the crowd was already so entranced they'd just think they were hallucinating. If they lived to remember this night at all. She had never tried to stretch her portals this wide before, but she couldn't think of a reason why she shouldn't be able to. Portals required no energy from her. It wasn't like a bigger one would be harder to make than a smaller one. As long as she was at the center of it, she could make it as wide as she wanted.

A flash of searing cold, and they started skipping around the world. New York to London, London to Pairs, Paris to Rome—snatching up maenads as quickly as Dionysus could point to the next spot on a map. The maenads didn't mind dropping everything to be gathered up with no warning. As soon as they saw Dionysus, they flashed their too-sharp teeth and eagerly followed him to whatever frenzy he had planned for them.

Hector watched the moon lower toward the horizon, his anxiety sinking with the light. Soon, the battle would begin and everything would be all right. He could relax when the lines were drawn, the fighting began, and choices were made once and for all.

It wasn't the pain or suffering of battle he craved, but the truth of it. Every combatant knew what side they fought for, and every confrontation had a winner and a loser. It was clean and real and it was honest in a way that the thousands of little deceptions and atrocities that were hidden behind the placid mask of peacetime could never be.

Calmer now, he could understand what the others were saying. For the past few hours they had been using the abilities of the Romans, Leda and Niobe, to evacuate the mortals on their part of the island. The Romans had been going door to door, telling a lie about a gas leak, and using their power to influence the mortals within, getting them to take shelter on the other side of the island.

"Tell Leda and Niobe to come back," Hector said. "Zeus will have them kidnapped and use them for ransom if they do not return to us now." He looked to his father and Daedelus, knowing they would be the most effected by such a ploy.

"Niobe is saying that there are still some people further down the beach," Jason said, holding his phone away from his ear to speak.

"She is to come back now. It's time," Hector said. He went to the case in his father's private study.

"I have the key to—" Pallas said, stopping when he saw that Hector was in the process of putting his fist through the front of it.

Hector took down his grandfather's war hammer. It sang in his hand.

"Arm yourselves," he told them, walking to another part of the house and another display case.

When did his family start keeping their weapons in cages? He broke a beautiful helmet and shield out of their prison. He put the helmet on his head and slid his other hand through the straps on the back of the shield. He felt anchored now, like he wouldn't blow away with the changeable wind.

He told them who was to fight and who was to stay inside the house and repel anyone who would come around from the rear to attack. A few of those told to stay inside the house did not like it, but they eventually obeyed. His mate had to be told several times, but when Hector made it clear that he would tie her up himself she settled down with the Healer, the Artist, the returned Romans, the Oracles, and the humans who were a part of this family. His family, Hector remembered, though it was like dragging his mind through mud to see them as people and not as chess pieces. Andy, Jason, Claire, Antigone, Cassandra, Noel, Kate, Leda, and Niobe. Those were their names.

The soldiers helped each other into armor and followed him outside to the battlefield. The quickest to ready themselves were his sister, who stood to his right, shining silver in the last of the moonlight, and Daedelus, who did not shine. He was not immortal, but Hector could feel his strength digging down into the ground like ropes of rock and clay. Besides his sister of the moon, this warrior of water and rock was the strongest among them. He was worthy of the front line. Behind him, Hector could feel the heat of his fellow Thebans, the sons of the sun.

From the shore came a strange outline. The torso of a man seemed to undulate toward them, surrounded by a halo of spikes. The dragon-man Ladon came from the sea to stand beside his brother.

Hector looked to the sky where he knew his goddess of thunder and lightning would appear. Then to the shadows in which he knew the Hand of Darkness listened and watched. They would come to the battle. But first, their adversaries would take the field.

The griffins were the vanguard, appearing on a cold wind. They had the head and wings of enormous eagles and the bodies of lions. Breathing fire and running right at the Scions with their claws scrabbling in the sand, Hector let his war hammer slide between his hands until his palm hit the knob at the end of the hilt. With his war hammer extended to its full length, he ran out to meet the shrieking creatures and swung away through their front line in sweeping arcs. Behind them were the centaurs and the giants—true giants, as tall as skyscrapers.

It was the giants Hector wanted.

His shield glowing from the fire of the griffins, Hector smelled smoke and blood and heard the battle cries of both family and foe.

It was heaven.

CHAPTER 8

Helen felt a little dizzy. A medium-sized amount of hectic. And a lot drunk.

One of the factors she hadn't considered was that the mere presence of the maenads and Dionysus had an inebriating effect on anyone who joined their ranks, and as Helen gathered up more and more maenads, she and Orion were starting to get caught up in their delirious magic.

"Yeah, sorry about that," Dionysus said when Helen lost her balance and swayed into him. "It's not something I'm doing *to* you, by the way. It's who I am. I can't turn it off."

"Just like Lucas," Helen said, but she didn't have the mental fortitude to elucidate further.

Helen couldn't fight a battle hammered out of her tree, and somehow as she portaled from place to place this became Lucas' fault. He always considered extenuating circumstances like this. Why hadn't he this time? When they got to Honolulu, their last stop in their trek around the world, Orion grabbed her arm, looking worried.

"I'm wasted," he confided. "Can you fix this?"

"I keep trying to, every time we portal," Helen said. "But it's not working. It's like each time we portal, I'm doing another shot."

"That's because you're taking me," Dionysus said like it was obvious. "You'll sober up once you put some distance between us."

The maenads were starting to do that spinning thing they did, grabbing each other by the wrists and whirling around until they suddenly let go and flung themselves into the crowd.

"They're just about to lose it," Dionysus warned.

Even drunk, Helen didn't need to be told twice. She portaled them to Hades.

"Lucas!" Helen called out, catching his eye through the throng of maenads. "You have to portal them. I can't do another shot or I'll barf."

Lucas looked momentarily confused, and then angry. "What happened?" he shouted at Dionysus.

"It's not my fault!" Dionysus argued. "I told her this was probably a bad idea."

"Let's just *go* before they eat the horses!" Palamedes shouted while trying to kick one of the maenads away from his mount.

"What a mess," Lucas mumbled, and then he told everyone to prepare themselves. The fighting had already begun. "I'm going to put you directly into the battle in the places I think you are the most needed. It will be shocking. Be ready."

He sent everyone but Helen. Then, he turned to her, catching her by the elbow.

"I can't join you," he said, not able to meet her eye. He was looking down at where his fingertips were barely grazing the curve of her arm. He pulled his hand away.

"I know," she replied, wishing he'd put his hand back.

No one would fight Lucas even if he did try to take the field. In fact, Zeus would probably portal his army away. If someone did somehow manage to kill or incapacitate Lucas, they would become the Hand of Darkness, and no one wanted his job. She wanted to say she was sorry for him, but she didn't let herself. She couldn't feel compassion for him, or she was as good as lost.

"I'll be watching from every shadow," he said.

Then, he portaled Helen into the sky above his house.

Hector felt the change on the battlefield as soon as they arrived. Though he had never seen these new combatants before, he knew instinctively they fought for his side. Which was good news for the Scions because they were vastly outnumbered and about to be overwhelmed.

Orion had appeared, fully armed, and back-to-back with Daedelus. His father had spun around, sword pointed. Daedelus allowed his posture to relax when he realized it was his son. "We brought an army."

"Fall back!" Hector ordered. They had formed a defensive circle and they were already surrounded. "Regroup with the new forces!"

He saw Pallas cut through a centaur and then pause to look around and get his bearings. Though they had only been fighting for a matter of minutes, his father was covered in singe marks and he'd taken several small injuries.

"Who are they?" Castor demanded, pointing his sword at the mounted soldiers now charging into battle.

"Arimaspi," Orion said, slightly slurring the word.

"Are you *drunk*?" Hector asked, shocked. "Fall back!" he ordered, not waiting for an answer.

The cavalry had to take the front line to be the most effective, but before anyone could make their way behind the Arimaspi, they heard blood-curdling shrieks.

Whirling pockets of snarling women were ululating and falling upon centaurs, griffins, and giants alike. It was only their positioning that made them attack the Scion's foes, though. They weren't aware of who or what they attacked. Like bombs, they simply went off where they'd been flung.

"Maenads?" Ariadne asked disbelievingly as she stared at them with a grimace of dismay on her face.

Hector glared at Orion.

"Okay. One army and six hundred maenads," Orion said. "But Helen said she could contain them with portals. Move them around if they got too close to one of us."

"Where *is* Helen?" Hector yelled as he and his family continued their fight toward the Arimaspi line.

Orion pushed a griffin back with his shield and then paused to look around for her. "She'll be here," he promised.

The centaurs were scrambling to form their own line to meet the Arimaspi, but the maenads were tearing through their ranks with abandon, making order impossible. Even with this new influx of fighters, Hector knew it wasn't going to be enough. Zeus had responded to the Scion's fresh ranks by sending more of his own army into the fray. Griffins were popping out of thin air, thousands of them, and behind them at the ocean's edge, the hulking outlines of giants were appearing so quickly they were starting to crowd out the horizon.

Helen appeared with a crack of thunder and white-blue streak of lightning. The lumbering line of giants turned to meet her, reaching up to snatch her out of the sky. Helen soared out of reach and sent forks of devastating lighting at them, instantly dropping the creatures where they stood. They fell down into the surf, still convulsing, but already dead. The Arimaspi sent up a cheer. Hector raised his arms above his head and bellowed his war cry with them. There was nothing Zeus could send that came close to Helen's power. The Scions had as good as won.

"You, there!" Hector called out to the front line of the Arimaspi. They turned to him as one, their awed faces reflecting back the glow of his godhead. "On me!"

Legs pumping, chest heaving, the pure joy of running into battle with the pounding of hooves behind him, and the smell of smoke and blood filling up his head was unlike anything Hector had ever known.

He had become exactly what he was always meant to be.

Palamedes hated war. That's why he'd invented dice.

Dicing was a civilized way to resolve disputes. There was skill and luck involved in equal measures, just as there was in war, but with none of the fear, pain, and death. That, and he'd been exceptionally bored on the beaches of Troy. War had been described to him as long stretches of tedium punctuated by moment of sheer horror, and Palamedes detested both of those things.

It had been thousands of years since he'd gone to war, but

he hadn't missed it or forgotten how to do it. Swing and duck. Keep your shield up. Stay on your horse. And if you see someone absolutely mowing down adversaries, get the hell out of their way. Honestly, it's not worth it. He'd seen the Hector of old fight and he'd had no interest in ever going near that monster. Nor would Palamedes get within fifty feet of this new Hector if he were on the other side of this beach.

The griffins, centaurs, and giants had no choice, however. This glowing Hector chased them down and slaughtered them in droves with his war hammer. He was thoroughly petrifying to behold.

Then, in the midst of all the chaos, the Scion goddess Helen appeared in a halo of lightning and a burst of thunder that shook the ground.

Palamedes had never seen Zeus in all his power. Zeus never came to the battle at Troy, though many had implored him to bring an end to the conflict that had lasted far too long. Nor had Palamedes ever seen the first Helen, so famed for her beauty, and yet ironically hidden away so that only a handful had ever claimed to have laid eyes on her. Here was this new Helen, the inheritor of both, and just as glorious as promised. And as terrible.

With a flash of white-violet light that made the hairs on Palamedes' head lift from his scalp, giants died where they stood, falling to the sand stiff and bucking as veins of lightning continued to crawl over their corpses.

Of all the warriors Palamedes had encountered in his long life, Helen Hamilton was by far the most disturbing. Something about the way the mighty giants crumbled before this breath-taking woman shook Palamedes in a way that he hadn't expected. He knew Helen fought for his cause. She wanted to save this abused world as much as he did, but seeing her lightning streaking out from her like a tree of ice in the sky was another thing entirely. This spine-tingling power of hers was destruction incarnate, and for the first time since meeting her, he believed Helen capable of ending this world.

And the *smell*. That was another thing about war that Palamedes did not miss in the slightest. War smelled absolutely awful. Corpses, effluvia, rot—and now this new scent of charred skin and burnt hair mixed with the scent of electrified ozone, it was *wrong*. Helen's power was disproportionate to any other being's ability, and therefore wrong to Palamedes' mind. There was no balance for her, no yin to her yang.

Trying desperately to calm his spooked horse, Palamedes watched as Hector lifted his war hammer, dripping with the blood of many unfortunate creatures, and shouted out his battle cry. Aflame with his blood lust, the Arimaspi echoed his adulation for their glowing goddess in the night and followed that big lummox right into the heart of the struggle.

Palamedes had no choice but take up the charge as well. He didn't want Plutus getting too far away from him. Though Plutus was favored above all by Lady Luck herself, Palamedes was determined to keep an eye on his husband and make sure he didn't get himself into too much trouble. For a while, Palamedes had his plate full just trying to keep his seat and not get himself eviscerated by a griffin's talon. There were suddenly griffins everywhere. Some of them were piled atop each other. Palamedes hadn't known there were this many griffins in the world.

Then, something extraordinary happened. All the griffins

(all the ones still living at any rate) jumped as one into the sky and streaked toward the young goddess. They flew up and formed ranks around her, surrounding her, but not attacking. The griffins hung in the air, thousands of them, as if waiting to see what she would do. The goddess floated in their midst uncertainly. Hector was shouting at her to use her lightning. Kill them all. The young goddess looked down at her new god of war, glowing beneath her.

"End this, Helen!" he screamed.

A globe of ball lighting enveloped her like a bubble. The light was white at its center, but it had an otherworldly halo of pink and violet—soft, blushing colors that belied their deadliness. *Like Helen*, Palamedes thought.

"She'll be the death of us all," Plutus whispered in awe. As usual, Plutus said aloud what Palamedes had been thinking.

From that iridescent bubble, rays of lightning forked out in every direction. The griffins fanned their wings wide, welcoming it, and *caught* the lightning. It crackled between their golden feathers as if trapped.

Then the griffins disappeared.

All of Zeus' army disappeared.

The goddess floated in the sky, dark now that her lightning had been drained. She was joined by another figure that Palamedes could barely see because he was all in black, but he had a halo of dark light around him, like a deep indigo aura. Palamedes knew it must be the Hand of Darkness.

The two Scions flew swiftly down to the battlefield, landing next to their god of war.

"Where'd they go?" Helen cried.

Lucas seemed to blink in and out of being, like he was vibrating between here and elsewhere.

"Everywhere," he said in a low voice that carried far though it was hushed by disbelief. "The griffins are everywhere. Spaced out in the air so that they surround the globe like a net. They're carrying your lighting."

"Can they do that?" asked Orion.

Lucas nodded.

"*My* lightning. That would mean I—" Helen began, but didn't finish. The fearful breath she held gave way to grief and she turned toward Lucas. "You were right," she said, tears jumping into her eyes as she realized she had just met her fate on the road she took to escape it.

The sky began to glow, like dawn breaking at the darkest hour of night. Palamedes reached out to his husband and took his hand. This was it. They'd done their best, fought their hardest, and ironically it had been *because* they had fought that they had brought about the end they had been trying to avoid. The Fates had won. Palamedes supposed he shouldn't be too surprised by that, but he was.

As Palamedes reached for his love, Lucas reached for his. He didn't crane his neck to witness the end, but rather, he watched Helen as she looked up to the unnaturally brightening sky that signaled their approaching doom, her eyes hollow with shame.

"I won't let this happen," Lucas said. He shut his eyes in concentration and lifted a hand. "Morpheus," he whispered under his breath. "Help me."

Palamedes felt a rush of otherworldly cold surround him like the hand of death itself reaching up from the Underworld to snatch him away.

CHAPTER 9

Helen and Lucas stood in the Fields of Asphodels.

She knew the place well, but something was different about it. She looked out over the darkened plain and saw shapes hunkered in the grass. At first Helen didn't understand what was going on. A gentle snore from one of the shapes confirmed in her brain what her eyes were telling her.

People were lying in the grass, sleeping. People everywhere, as far as Helen could see across the seemingly endless fields.

"What did you do?" she asked Lucas numbly.

Lucas was looking around at the vast number of slumbering bodies laid at his feet, allowing the enormity of what he'd done to register. "I took everyone before the lightning struck," he replied.

"Everyone?" Helen repeated disbelievingly. "Like, everyone in the entire world?"

Lucas nodded. "I've been trying to figure out how the whole world could end up in Hades at the same moment, and I realized there's no way that could happen unless I did it." He seemed to make peace with his decision. "And we need time, Helen. Time to figure this out. This is the only thing that makes sense."

Helen stared at the peaceful faces, not sure she agreed with him yet. "Morpheus put them to sleep?" she guessed. "How long can they stay down here?"

Lucas lifted a shoulder. "Forever if we need them to," he replied. "Hopefully, we'll figure out where the Moirae are before that though, and we'll find a way to change this."

Helen thought about what it was the Fates could possibly do to change what Helen had already done, even if she did manage to find them, while she looked out, trying to see an end to all the bodies. Though they seemed untroubled, to see billions of people lying motionless among the little white flowers was eerie.

"What about Hector and Orion?"

"They're fine," he snapped.

She'd meant to ask about everyone. Hector and Orion were simply the first names that popped into her head, but before she could amend her question, Lucas flicked his fingers in annoyance and they were suddenly inside his palace, in the suite of rooms adjacent to his bedroom.

Their families were there with the Arimaspi leaders, the Servants of Tyche, Morpheus, and Dionysus. They seemed to be in the middle of several conversations, all of which ended as soon as Helen and Lucas arrived.

There was a moment of silence, then a swarm of questions.

"What happened?" Castor asked.

"Is the world, like, over?" Claire asked.

"Are we going to be stuck here forever?" Kate asked.

"Where are the rest of my soldiers? Are they dead or sleeping?" Geryon, the Arimaspi king asked.

"We have to go back right now!" Hector demanded. Everyone stopped at that.

"Back?" Palamedes asked, incredulously. "So we can be incinerated?"

"I think you need to put the big guy to sleep," Dionysus whispered loudly to Morpheus, pointing at Hector.

"This fight's not over," Hector said, ignoring them. "Helen. Send me back."

"No—just *no* Hector! No one is going back until Lucas and I have figured out where the Fates are and we... you know... change it!" As usual, Helen's public speaking skills left a lot to be desired, but she got her point across.

"You think you can change the fate of the world?" Morpheus asked her. She couldn't tell if he was challenging her, or if he honestly wanted to know if she had information that would make this possible.

"We don't have a choice," Lucas replied. "I brought everyone here right before the absolute destruction of all life on the surface of the planet. I suppose the immortals among us would technically survive, but there's a difference between living and just existing, and once that lighting hits, existing is all anyone will be able to do."

A heavy silence descended.

"I'm going to make this right," Helen promised.

"How, Helen?" Leda asked kindly. "It doesn't sound like enough time to fix much of anything."

"We have all the time in the world here," Lucas said, slipping too easily into the role of host. Food and drink appeared on the tables, making almost everyone startle at the suddenness of it. "If anyone needs to rest there are hundreds of rooms for you to choose from. Settle in. Make yourselves comfortable."

"A word before I go," Morpheus said, and he and Lucas went out onto the terrace that led to Lucas' cosmos-reflecting pool to speak privately.

Helen couldn't help but notice Noel staring after her son. It was like she didn't even recognize him anymore. Castor was still frowning at the magically summoned food. Though Castor had spent his whole life surrounded by Scions would could do the impossible, not even they could conjure food out of nothing. His son was now something different. Helen understood how Noel and Castor felt and it occurred to her that this was how people looked at her sometimes.

After seeing her lightning, Palamedes and Arne now regarded her with fear and suspicion. Helen supposed she deserved it, much more than Lucas did. Unintentionally or not, she had proved herself to be the worst thing that had ever happened to the world. And she'd always thought she was the good guy. The anti-Helen of Troy. The one who was going to break the cycle, not complete it. The shame almost swallowed her whole.

"You're spiraling," Orion said in her ear.

"Uh-huh," she replied, and walked away. She couldn't talk about her feelings. There was no amount of talking that could make what Helen had done any better.

She hadn't been invited, but she followed Lucas and Morpheus outside anyway. When Morpheus spotted her, he raised his voice and included her.

"The Moirae do not dream. I cannot tell you where to find them." Morpheus looked more serious than Helen had ever seen him before. "Your only hope is to solve the riddle the Graeae gave you. And do it soon."

Morpheus looked sadly at the Sleepers, and the disappeared.

"Why soon?" Helen asked Lucas. "Don't we have all the time we need here?"

Lucas was thinking too much. Usually that meant he was trying to figure out how to lie to her or hide the truth without her Falsefinder talent catching him out.

"Let's skip the part where you try to keep the worst of it to yourself, and then we fight about it, and then I end up finding out through some other way after we've already wasted a ton of time, and just tell me, okay?" she said, exasperated.

"Is that what we do?"

"Yes! And I'm sick of it. You think you're protecting me, but actually you're belittling me. I'm not some fragile child who can't handle the whole truth, you know."

He regarded her for a while, really looking at her. It had been a while since he'd done that.

"You're right," he said.

Helen shifted from foot to foot, doing her best not to say thank you. She knew she shouldn't say thank you for this. It should have been a given the whole time they were together, though this new concession showed how much Lucas had changed. They were staring at each other again.

"The Sleepers," she prompted.

Lucas nodded, getting back on track. "There was a Chinese philosopher once who had a dream about being a butterfly," he said. "When he woke, he asked himself if he was a man who had dreamed he was a butterfly, or if he really *was* a butterfly that was dreaming he was a man."

"Oh crap," she whispered, understanding immediately. "So basically, everyone will lose their minds?"

"They'll lose their grip on what had really happened to them in their lives and what they had dreamed," he specified.

Helen put her hands in her hair, mildly panicking. "How long do we have?"

"Months? Morpheus said he'd warn me when it was coming." He hesitated before adding, "The children will lose themselves first."

Helen groaned and turned away from him, her gaze guiltily seeking the children among the Sleepers. "We have to find the Fates."

"Yeah," Lucas said, sighing in frustration.

Helen saw a distortion in the air right over Lucas' shoulder. "What's that?" she asked, pointing. The distortion seemed to ripple in the darkness and take a ghostly shape momentarily. She saw an older man with a beard, wearing a long cloak. Then, he disappeared.

"That was Minos," Lucas replied in a subdued tone. "One of the judges of the dead, informing me that I have to go."

"Go where?" Helen asked, stepping toward him. "What do you have to do?"

Lucas looked tired. "My job." Then, the shadows seemed to grab him and he was gone.

Hector felt like something was missing. Everyone kept telling him that the fighting was over, but no matter how hard he tried to believe them, the unfinished way they'd left it made him restless. It was like he was trying to remember the tune to his favorite song, but it kept eluding him because another song was blasting in his ear. The fighting wasn't over. It was just on pause.

He watched Lucas, Helen, and Morpheus speak with each other by the mirror pool with the Sleepers lying around them. Those three were gods of worlds. They could make whole realities for others to live in, and as such they were going to be creating the rules that the smaller gods like him, Jason, Ariadne, Claire, and Orion would have to deal with. Hector understood hierarchies, and he knew one had already formed. It didn't bother him in the slightest, either. In fact, that was how it should be. Hierarchies were the only way wars got won. Someone was the big leader who told the practical leader on the field what they wanted done. He knew Helen would be the big leader once it all shook out, and Hector wasn't really interested in being the boss any place but on the field. He also knew that as long as Helen was in charge, he would always be her god of war. They trusted each other.

Helen had come inside after Morpheus and Lucas had both disappeared, looking worried and anxious. She hadn't told the rest of them what they'd discussed out there, but she did tell them the riddle given to her by the Graeae—that the Moirae lived in what they were made to tame—and then repeated her mission to find the Fates. Hector didn't know what she was going to do when she found them, and he didn't think she did, either.

He'd totally kill them for her, but he wasn't sure it worked like that. Maybe she was trying to come up with something to offer them? Something they wanted in exchange for making the world right again. Hector didn't think that was how it was going to go down, though. What can you offer the three ladies who already have *literally* everything? The Fates have always controlled the cosmos, and this ending of it was what they wanted. There was nothing to offer them. Hector knew that even if they found the Moirae there'd still be that giant piece missing, but whatever. Figuring that out was above his pay grade.

"I'll find them for you," Hector offered. "Tell Lucas to give me a map, and I'll get a squad together."

Orion looked at him doubtfully. "This place is always changing," he told Hector. "There's no way to map it because it alters based on the thoughts and feelings of the person traveling through it."

"Then I'll think and feel like I'm going to find the Fates and I will," Hector said, smirking like that was obvious because to him it was.

"You mean, just have faith?" Claire asked uncertainly.

"More like, overconfidence," Jason commented, giving his brother a wry smile.

Orion looked at Helen, cautiously optimistic. "Would that work?" he asked her.

"I don't know. Maybe? I mean, we can try it," Helen said. Then she started pacing around, worrying again.

Hector crossed his arms, leaned up against the nearest wall, and settled in. He wanted to get moving, but he knew he was going to be stuck in this room while everyone fretted for the next hour until finally, they'd argue their way back around to this same point and someone would tell him to do what he'd already decided he was going to do anyway. He tried to be patient, but patience was not a virtue that came naturally to him.

"Why don't we ask Hades where they are?" Leda suggested. "He *is* this place, and you just said that all worlds border Hades, so in theory he would know where they are."

Orion looked at his mom, surprised she'd made such a lucid suggestion. He didn't know yet how to relate to her in any way but as the crazy lady who might come after him with a kitchen knife, which Hector had always thought was so sad. But she wasn't crazy anymore. In fact, to Hector she seemed as clever as they come. Looking over at his uncle and dad, Hector could see that they weren't surprised at all. They'd known Leda back when she'd had all her marbles. It still cracked Hector up that his uncle had had a fling with her, but whatever. She was smoking hot. Not as hot as Andy, but he couldn't let himself think about that right now.

He let his attention shift momentarily to where Andy listened quietly from the other side of the room, missing nothing, of course. He had a vague recollection of telling her she was his, but he didn't know if she'd agreed to it yet. Or if it was even safe for her to agree to it. Some of the changes he'd gone through recently still freaked him out. Not on the battlefield. There, he felt totally at home. But being with Andy worried him. He was never going to hurt her, even if that meant he had to stay away from her altogether. Andy must have felt him starting at her. She looked over. He quickly looked away and focused on the conversation again.

"Lucas mentioned something about not having seen Hades in a while," Helen said. Then she shrugged. "But I think it's worth a try to find him. He's always been nice to me."

"Your mother liked him, and so did Adonis," Leda said, like what Helen said tracked. "He's helped both of them in the past."

Daedelus was getting antsy at the mention of Adonis. From what Orion had told Hector, Adonis was the thing that usually triggered Leda, but she looked calm to Hector.

"Hecate knows where Hades is," Plutus said. Hector really liked the god of wealth and his husband, Palamedes. They were a lot of fun.

"Yes," added Geryon, king of the Arimaspi and one hell of a javelin thrower. "Hecate had dealings with Hades. She got permission from him so that we could use the Roads of Erebus."

"So... where's Hecate?" Daedelus asked. What a swordsman that guy was. Hector had already decided to train with him. Orion was impressive, but his dad was a damn poet with the gladiolus.

"I'll handle that if it comes up," Helen said reluctantly. She rolled her eyes. "I'll probably have to do another three tasks for her."

"What kind of tasks?" Ariadne asked suspiciously.

"Who knows? But you can bet she'll make them extra difficult," Helen replied. "You can come. It'll be great."

"Cassandra? Antigone?" Castor said. "Have either of you seen anything that could help us?"

The two Oracles shared a look that had about a million words inside it. Hector stayed still, watching them. Sometimes, if he drew attention to himself, people got spooked and decided that they couldn't say what they were going to say in front of him. Although that annoyed him, even he had to admit he had a habit of going into kill mode when he heard about something that was a danger to his family. No one wanted him to hear distressing things that might set him off, which meant they often tiptoed around him. His best bet at hearing all the news, and not just the watered-down version of it, was to stay quiet and let them all talk.

"That depends," Cassandra said. "Right now, I think I'm only seeing what they want me to see. Which is the end of the world."

Antigone looked at her partner, Ladon, who was a total badass. During the battle Hector saw him throw a centaur halfway across the frigging beach with one arm. What an animal, and not just because of the dragon thing, although that made him even more of a badass in Hector's estimation. But Antigone wasn't looking at him because of his raw monster awesomeness. She was trying to figure out what she had seen and probably discussed with him.

"It's confusing," Antione said. "Dizzying is a better way to describe it. I saw the world ending, and then it was fine, and then it was ending again. I don't know what it means."

Cassandra nodded. "I saw something like that too. It flashed by so quickly—too quickly to keep track. But it always ended on the end."

"That doesn't mean anything," Antigone said.

"Of *course* it does," Cassandra insisted, like she thought Antigone was nuts.

Two Oracles arguing. Hector thought that must be weird

for both of them. They're so used to be right all the time, what do they do when they can't agree?

"Okay," Orion said, taking Cassandra's hand and pulling her down next to him before the Oracles started to yell at each other.

Not that sitting made much of a difference. Cassandra was so tiny Hector sometimes couldn't tell when she was standing up. Though, he had to admit she'd grown recently, and not just up. Orion had noticed, but he pretended he didn't, which Hector thought was hilarious.

As clued in on everybody else's emotions as Orion was, he was pretty stupid about his own. Even Hector understood that Orion stayed available for Helen because he knew he'd never actually get her, and that way he wouldn't have to deal with a real relationship. Yet, he avoided Cassandra because he knew as soon as he started with her, that'd be it, and he didn't want to commit to someone the way his dad had committed to his mom—especially not someone who had every likelihood of losing it like his mom did. Oracles were fragile. Orion didn't trust fragile, and for good reason. But seeing how Ladon and Antigone had made it work had shaken something in his best friend. It had made him more scared of being with Cassandra, not less, and Hector was going to have to ask him about that eventually. But not now, obviously, because everyone was still talking a lot of nonsense.

"So, are we going to go get Hecate or what?" Hector finally asked when he couldn't take all the jabber about the difference between prophecies and visions. Why didn't people just keep their thoughts to themselves, like he did?

Personally, Hector didn't trust a word the Oracles said

anymore, with or without their Shields supposedly protecting them from the Fates. Hector knew visions were supposed to be what the Fates knew that they didn't want the Oracles to see, but still. Where did these visions come from in the first place? The Fates.

"Yeah, I'm ready," Ariadne said, standing. "Let's do it."

He could always count on Ari to get her hands dirty. His little sister was such a bruiser. He turned to Orion. "Well, come on. Helen can't go anywhere without you. Cass, you stay with Ladon."

"What are we supposed to do?" Jason asked, indicating himself and the large group that were now refugees in the Land of the Dead.

Hector was feeling feisty after standing around for so long. "Put your feet up," he said, just to see Jason's face get red. Jason hated being left behind, but because of his talent, he usually was. Healers needed to be where you could find them. That meant they had to stay put more than Jason liked. And honestly? Ari was a better fighter, and Jason was a better Healer. Case closed.

"Hector," their father said warningly.

"Just kidding, Dad," he said, turning quickly to Helen. "Can you portal us?" he asked.

"I can't. It would start time up again because my portals go through Everyland," Helen replied.

He just let that information hang there for a second, smirking at her.

"What'd I tell you?" Hector said, baiting Helen.

"I don't want to hear it," she replied, holding up a hand.

"When are you just going to admit I was right? You should have made Everyland timeless," he said, grinning.

"Oh my god," Orion muttered. "Just ignore him."

Helen went through the French doors, grumbling under her breath, but at least she didn't look afraid anymore. Mission accomplished.

Helen was lost. That meant everyone was lost because they were following her lead.

Lately, Lucas turned up when she didn't want him to, so of course he wasn't here when she needed him. Helen knew all she had to do was whisper his name and he would show up, but she didn't want to do that. Because she knew that *he* knew she was lost. This was his land, now—or it mostly was. Helen wasn't sure if it was a fifty-fifty split with Hades or what, but Lucas certainly acted like the place was his. So, he had to know she was lost, and still he hadn't come. He was waiting for her to ask for his help.

"Why are you such a pain in my ass?" she whispered. Lucas slipped out of the shadow next to her.

"I didn't want to interfere," he said.

Helen stopped walking and faced him. "Were you keeping me from getting to her on purpose?" she asked indignantly.

"Of course not," Lucas replied. She could hear that he wasn't lying.

"Then why can't I find a crossroads?"

He went back to trying to repress a grin. "Because there are no crossroads in Hades."

"Such a jerk," Helen whispered, turning away from him. He caught her arm.

"Why do you want to find Hecate?"

"To find Hades! *You* don't know where he is!"

"Yes, I do. Or I know where he might be."

"Why didn't you just say that before?" Ariadne asked. "We've been walking for hours."

"No, you haven't," Lucas replied. "You've been walking for what on earth would be about forty-five minutes."

"Still, why'd you let us walk around for so long?" Orion asked, his eyes narrowed.

Orion and Lucas had plenty of reasons to dislike each other, Helen and Cassandra being the biggest reasons, yet the two of them had always gotten along for the most part. Lately though, Helen had noticed that Orion was beginning to doubt Lucas. He didn't trust him anymore.

"Because I was busy and you didn't wait for me for come back. If you had, I would have saved you this entire trip." He looked at Helen. "I can't force you to include me when you make decisions, but you might find it useful to do so in the future."

Helen glared at him. "Point taken. Still, it was a *waste* of *time*."

They had maybe a month to figure this out, but she and Lucas knew—though the others didn't—that they didn't have forever.

"If you hadn't said something soon, I was going to come anyway. You're so stubborn." Lucas flicked his fingers and they were transported to the gateway of a lush garden. Helen had been here before.

"Persephone's garden," she said.

"She's not here. It's spring. She's back on earth," Lucas said, opening the gate and letting them in.

The lush garden, once so full of life, was dying. The flowers drooped. The trees looked wilted, and the perfume coming from the browning blooms was tinged with the must of rot.

Ariadne crept in last, and shut the gate behind her respectfully. "Is this okay, just barging in? I mean, it is Persephone's space."

"She's moments away from dying," Lucas said. "Isn't that right?" he said louder as he strode toward a shaded nook just off the path.

"It is," Hades replied.

There they found Hades sitting on a marble bench beneath a myrtle tree, wearing a black chiton tied over one shoulder with no helm on, looking so much like Orion that Ariadne, who was the only one among them who had never met him before, glanced between them repeatedly.

Helen couldn't recall ever seeing Hades seated before, or without his Helm of Darkness, but this was obviously no holiday for him. Hades looked sad.

"You've brought your best warriors, Helen, but there's no fight here," Hades continued. He seemed tired.

On impulse, Helen asked her friends to give her a moment alone with him. "I think it would be better if I just talked to him," she said, winging it.

Hector and Lucas didn't want to leave her, but Orion and Ariadne thought Helen's approach was best, and the two of them coaxed Hector and Lucas a bit down the path to give them some privacy. They kept Helen in view, though, and Helen had no doubt that Lucas would be listening from the shadows. She didn't know why they were so suspicious. Hades was not their enemy, nor had he ever been. She figured they just didn't like being left out. Helen sat down on the bench next to him.

"Why don't you open a portal and bring Persephone here?" she asked.

"Here or there, it doesn't matter. All the gods and goddesses of the earth, like Persephone and her mother Demeter, are going to die with it," he replied. "If I open a portal, time will move there again, and the earth will die."

"But—maybe you could stop it."

He shook his head. "The time of the gods is over. We have known this since your birth, Helen, though my brothers and sisters tried to fight it."

"You knew?" Helen thought about that. The gods knew the Scions were going to replace them in her lifetime. "That's why you allowed Lucas to trade himself for you. Because you knew it would be over for you soon?"

"I wanted him to have a chance to train first, as I trained you. There will always be dead, and they need a guide. Lucas makes a good one." Hades regarded her with something approaching admiration. "You will do well, Helen, in your new world. You will make a beautiful place, and hopefully the humans you bring to fill it will be worthy of it."

Helen had never felt so alone. "I don't want to be a goddess."

"You don't get to choose. The Fates already did that for you. None of us really get to choose. I certainly didn't when I drew the lot for the land of the dead."

A thought occurred to Helen. "You can't die. What will you do?"

He smiled unexpectedly. "Maybe I'll ask my father to swallow me again."

Helen chuckled quietly at his joke. They sat in amiable silence for a while. "I'm not ready to give up. I can't. The earth is our home. Humans have done a pretty terrible job taking care of it, but we all still love it," Helen said. "Tell me where the Fates are and I'll figure out how—"

"The Fates are not in a place," Hades interrupted, spreading his hands out helplessly. "They are in a state of being you must get to in order to have an audience with them."

"What state of being?" Helen pleaded. "Help me."

Hades made a frustrated sound. "They live in what they hate. The uncertain. The unpredictable. Chaos, Helen. They live in chaos. That's what you must find."

Helen dropped her head in her hands and groaned. "What does that mean, exactly? How do you find chaos? It's like telling someone to find peace or forgiveness. It doesn't mean anything."

"I don't know," Hades said, shaking his head vaguely. "But I do know no one can find any of those things for you. You have to figure it out for yourself."

Chapter 10

Palamedes couldn't remember the last time he'd enjoyed such stellar accommodations. Their rooms were palatial. The food was five-star. The closets were perpetually full of the finest clothes. Even the company was intriguing; Ladon and Kate had become particular favorites.

Palamedes sipped his excellent cappuccino from the gilded edge of his porcelain coffee cup, enjoying the last nibble of his croissant. This would have been the ultimate romantic getaway for he and Plutus, but for two things. The grounds were covered with bodies and they were prisoners in Hades.

"We should try to speak to Noel about him," Palamedes suggested. "Mothers have a lot of influence over their sons."

"And say what, exactly?" Plutus replied, still pacing the terrace outside their rooms. "By our calculations we've been here for three earth weeks, and your son won't let us leave?" he said, testing it out sarcastically. Then he cast an arm wide to include the inert bodies. "And can you ask him to do something about all the Sleepers? They're ruining the view."

Palamedes grimaced, thinking that he might actually suggest that last bit, though he knew that the view wasn't what Plutus found disagreeable. What he found disagreeable was that the earth was, for all intents and purposes, dead. The Scions simply hadn't admitted it yet, and holding the rest of them prisoner until they figured it out was futile.

Plutus sighed heavily. "Not that we can even *find* Lucas lately."

"He's quite busy, it seems," Palamedes agreed.

"Busy with what? It looks to me like everyone's already dead!" Plutus burst out, frustrated.

Palamedes turned in his seat, sensing someone joining them. "He's busy searching for the Moirae," Leda said. She lifted a doubtful eyebrow. "Or so I've been told."

Leda sauntered toward them out of the star-spangled darkness wearing a flowy sort of gown, her bare feet padding across the marble tiles. She wasn't trying to be seductive; she was just one of those women who couldn't help but saunter when they walked.

Plutus shot Palamedes a look. The Scions were a complicated mixture of friends, family, and former enemies, and navigating what they could say to whom had become increasingly difficult as they had started to question the fact that Lucas was essentially holding everyone captive.

No one could leave Hades and go to any other realm. The split second it would take for Lucas to leave Hades in order to portal anyone to another realm would be the split second that the earth had left before being annihilated by Helen's lightning. Plutus and Palamedes were Servants of Tyche, but to bring them back to Tyche where she dwelled on Olympus would require Lucas to break from timelessness, and doing so would end the world.

It wasn't that Palamedes and Plutus wanted that. They had fought against the world's end. And they had *lost*. What Lucas and Helen refused to accept was that a split second was not enough time to fix it. It was over, and Palamedes and Plutus were not prepared to spend eternity in Hades where they didn't belong.

Nor were Geryon and Arne. The Arimaspi had a realm of their own. It was one of the many subterranean shadow lands that bordered the Underworld, but it wasn't Hades, which meant that Lucas would have to portal them there, and he had refused to do so when they had asked. He'd been understanding about it the first few times the subject had been raised. Then slowly, in the subtlest of ways, even speaking about returning to the realms where they belonged had become verboten. The shift had been quiet, but unmistakable.

Lucas was impossible to argue with, not just because he was as clever and smooth-spoken as the best and worst of politicians, but because over his shoulder stood his great, big, golden cousin who just happened to be the god of war.

And that was when they could actually find him. The Hand of Darkness always seemed to be busy.

Palamedes and Plutus didn't know where Leda stood in terms of her loyalty, but they knew that she had no blood tie to Lucas and that she had no particular reason to side with him. On top of that, her son seemed to be attached to Helen. Still, it was a dangerous subject. One that required the upmost tact. So, of course, Plutus blundered in with all the subtlety of a greedy baby.

"When are they going to give up that fantasy?" he said irritably. "I don't like the outcome either, but it's time we faced the music, yes?" Plutus gestured to Palamedes. "When we leave here, we are bound to Olympus, and possible punishment from Zeus, and yet we know that is our duty. It is the duty of the Scions to accept their defeat."

Leda turned her poker face on Palamedes. "Are you so eager for punishment?" she asked.

Palamedes fiddled with his coffee cup. The thought of Zeus and what he might to do them was terrifying, and yet they needed to return to their mistress.

"We don't belong here," he said simply. "Sooner or later Lucas is going to have to admit that none of us do." He gestured to the Sleepers. "This is wrong. You know it too, I suspect."

"What I know is that there is a perfectly good world waiting in the wings. Everyland," Leda said.

Plutus took a seat across from Leda eagerly. "Yes. We've considered this, too."

"Helen could portal all the Sleepers there. It would be shocking for them when they woke, but better than dying," Palamedes said.

"Why hasn't she done that?" Plutus asked.

Leda frowned, staring at her hand resting on the white tablecloth. "I don't know. I think she's scared of something."

"Can your son speak to her? Convince her?" Palamedes asked.

"He does seem quite convincing, doesn't he, my love?"

Plutus commented, teasing Palamedes, who couldn't help but blush every time Orion spoke to him, or looked at him, or even just entered a room. Orion was embarrassingly attractive and Plutus was probably going to tease Palamedes about his inability to form a coherent sentence around the young man for the rest of eternity. However long or short that turned out to be.

Leda grinned, enjoying the couples' harmless sport with each other. "He has. Helen tells him that Everyland is not ready. She doesn't know if her world will work."

"What does that mean?" Plutus asked.

Leda lifted a shoulder and let it drop. "Something about self-sustaining ecosystems and butterflies flapping their wings." She rolled her eyes dramatically. "She's a worrier."

Palamedes and Plutus shared a confused look. "She's a *goddess*. She can make anything work, right?" Plutus asked.

"There are rules even the gods can't break," Leda replied.

"What can we do about it?" Plutus asked.

Leda's face became stern with thought. "I remember her mother and I discussing the subject of luck. Something—" she trailed off vaguely, not able to remember. "We had a plan. I was to give her the last piece, but I think—no, I *know* because I know Daphne was working with Nemesis—you two are here to give her another. It must have something to do with luck or chance," Leda said, getting to the heart of her visit. "How do you give someone luck, anyway?"

Though they had been the servants of Tyche, and had been withholding or bestowing her bounty to humanity for thousands of years, luck was not something either Plutus or Palamedes were very good at explaining.

Mortals had often described luck as fickle, but it was something more worrisome than that. If you looked at it for too long it changed. Sometimes it morphed to become whatever you believed it to be, good or bad. Never predictable, it still followed precise mathematical rules, as it did in games of chance. Until it didn't. Sometimes good luck came disguised as bad, and the worst luck was sometimes hidden inside a great windfall that proved ruinous over time.

"We may give her luck, but the result might not be what any of us expect," Palamedes said. "It's difficult to explain."

"Try," Leda urged. "Or you can always lie and say she has it."

"No one can lie to her," Plutus said, frowning. "She's a Falsefinder."

"But you can lie to my son. Convince Orion that luck is on Helen's side and he will convince her."

If Palamedes ever doubted that this woman was capable of running the most conniving of all the Scion Houses, those doubts were put to rest. Leda had no misgivings about crafting a deception that involved her son.

"Will simply thinking she's lucky be enough to make her risk it?" Plutus asked.

"Like you said, my son can be very convincing. Make him believe it's enough, so she will believe it." Leda stood, pausing before she left them to add, "Lucas has nothing to gain by letting us go, and everything to lose if he does. Including Helen."

. . .

Helen didn't want to go to the pool for breakfast. She didn't want to have lunch in the inner courtyard by the fountain, or eat dinner in the grand hall.

Meeting for meals was still a Delos habit, though Noel no longer cooked and there was no kitchen. Over the past three weeks certain social patterns had emerged. Breakfast by the pool, a snacky-lunch situation around the fountain in the atrium, and dinner in the grand marble hall, complete with the fanciest attire they could mentally conjure from Lucas' infinite wardrobes. Claire had the most fun with that. Her artistic skills had turned her into the most sought-after designer in Hades, but Helen had grown tired of playing dress up.

Whenever Helen used to read books or watch movies that centered around nobility from the past, she always used to wonder why fancy balls were such a big deal to them. Three weeks in Hades with nothing to do—no job, no school, no future to secure—and she understood. Socializing became vitally important when you were lacking genuine employment. To want for nothing meant you had to invent things to want.

Dionysus had something to do with the perpetual partying as well. That guy made an event out of everything, and if he stopped by someone's rooms, it didn't matter if they felt like being alone. He drew everyone out. It was part of his magic, which he insisted was not a spell he cast, but his essence. Though his intoxicating effect was somewhat diminished in Hades, everyone still ended up getting drawn into his revelries.

Dionysus had introduced many games into their daily routine. Croquet in the dark, under Lucas' stars, of course, was a favorite of his. They all got into it. Billiards was another thing that everyone joined in on, especially Castor and Daedelus who were working out some decades-old rivalry. Cassandra and Antigone played chess against each other, to everyone else's amusement. Watching two Oracles trying to outmaneuver each other was quite thrilling, especially when they played speed chess. And of course, the Servants of Tyche were ready to throw dice or play cards at any hour.

But Helen avoided Dionysus, and had done so since they'd all been thrown together in Hades. Not only did she need to keep a clear head, but all of the dallying he inspired chaffed on her nerves. An idle life did not appeal to her. She'd never *not* had a job. In fact, she'd never had a real vacation. She never went to camp or spent her summers on the beach. Summers were the busiest time of the year in her dad's shop with the tourists on island. Sometimes she would even dread the end of school because it meant she had to work double shifts at the News Store, and watch all the tanned and happy people traipsing in, shedding sand from their flip flops while she broke down boxes in the back or hauled garbage to the dumpster.

But when she did manage to get an afternoon off in July or August, it was amazing. She and Claire would lay on their blankets, sunning themselves and listening to music. They'd drink endless iced teas, and Helen would bask in the luxury of doing nothing. Because she'd earned it. It was no fun unless you'd earned it, in her opinion, and this endless parade of gowns and games was far less interesting than it had seemed when she was stuck inside doing inventory on a summer's day.

Then there were all the Sleepers. During croquet games as they knocked their balls past the Sleepers' splayed limbs and slack hands, Dionysus told anyone who was troubled by them to look at their faces. The gently smiling Sleepers did look happy, each of them snuggled into their nests, cupped in the tender palm of Lucas' night. What disturbed her was that sometimes it seemed like the rest of her party would have been content to leave the Sleepers as they were, forever lying in the flower-speckled grass under the softly glowing cosmos, dreaming their most cherished dreams. But Helen knew something the rest of her party didn't. She knew that if she didn't do something soon, the Sleepers would be too far gone to wake.

Helen paced her rooms, wondering where Lucas was. No matter how far she walked down the hallway from his suite each night before she went to bed, she always woke in the room adjacent to Lucas' bedroom. When she questioned him about it, he'd told her that he wasn't doing it. She heard no lie, which meant that somehow either the palace was doing it of its own accord, or Helen was. A few times Helen had even awoken in Lucas' bed. Luckily, he didn't sleep anymore and he wasn't there. Since it had happened while she dreamt, Helen began to wonder if it was Morpheus' doing.

As Helen was thinking about Morpheus, doubtful that he would do something like that to her, she noticed one of the elven people who live in the land of dreams out among the Sleepers. She seemed to be counting them, or possibly tending them, like a flock of sheep. Occasionally, the elven woman would bend down, lean her tall, pointed ear close to a Sleeper's mouth and listen. When the elven woman spotted Helen watching, she raised a hand and gestured for Helen to join her. Helen snuck out of Lucas' palace and picked her way among the bodies, hoping that Dionysus didn't spot her from the wall of French of doors and come after her.

Helen looked around for Orion. They tried to stay together

most of the time to shield Helen from the Fates, but as time had passed and she had come no closer to having an idea, they had slacked off and occasionally wandered away from each other. This was one of those times he had wandered away and, anxious about missing this opportunity, Helen decided to follow the elf without him.

As Helen approached the skittish elf, she moved away. Helen stopped and the elf stopped. Helen called out to her, but the woman only moved more swiftly, beckoning in Helen's direction. Helen assumed the elven woman wanted her to follow. Keeping her distance, the elven woman soon brought Helen to Morpheus' pavilion. From a distance Helen noticed that there was more activity among Morpheus' marble columns than she had ever seen before. The braziers that always glowed with scented fires were ablaze, and the silken draperies that were hung like banners between the marble arches snapped in what was once gentle breezes, and was now a tumultuous wind.

Morpheus was not in his enormous bed, but rather he stood among the columns, receiving elves who ran to him, delivered messages, and then ran away, too busy to dance among the glowing mushroom and nodding poppies anymore.

"Did Morpheus send for you, too?" Lucas asked, appearing from the darkness on the edge of Helen's vision.

She gasped and pulled back, startled. Though she had seen him shadow travel many times now, it still sent a thrill down her spine to see him slip out of the darkness as if he were made of it.

"Sorry," he said, halting his progress toward her. He seemed to glow. Not with the golden light of sunshine she always associated with Lucas before, but with the cold sparkling light of distant stars. He kept his hands where she could see them and waited for the rush of adrenaline she'd felt to dissipate. "I didn't mean to scare you."

"You didn't," she lied. He gave her a knowing half-smile and, doubling down on her fib, she took a step toward him. "I was just surprised, is all."

"Okay," he said, letting it go.

They walked slowly toward the pavilion side by side. Helen stole glances at him, and she was sure he was aware of it, but she couldn't stop. She was waiting for him to speak, or maybe do something that would release the tension between them, but he didn't. As they approached Morpheus, the elven attendants scattered before Lucas and Helen could get close.

"They're very shy," Lucas told her when Helen tried to catch one's eye and wave. "They've never allowed me to get close enough to speak to them."

"Who are they?" Helen asked.

"I'm not sure," Lucas replied. "I assume they work for Morpheus somehow."

Helen recalled the ghost-like Minos whispering to Lucas. "Do you all have staff down here?" she joked.

He smiled warmly, and Helen realized that's what she had been waiting for, a feeling of familiarity between them. "I suppose we do. Don't you have staff in Everyland?" he asked.

"I've always been more of the servant type than the type that gets served. You know that."

Lucas didn't exactly laugh, but he smiled at the ground, still thinking deeply. He was always thinking now, but not in a frantic, frustrated way like he used to, his mind spinning faster than everyone else's, and a bit annoyed that no one could keep up with him. He was calmer and more deliberate in everything he did. Helen couldn't stop watching him. He was magnetic if a bit unfamiliar.

They reached the nightmare tree and Helen stopped. "Aren't we crossing into another land if we go to Morpheus?" she asked.

Lucas considered. "Time will stay halted on earth." He searched for words. "It's difficult to explain, but the edges of Sleep and Death have always overlapped. You can be in both places at once if we allow it. Does that make sense?"

Helen tilted her head in reply, not wanting to think too much about the fact that to sleep was to tread on the edge of death every night.

"Is that why you don't need to sleep anymore?" she asked. Lucas looked a little surprised she'd figured this out.

"Yes," he said quietly.

Morpheus greeted them as they arrived, looking almost hassled, which Helen found unsettling and strangely sad. Morpheus had only ever seemed laid back and dreamy, and now a crease had developed between his dark brows.

"I am sorry to say we have less time than I had hoped," Morpheus said while his elven people moved away among the snapping banners and licking flames of the braziers.

Lucas' face fell. "How long do we have left?" he asked.

"Days," he replied shaking his head to indicate a guess. "Have you found the Moirae yet?"

"No," Helen admitted.

"Then maybe it's time you considered that the only way to fix this might be to make it so it never happened," Morpheus said.

Lucas and Helen shared a confused look.

"Cronus owes you, whether you made a deal with him or not," Morpheus continued, looking at Helen. "The Titans have a very exact understanding of these things, and he knows he's in your debt. If you go to him, he just might break a few rules for you."

Lucas' expression darkened. He didn't like the advice Morpheus was giving him, but Helen immediately latched onto it.

"Wait—you mean Cronus might let us go back in time? We can undo this?" she asked, feeling like a boot was being lifted from her neck. Finally, an inkling of hope.

"We can't change what's already happened," Lucas argued, shaking his head.

"Why not?" Helen demanded. "Who wrote that dumb rule, anyway? Look, it's not like I can screw up the cosmos any more than I already have. What have we got to lose?"

Morpheus raised his eyebrows at Lucas. "Normally I would avoid suggesting this course of action at all costs. But it appears all costs have come due," he said gravely.

"There's no way to know what chain of events we'd be setting off," Lucas cautioned.

Helen made a frustrated sound. "Can you think of anything worse than what I've already done?"

Lucas wanted to say that he could, but he knew she'd hear his lie and stopped himself.

The elven host who had stood back for this exchange inched closer and now seemed poised anxiously on the edge of some invisible circle. Morpheus nodded to let them know he was coming.

"I'll leave you two to decide," Morpheus said, then hesitated. "But you must do so quickly. We can only coax the straying minds back so many times before they'll stop listening to us." He hurried deeper into his pavilion, immediately surrounded by his attendants.

"Lucas—" Helen began.

"Helen—" he said at the same moment.

They both stopped.

"I have to try," she said. She didn't say please or ask for his permission. Permission wasn't his to grant anyway, and they both knew it. But she did want his support.

He nodded. "Okay."

They appeared by the banks of the River of Joy.

It had been weeks since Helen saw the sun, or the Elysian Fields' much better rendition of it. The gently rolling hills, puffy clouds, and glossy grass swaying in the warn, fragrant breeze were only the visual aspects of this version of heaven. There was something past visual that made this place so pleasing. It felt like peace swelling up from the ground and rushing past in the air, and Helen felt her heart flood with it. She nearly reached for Lucas' hand, but snatched it back, too aware of how strongly she felt herself pulled toward him. It had always been like that between them.

"Just us?" Helen asked.

Lucas nodded, not looking at her. "If you'd rather I bring someone else," he began stiffly.

"No, it's fine," Helen said, cutting him off. They didn't need a chaperone. She looked around so she didn't have to look at him. The River of Joy burbled happily alongside them. "Do you ever come here and just drink buckets of that stuff?" she asked. She'd only dipped her fingers in it once, and the elation she'd felt was indescribable.

"No," he said, smiling at the ground in thought as he started walking. "It doesn't affect me."

Helen considered this. It made sense, but still it seemed like he was being cheated out of even this one comfort. "Do any of the rivers affect you?" she asked, rather than feel sorry for him.

"Styx," he answered immediately. "If I swear on it, I can't break my vow." He outpaced her slightly, and she followed him to a bridge that spanned the tranquil waters.

"I'm surprised it's not surrounded by the dead, chugging away," she said, catching up.

"They only need to drink from it once. Anyway, it's Lethe most of the dead want."

"They want to forget?" she asked, but he didn't answer.

He looked at her cautiously, like he was weighing whether or not he wanted to continue this conversation. Helen searched his profile, trying to discern why this topic was a loaded one for him. She glanced at his chest but, as usual, Lucas' emotions were a complicated tangle that he snatched away before she could tease them apart, though she could see fear, dread, and anxiety the most. Maybe he was wary she would bring up seeing her father again. She almost did, but stopped herself. Helen knew what his answer to her request would be. Right now, she needed his help and an argument about her father would probably drive them apart.

"It should be here," he said, stopping and looking around. He lifted a hand, like a mime feeling an invisible box in the air.

His expression went from confused, to chagrinned. "Cronus won't let us in."

"That can't be right," Helen said, trying to find the edge of the invisible box that Lucas seemed to sense, but that she couldn't. When she failed to feel it, she paced around in the dulcet air of the Elysian Fields, getting angrier and angrier while Lucas inspected the area.

"This is where the Elysian Fields meets Cronus' land. He's not letting us in," Lucas said.

"Does he know we're here?"

Lucas nodded, but didn't need to. Helen knew that if someone was literally knocking on the borders of Everyland she would know. She kept pacing around, thinking it had to be a mistake somehow.

"We can try Cimmeria again," Lucas suggested. "Or we could ask Ocean if he knows where the Moirae are."

"You want to give up?"

"On this? Yes," Lucas admitted. "I don't think messing with time is the answer. We need to focus on finding the Moirae."

Helen considered this. "Does Ocean speak?"

Lucas' expression said no. That left them no closer to finding the Moirae, no closer to fixing Helen's calamitous mistake.

Helen paced, unable to let it go. She didn't realize how much she'd already invested in this option. How she'd decided inside herself that this was going to be the way she rectified her biggest mistake. She'd time traveled before and saved a Titan from suffering without destroying causality, why not save the world by doing it again? It was only now that she let herself hope, and now that this option was evaporating in front of her that she had to face what she'd done. And she simply couldn't.

"Let me in," she said speaking quietly to the invisible world she knew was hidden one step away. "You use me to secure your family's safety, and then leave me to lose everything I've ever loved?"

"Helen. There's no way in, unless you want to challenge him for his world," Lucas said gently, trying to talk her down.

But she wasn't finished. "No. It won't end here," she said, her body shaking but her voice strangely steady. "He can either do the right thing and help us, or I'm calling him out."

Lucas' eyes widened. "You don't know what you're saying," he warned.

"Yes, I do!" Helen shouted.

He grabbed her by the shoulder, but let go just as quickly, shocked. "Don't challenge him," he said.

Sparks began to spill off of her and bounce across the grass. Lucas took a step back and shielded his eyes from the brightness of the lightning that was starting to encase her.

And then they were inside Cronus' grove.

The Titan sat cross-legged on the ground, under his old and newly blooming olive tree, flanked on both sides by his fellow Titans. Hecate and Atlas she knew, but there were more, and most of them were difficult to see physically. There was one who glowed bright golden like the sun, and Helen had to turn her face away from him. *That must be Helios*, she thought.

"It is always good to see you, grandchildren," Cronus said.

Helen hadn't expected his tone to be so genuinely welcoming, but she supposed he must have known that she was coming. He even must have known she was going to yell at him. He knew everything.

"Why shut me out if you knew you were going to let me in?" she asked.

He smiled, but his galaxy eyes gave away nothing. "There are many ways this will had been happening. It is for *you* to decide which it is."

Helen actually understood him. The choices she made showed him who she was. "Are there other ways that are happening now? Like, a way that doesn't include me ending the world?" she asked.

"Many," he replied. "Forever is a very long time and the universe is very big. Everything will have happened somewhere eventually."

Helen glanced at Lucas, letting herself hope again. "Can we —er—try one of those other ways?"

Cronus paused. She couldn't remember him ever taking so long to answer her before. It was as if he didn't know what he should say, which was impossible because Cronus was supposed to know everything that had and would happen.

"You confuse mistakes with choices. Mistakes, wrong words spoken, silly behavior you regret—these things do not change our paths. Choices do, and what has been chosen cannot be unchosen. Everything is as it always was," he finally decided.

Basically, a big fat no. Helen stared at him, the wind knocked out of her. What did he care? It wasn't his world. He'd stay here in his grove, murdering tenses for eternity, and in the meantime, Helen would never sit on the beach again. Never walk to the News Store, freezing her butt off in January, and be enveloped by a wall of warm, sweet air. She'd never hear the murmur of conversation in the background while she put up stock or counted out her drawer. She could recreate all of this in Everyland, right down to the hissing sound of Kate steaming milk for a cappuccino, but it wouldn't be real. It wouldn't be her town, her beach, her neighbors. Not really. And it was all her fault.

"Grandfather. You said just now that our choices decide who we are, but how can we ever really choose if we are fated?" Lucas asked.

"Free will is what is at stake here," Cronus said, as if Lucas had finally hit upon the matter. "Free will must be preserved into the next turning of the Wheel. That is why you suffer, grandchildren."

Helen and Lucas shared a look, and she was relieved to note that he seemed as perplexed as she did.

"The world is ending to *preserve* free will?" Helen asked, choosing her words carefully. "Then, I want to choose again."

"Would you choose differently than you have?" Cronus asked.

"Yes!" Helen practically shouted.

"We want a chance to choose without being railroaded by fate," Lucas said. "You still owe Helen for what she did for your brother. Give her this and we'll call it even."

Cronus smiled at Lucas, and then his smile turned into a chuckle, then a belly laugh that all the Titans shared.

"Your bargains are always amusing, grandson. You will have always made the perfect Hand." The laughter died down and Cronus frowned suddenly. "So here is your favor returned. Look. Look and tell me how you would have chosen differently."

. . .

...Helen was at the News Store, but it was strange. It was nighttime so it took a moment for her to understand that it was the News Store before they had rebuilt most of it. It was the News Store before that Halloween when it had been nearly destroyed in the riots caused by Eris.

Helen walked slowly through the aisles, past the humming refrigerators where bottles of single-serving drinks stood in rows like toy soldiers. She went behind the counter and saw her dad's stuff stored beneath the register—work gloves for unloading heavy crates, and his apron, folded neatly. She put her hand on top of it, her throat tight. If she went home right now, would he be there?

She heard a faint shuffling sound from the storeroom. The hairs on the back of her neck stood up. She crept to the storeroom and saw Kate, lying unconscious on the floor.

Helen knelt beside her, and her vision was suddenly swallowed up by stifling darkness as a cloth bag was put over her head. She felt arms wrap around her, restraining her.

Helen had always been strong. Not strong for a girl. Strong for a bear. The person who had her was strong as well, but Helen would not allow herself to be taken. Kate could die if she didn't get to a hospital soon.

Then Helen remembered. This was the moment. Her attacker was Daphne, trying to save her from all the heartache that was to come. It was her mother, doing exactly what Helen had asked her to do just weeks ago. But right now, in the past, Kate was hurt. Maybe dying.

Helen flexed her back, planted her feet, and felt her white tennis sneakers shred with the force of her step...

. . .

Helen was back in the olive grove, staring into Cronus' galaxy eyes.

"That's not fair!" she shouted at him.

"It is as it always was because you chose to save your friend. Then. Now. Always,," he said. "It is who you are, Helen. This choice. You cannot un-choose it without becoming not you."

Then Cronus looked at Lucas, who stood next to Helen with a stricken look on his face. "And you grandson—"

"I know what I chose," Lucas said. He glanced at Helen out of the corner of his eyes. "And I would choose it again."

Cronus nodded sadly. "Everything is as it always was, grandchildren, not because you had been forced by fate to make the choices you did, but because the choices reveal who you are. The question is what are you going to do next? Who are you choosing to be now?"

Helen strode through the Elysian Fields, eyes down so she didn't step on a Sleeper, and jaw tight to keep from crying.

She was not going to cry. Crying was for people who'd lost something, but *she* was the one who had taken everything away from everyone else. All of these people she weaved past, limbs flung out at odd angles in the tender grass, she'd taken everything from them. Their whole world. She didn't deserve the comfort of crying.

"Helen—"

"Don't," she warned. She had no idea what he was going to

say, but Lucas' tone had been consoling, understanding, *caring* even, and Helen didn't deserve any of those things.

"I failed," she said, the words tugging on her throat as she said them. "Again. I could have fixed it and I didn't."

Lucas was a quiet for a while. "What choice did Cronus show you?" he asked.

Helen debated answering. Every truth she'd ever told him about herself had only brought them closer together, but this one wouldn't.

"The night before I met you Daphne tried to kidnap me, but Kate was injured," she said.

He nodded. "Getting away from me or saving Kate. Well, at least I'm not worse than Kate's death," he said ruefully.

Helen couldn't help but give a little laugh. "Not quite." She found herself watching him again. He always drew her gaze. "And you?"

He gave her a half smile. "Guess."

"Trading yourself for Hector," she said, certain of it. She gestured widely to the sparkling beauty of this unchanging paradise, marred by the mounds of sleeping bodies. "But then you wouldn't be king of all you survey, and what's not to love?"

He chuckled at her sarcastic comment, then pulled his lower lip through his teeth. "That wasn't it," he said after a pause.

She wanted to know, of course she did. But she shouldn't want to know anything about Lucas anymore. He shouldn't fascinate her as much as he did. It was yet another example of how she couldn't govern herself. How was she supposed to be a goddess, in control of the whole world, if she couldn't even control herself?

"Well, I guess it just goes to show that I never knew you very well," she said.

What she said hurt him as much as she knew it would. It hurt her, too. They were stuck in a feedback loop that kept getting louder and more intolerable the longer they were near each other. It was never going to get better, either, because no matter how much Helen hated Lucas for keeping her father in Hades, she still loved him.

"Why couldn't you have just given him back to me?" she asked.

Lucas walked beside her, looking forward, vaguely shaking his head.

"At least tell me why," she persisted.

"I *can't*," he said, nearly choking on the word.

Helen faced him, she wasn't going to let him off the hook again, then she looked down, realizing that their progress had been halted, and not by a Sleeper. There were no Sleepers here. They had come to the banks of another river, but it wasn't the River of Joy. Helen couldn't quite put her finger on it, but she had a feeling she'd been here before. Which was impossible, because how could she forget a river that had pale fish bumping around inside it like they couldn't remember how to swim?

"Where are we?" she asked.

"The river Lethe," he replied. "It was thinking about it so we ended up here."

She stared at those fish, thoughts slipping her mind in the same way she knew they would slip through her hands if she tried to grab one.

"It's not actually a place of forgetting, but of memory," he said. "Spirits wash their memories away here, but they're all there. Stored in the river."

"Yeah, I knew that. You were a knight once," Helen said absently. She looked up at him. "Why do I feel like I miss you?" she sighed more than said.

It seemed silly that he was so far away from her. Were they fighting? Helen couldn't remember, and therefore she decided that whatever had parted them was insignificant. They should always be touching. She stretched up and put her arms around his neck. His hands automatically went to her waist. He tried to move her away from him.

"Helen, don't," he said.

"Why?" she asked.

"It doesn't affect me, but being near the river is dulling your memory. You don't know what you're doing."

She pressed herself up against him. "I don't know what I'm doing so far away from you," she said, smiling at him cheekily until she got the laugh he was trying so hard to quash. She could always make Lucas laugh. "There was, like, a football field between us. That's unnatural."

"It is." He held her tighter for a moment, and then pulled away with a little groan. "We should go back."

"Uh-huh," she murmured, placing her head on his shoulder, and brushing her lips against his neck. "Just a sec."

He put a hand in her hair, moving her head away from him so he could look at her. He was just about to kiss her. Then they were in his private rooms in the palace and he was already walking away from her.

Helen remembered everything again. She really wished she didn't.

When her legs stopped shaking, they flooded with energy. Not ready to join everyone else, she paced about his suite. In an adjoining room she found a large, carven desk with papers scatter all over the top of it dominating the space. The papers looked old and thick, like parchment.

Helen went around the desk, noticing that the papers were filled with lists and lists of names in every language imaginable. Looking at all the dots and squiggles, the letters and accent marks that didn't exist in English, she wondered if Lucas could pronounce all those names. As soon as she asked herself that question, she knew the answer. Not only could he pronounce all those names, but he could speak every language in the world. He had to, in order to be able to communicate with any spirit that came before him.

She touched his fine fountain pen and his onyx paper weight, wondering if he ever had any reason to use either. She knew she had no right to touch his things, or poke through his rooms, but she couldn't help it. She browsed the books on his shelves, not recognizing any of the titles. Had they ever read the same books, she wondered?

Suddenly very tired, Helen went in search of a room of her own. She picked one that had access to the terrace. She immediately crossed to the French doors and closed the curtains. She knew the bodies in the grass were sleeping and that no violence had come to them. Still, it looked like the whole world was dead.

CHAPTER 11

Hector and Daedelus hacked away at each other, the sound of swords clanging on shields rang out in Lucas' marble hall, underpinned by the sound of huffing and grunts. Everyone was enjoying the entertainment. In Hades, all of their godly skills were vastly diminished, and that gave them a chance to gauge their true abilities. Hector was beside himself with glee at the chance to spar with Daedelus.

Helen had barely slept an hour after her visit with Cronus, but sleep didn't matter anymore. Her mind was turning on a wheel that led right back to where it started. She had a day, maybe two left to figure out how to get to the Fates, and she still had no idea how to do that.

She saw Dionysus glancing at her as he spoke and laughed with Kate. Helen knew any minute now he'd be making his way toward her. She slipped out. She didn't want to get sucked into one of his diversions. She needed to focus, and Dionysus' presence was not good for problem solving.

"Are you running away from Hector or Dionysus?" Orion guessed, hurrying to catch up to her as she crossed the terrace and went out among the Sleepers.

"Both," Helen admitted. "It's like both of them need to be doing something every second or they'll implode."

Orion didn't laugh like she thought he would. "Hector needs to keep himself distracted so he doesn't start screaming. He feels guilty."

Helen pulled a face, surprised. "For what?"

"For telling you to use your lightning on the griffins. He thinks it's all his fault."

Helen bumped into a Sleeper, repositioned herself, and continued on sputtering at Orion. "That's just *ridiculous*."

Orion shook his head. "If he'd taken the time to learn that they could conduct lightning he would have told you to fight them hand to hand, knowing you still could have beaten them that way. Ecpyrosis wouldn't have happened. That how he sees it, anyway."

"It's not his fault, and I couldn't have beaten them with my fists. Zeus would have just sent more," she mumbled, dismissing the notion.

"It's all our faults, and it's none of our faults. This started way before we were born. My dad thinks it's *his* fault."

"How does he figure that?"

"If my mother and father didn't have me, two Houses wouldn't have joined. You and I wouldn't have shared blood. The gods would never have left Olympus." Orion gave her a sidelong look. "See? We're all to blame. And also, none of us are. I don't think we've figured out where it began yet, and until we do, we won't find a way out. It's a good thing we've got forever to figure out how to fix the end. We're going to need it. That and a lot of luck. Good thing we have Plutus and Palamedes. He said luck is on your side."

Helen huffed a laugh in reply. It came out weak and strangled. Orion frowned.

"What is it?" he asked.

"I don't know how much I agree with that. We don't actually have forever," she admitted. She didn't mean to burden him by telling him everything, but it all came tumbling out anyway.

Orion had stopped walking. He was staring dumbstruck at the Sleepers at their feet. "So, they're all going to lose their minds?"

"Morpheus said if we wait much longer, they won't be able to tell the difference between what they've dreamed and what's happened to them in real life. Everyone will have a different reality." She gestured to the nearest Sleepers. "*He'll* be convinced he really was a rock star or an astronaut or whatever it is he's been dreaming. *She'll* be convinced she has a talking pet giraffe, or an alien in her handbag. They won't be able to understand that those things didn't really happen to them. That they were just dreams."

"That's very bad."

"It'll be chaos." Helen heard the word as it came out of her mouth. She grabbed Orion's arm in excitement. "Hang on."

"Please tell me you've figured it out," he said desperately.

She didn't want to let herself get too carried away, so she contented herself with squeezing Orion's hand. "We need Morpheus."

They started running as best they could through the seemingly endless carpet of bodies. Helen had learned to trust the landscape to bring her where she envisioned going, and in moments she saw the nightmare tree. Beyond it, was Morpheus' pavilion. A few paces more and they were climbing the steps to where he stood between two burning braziers.

"Are dreams a way into chaos?" Helen asked him, blurting the words out as soon as they had formed in her head.

Morpheus looked stunned for a moment, and then pensive the next as he considered. "I suppose they could be," he ventured, looking concerned. "But Helen, I don't know if dreams are the *safest* way to chaos."

"Well, it's the only way I can think of," she said, not bothering to hide her desperation. "Will you help me?"

Morpheus had obvious misgivings. He looked at Orion with a combination of worry and appraisal. "If he consents to go with you as a safeguard, I will."

"Go with her?" Orion repeated. "Inside her dreams?"

Helen could tell he was both frightened and intrigued by the prospect. To see another person's dreams would be like looking inside their heads.

"Inside a series of dreams," Morpheus corrected. "She'll need someone there watching her, ready to pull her back if she goes too far."

"Hold on," Helen said, suddenly having doubts. "Are these going to be my dreams, or dreams you make up for me?" she asked Morpheus.

He gave her a sympathetic look, understanding her sudden reservations. Danger, Helen could handle. Mortification over Orion potentially seeing her most private and intimate thoughts was a different matter.

"Both," Morpheus replied. "It's only chaos if you start to

question what is real." He gave them both a knowing smile. "This is not going to be easy on either of you, but if you're determined to try—"

"I am," Helen said with far more conviction than she felt.

Orion nodded, despite the fact that he looked petrified. "Yeah. Okay. We're doing this," he muttered, trying to psyche himself up. "I'm not going to lose my grip on reality too, right?" he asked Morpheus.

"You must do your best not to, and call to me if you feel as if you are losing your sanity," Morpheus replied, leading them into the interior of his pavilion. "I can't go with you, but I will hear you when you are ready for me to pull you out."

He brought them to his giant bed and motioned for the two of them to get in.

"Have you noticed we always end up in bed together?" Orion said.

"Oh yeah," she said ruefully, scooting down between the smooth sheets. "I've noticed."

Helen and Orion lay on their backs, side by side, their shoulders touching. Helen had to admit to herself that she would have felt no difference if it were Claire or Ariadne lying next to her. There were no butterflies in her stomach, no half-scared hope he'd reach for her under the covers.

She could tell he felt the same about her. For all the near misses and false starts, they were never going to be together romantically. They had forged a true friendship that was now devoid of attraction for both of them, and though Helen was briefly sad that she had missed out on being with someone who would make a fantastic partner, she was more gratified in knowing that the two of them would always be friends, and that neither of them resented the other for it. How that had happened would have struck Helen as some kind of miracle, but for the fact she knew it wasn't divine intervention. It was because Orion really was that remarkable. Or maybe she was that lucky.

"Thank you," Helen whispered to him, turning her face in his direction.

He turned to look at her as well, took her hand under the covers and squeezed it in reply.

"Timing will be of the essence for you, Orion," Morpheus warned. "Call for me too soon and it won't work, too late and —" He trailed off, not venturing and answer.

"And *what*?" Helen demanded. If she was going to do this, she was going to need some particulars.

He mulled it over for a moment. "Maybe you will suffer the same lack of understand that awaits the Sleepers if they stay under too long?" He shrugged. "I'm not sure, Helen. That's the risk, but it's compounded because you are a Worldbuilder. You can make your dreams a reality for others if you see fit."

"Wait," Helen said, sitting up suddenly in a panic.

"Don't worry. You can only change things in Everyland. Here, and in Hades, Lucas and I can rein you in," Morpheus said. "Still, it is a risk."

Helen looked down at Orion. "What do you think?" she asked him.

Orion took a moment before replying. "I think in order for you to find chaos it's going to be dangerous no matter what, because of who you are and what you can do," he decided. "I know you don't want to hear this, but maybe we should have Lucas here—"

Helen flopped back down in the bed. "I don't need Lucas to make decisions for me," she huffed.

"That's not what I meant."

Helen didn't give him a chance to finish. "Let's go," she said to Morpheus. She looked back at Orion. "Are you still going to do this with me?"

"Of course," he answered, frustrated.

Helen fussed with the covers, trying to dispel her annoyance both at Orion for mentioning Lucas, and with herself for her overreaction at hearing his name.

"Okay. I'm ready," she said, closing her eyes.

She heard Morpheus guffaw disbelievingly at her comment. She opened her eyes to make some kind of retort, only to find she could neither see, hear, nor feel anything anymore.

Hector liked cleaning his own equipment after a fight, and it bothered him that there was no need for him to do so in Hades. He preferred his actions to mean something, to have consequence, even in the basic, quotidian way of having to clean up his own messes.

Ignoring the fact that Helen had said something that was annoyingly close to this line of thinking while they'd been arguing about her insistence on including hangovers in Everyland, he went about his usual routine of buffing his armor. It relaxed him. Grounded him. And he needed grounding right now. He had been pretending to be patient and he'd played along with all of Dionysus' games, watching Helen agonize and Lucas strategize, but he'd reached his limit. If he didn't do something soon, he was going to start screaming.

There was a knock on the door to the secondary room of his suite. Someone like Lucas would have a library or an office in this space adjoining the bedroom, but for Hector's tastes and inclinations it had become a fancy locker room where he stored all of his work-out gear, armor, and weapons. There were benches to sit on while changing, all sorts of different sized mounts and shelves for the various bits of armor, and drawers beneath them with the corresponding tools, rags, and solvents necessary for keeping all that leather, bronze, and steel in the best condition. All that was missing were the actual lockers. He could never put his armor in a cage. That was barbaric.

"Come in," he called, and Andy entered.

He stayed where he was, one hand hovering over his work, frozen. It struck Hector that even though she could wear anything she wanted as easily as jeans and a t-shirt—jewels, gowns, high-end couture—she still chose to wear jeans and a t-shirt. He loved it. She had one of those bodies that looked extravagant no matter what she wore, and even in the simplest clothes she held herself in such a confident way that it was as if she was wearing high-end couture. He didn't know what couture was anyway. For all he knew, she *was* wearing it.

This was the part where he was supposed to say something.

"You're avoiding me," she said, not at all cowed by his frown or his silence.

"I am," he admitted.

"Are you still angry with me?"

"No."

She shifted her stance into something less confrontational. "Then what is it? I know you still love me, and I've made it pretty clear how I feel about you."

He looked back down at his armor and gave it a few swipes because he didn't know how to say what he wanted to say. She came to him and took the brush out of his hand. As soon as she touched him, he jumped up and started throwing his things haphazardly onto the shelves.

"You should go, Andy," he said.

She got in his face. "Make me."

He turned away from her. "I don't want to hurt you," he said, shaking with the effort to keep his hands to himself. She watched him carefully for a moment.

"*That's* what this is about," she said, relieved. She laughed under her breath and moved closer to him, putting a hand on his bare arm, and sliding it up to his shoulder. "You won't."

He jumped back. "You don't understand. I—something happened to me."

She just smiled as she came closer. "Uh-huh. I know. The blood."

"Wait—" Hector began, confused. He didn't know how to frame his next sentence.

"You don't scare me. You *do* know what sirens like, don't you?" she asked, shaking her head at him.

Now he really didn't know what was going on, because it almost seemed to him like she was saying that she liked the blood, too. Before he could figure out what questions to ask her and how to ask them without sounding like a freak, Cassandra called from outside the door and Hector, grateful for the interruption, moved away from Andy and hollered for his cousin to enter.

"Orion isn't with you?" Cassandra asked as she swept in, though she could see plainly enough for herself that he wasn't.

JOSEPHINE ANGELINI

"He's not out there?" Hector asked.

Cassandra shook her head. "I think he went somewhere with Helen." Knowing that what she said was putting them into the awkward position of having to tiptoe around what Helen and Orion might be doing while sneaking off together, Cassandra made a frustrated sound. "No, not like that. There's something very confusing about to happen. Something that I don't know how to explain."

"Did you see something?" Andy guessed.

"Maybe?" Cassandra replied uncertainly. "It's like a dream, or a nightmare, and I can't quite figure it out, but I think whatever it is they're about to do is a bad idea. I think it's going to make things worse, and we should find them and stop them."

Hector nodded. Finding people and stopping them were things he was very good at. "Lucas!" he called.

"I already tried that," Cassandra said. "I don't know where he went, but it must be outside the borders of Hades, because he's not answering."

That worried Hector. Cassandra was just about the only person Lucas had always listened to, and if she called him, he would certainly come, unless something was stopping him. They could ask Hades the god for help, but Hector had a feeling he wouldn't answer, either. Hades had seemed completely checked-out that last time they'd gone to see him.

"Where are those ghost guys?" Hector asked. "The judges."

Hector had died once. He had come to Hades and had his heart judged. He remembered three shadowy figures with crowns on their heads, placing his heart on a scale. Not much had ever scared Hector, but in that moment, he'd felt true fear.

He'd never forgotten them, though he hadn't been told their names.

"Minos, Rhadamanthus, and Aeacus," Cassandra replied. Of course, she knew that. She was as big a geek as Lucas.

"Call them," Hector said. He was still too spooked to do it himself. He'd pull it together once they arrived though, as long as he wasn't the one who was supposed to talk to them.

When they appeared, their vague shapes seemed as foreboding to Hector as they had when they were weighing his heart. The three judges wore chitons, cloaks, and crowns. One had a long white beard, one a long black beard, and the third was clean-shaven. Apart from the facial hair, Hector found them almost interchangeable. They spoke only in whispers, and wouldn't let either Hector or Andy approach. They wafted away when anyone but Cassandra or Lucas tried to get nearby, which was fine by him. Hector kept his distance while Cassandra conversed with them. The ghosts waited a way off while Cassandra shuttled their message back to Andy and Hector.

"Well?" Andy asked.

"Helen and Orion are with Morpheus in the Land of Sleep, and Lucas is gone. No one knows where he went. The dead are agitated. The judges say that Lucas is endangering his promise to them," Cassandra said, frowning.

"What promise?" Hector asked.

"It can only be his promise to care for them," Cassandra said, taking an exasperated guess. "They aren't very forthcoming."

Hector nodded. "Right. First things first. Let's go get Helen and Orion." He gestured to the three judges. "Can they, uh…"

"*Get* us there?" Cassandra finished for him. She nodded. "They offered to shadow travel us."

Andy balked. "Orion told me about that. Shadow traveling is supposed to be super creepy," she said.

"You and Orion talk often?" Hector asked, bothered by it.

Andy shrugged. "Sure."

"How often?"

"Like, all the time," Andy said, throwing up her hands. "There are about a dozen people awake in the world, if you hadn't noticed, and he's very easy to talk to."

"Yeah. Oh. I'm *sure*." Hector was just flinging words out of his mouth like they were insults, even though they weren't very insulting. He felt something fluttering in his stomach. Not a butterfly. More like a bat. An angry, nasty, irrational bat.

Andy smiled slowly, enjoying the show. "If I had *you* to talk to, I wouldn't have to talk so much to Orion," she said tauntingly.

"Easy to talk to," he grumbled under his breath. "Not so easy to talk to with my fist in his—"

Cassandra whirled away from them and went back to the three judges. What started as a discussion quickly became more like an argument. From what Hector could gather, the three judges didn't agree with the Scion's choice to go after Helen and Orion instead of Lucas. As Cassandra argued, the judges became more disturbed. Hector could feel the air pressure around him changing, like a bunch of people were crowding in close, though there were no bodies present. There was a sudden chill in the air, and he saw Andy shiver and hug herself. Instinctively, he stepped closer so she could shelter against him. Her arms were covered in goosebumps and he tried not to enjoy the feel of them. The dead were getting angry, and Cassandra was just being stubborn. Despite how she'd brushed it aside, she still wanted to interrupt whatever Helen and Orion were up to.

"We can't win this one, Cass! Let's just do what they want and get Luke first," Hector called out. Cassandra faced him, her mouth agape in disbelief at his defection, but Hector wasn't going to feed into this nonsense and talked over her. "It's not like we can fight these guys. They're driving, not us," he added, gesturing to the three judges.

"Okay!" she snapped and stomped over to Hector and Andy. "Bring us to where you last sensed my brother," she called out to the three judges.

It felt like hands were crawling all over him, and not in a sexy way. Everything was dark, and Hector was overcome with a sensation of powerlessness. It was not something he was either used to, nor willing to become used to. The only thing good about it was that it was over quickly.

They appeared—jolting out of the darkness with various shouts and sounds of protest still burbling from their mouths— in the shadows of a rocky overhang. Across a stretch of black sand was a huge body of silvery-gray water that oozed and sloughed onto the shore, behaving as if it was as dense as mercury. Cassandra wandered to the mouth of the indentation that was sheltering them, staring at the body of liquid.

"It's Ocean," she said, awed. Then she strode out purposefully toward the water and turned around to look at their environs. Her expression was blank with shock and mounting horror.

Hector hurried out to see what Cassandra saw, with Andy close behind. The indentation that they had appeared inside was part of a crumbling, saw-toothed mountain of obsidian-flecked volcanic rock. The sky was a livid shade of dark red brown, like dried blood. There was no sun, no clouds, and no moisture in the air. Hector could feel the malevolence of this place, staring down on him like an eye in the sky. Even the acrid air scoured the skin with bits of glass-flecked sand.

"Tartarus," he said.

"Why would Lucas come here?" Andy asked.

Cassandra shook her head, dazed. "He must have come here looking for answers."

"Who's the boss around here?" Hector asked.

"Erebus and Nyx," Cassandra replied. "Darkness and Night," she said more quietly.

Hector scanned the horizon. There were duplicates of the sharp, volcanic mountain that they stood near shooting up periodically across what was otherwise a completely flat landscape, but one of the shapes he could make out was a little too regular and smooth to be a mountain.

"There," he said, pointing at it. "Is that a building?"

"The Mansion of Darkness," Cassandra said, naming it. She looked at her cousin and nodded. "It's the home of Erebus and Nyx. I bet Lucas went to see them."

"He's probably trying to make a deal with them," Hector said. Lucas was probably trying to bargain with the lords of Tartarus, and probably at his own expense. "Let's hope we can stop him before he ends up stuck in Tartarus."

They started walking toward the mansion.

.   .   .

Helen was in Mr. Hergesheimer's class. He had on his favorite yellow scarf today. Matt was talking passionately about *Catcher in the Rye*.

Helen had almost finished reading that book, but not quite because she'd had to work the night before, and after Holden Caufield rented the hotel room, and was thinking about calling a sex worker, Helen had lost interest and turned out her light. Sleep was more crucial than reading about a whiny, over-privileged white guy who, in Helen's opinion, needed to get a frigging job. Maybe if he had to uncrate an entire shipment of beverages, all in slippery glass bottles, he'd stop complaining about how everyone was so "phony". Some dead-arm from the repetitive motion of lifting and pushing back bottle after bottle into a refrigerator—and for minimum wage—was exactly what that guy needed.

Anyway, Matt loved the book. To him, Holden Caufield was a hero of individuality. He believed Holden was fighting against his over-privileged up-bringing, and not indulging in a no-consequences drunken spree afforded him by his rich boy status, like Helen did. But she didn't want to get into an argument with Matt in class. Especially since she had no idea how the book ended.

"Miss Hamilton. You look like you have something to say," Mr. Hergesheimer said leadingly.

Crap. She hated it when Hergie put her on the spot like this. He was definitely going to ask her about the ending, too, she just knew it. And then she'd be caught out. Again. She almost never finished the books for this class, but it wasn't her fault. There just weren't enough hours in the day. Between track, and chores, and work, she had no time. The bell rang.

Helen tried not to laugh out loud at the look of consternation on Hergie's face. "I thought he was an idiot," Helen said over the sound of everyone gathering up their stuff, and she ran for the door before Hergie could make her write a paper on *why* she thought Holden was an idiot.

She walked to her locker—or at least, she tried to. Everything was strange. It was definitely the right hallway, but when she tried to turn the corner past the art room, she couldn't find her locker. It simply wasn't there. Helen looked at all the lockers on the wall. There seemed to be thousands of them. But they were the wrong color and the dials had strange mathematical symbols on them, and for the life of her, Helen couldn't solve the equation and open her locker, but maybe that was because the locker wasn't even hers, but it should have been.

How could she have forgotten where her locker was? She was so late. No one was in the hallways anymore. She ran for it, thinking it would be better to show up without her book than not at all. She ran down steps, up others, down hallways that were now the hallways from her elementary school. Yeah, she was in the wrong school now and there was Matt as a little boy, walking with Zach, and then she turned a corner and she was in a huge mall, skylights everywhere, and she was running down a wide staircase that led to an indoor courtyard that was filled with tables of people sitting down to eat.

Was she in an airport? Maybe it was an airport, not a mall. She ran because she knew she was supposed to meet someone. Someone was supposed to be here with her. Oh! Maybe she was supposed to pick up her dad? That was it. She must have forgotten!

His plane already landed and she was at the wrong gate. She

had to run, but if she went too fast, she couldn't read the gate numbers. She was lost. Her dad was going to be so angry. He always told her, "On time is ten minutes early," and that she shouldn't leave the house at the last second but she had a list of things to do every day. Things she didn't even want to do. She had so many responsibilities, things she had to keep hidden, and it was all her fault, and how the heck was she supposed to leave ten minutes earlier if she didn't even get out of school until ten minutes later than she should have left?

She had to find her dad and make sure he never found out she was late. If he found out about that, he'd know about all the terrible things she'd done and he'd never love her. How could anyone love her if they knew what she really was? She looked for him, but she couldn't see anything clearly. No matter how hard she squinted from her hiding place she couldn't make out the gate numbers. She wasn't even at the airport anymore. She would never make it in time to get her dad. Nothing was familiar, nothing made sense. Hallways ended in walls. She was running, running, endlessly running.

She pushed through a door and into a dusty warehouse that stored all the strange-looking vehicles that moved baggage and planes. She tried to drive one to get back inside the airport, but the control panel was rusted and she couldn't push the buttons. There were bad people everywhere now. She was trying to push her way through a crowd but there were men who touched her and pressed up against her. No matter how hard she screamed at them—they had no right to do that—they just smirked at her. What was *she* going to do about it, they asked with those satisfied smirks. She couldn't hurt them or make them stop even if she punched and kicked. She screamed and screamed.

"Helen! This isn't chaos, it's a nightmare!" someone yelled.

That someone was a friend. But her friends didn't trust her. Her friends had found out about all the shameful things she'd done, they'd found out about those men and their smirks. They knew she wasn't the sweet, innocent girl they wanted her to be. The one they liked. The one she pretended to be. Her friends had turned on her.

No one loved her. No one ever could. She'd chased Lucas for months, but it was only after she'd slept with him that he'd bailed. He must have discovered the truth. She just wasn't worth it. Smirk.

CHAPTER 12

Palamedes was always willing to throw dice, but he felt like he should be somewhere else. Or maybe he was expected somewhere, or he was supposed to be doing something else? Dionysus kept reminding them all that there was plenty of time.

Plenty of time for what? Palamedes wondered.

Dionysus threw an arm over Palamedes shoulder and they both started laughing. Palamedes had no idea what was funny, or even what was going on, but he was braying like an ass anyway. Dionysus had a three-martini aura and Palamedes had been standing next to him for too long. He had to get away before he passed out.

"You win!" Palamedes relented, begging off. "Here. Take these."

Palamedes shoved the chips they'd been using as money at Dionysus hurriedly, pocketed his dice, and staggered as far away from the party god as fast he possibly could. He poured himself a glass of water and hoped he didn't have sleep with one foot to the floor again.

"Did you win, or... nope. You lost," Plutus said, scanning his husband quickly and noticing the glassy eyes and sloppy smile. "Come here. Sit. Drink your water."

Plutus led Palamedes over to a couch where Noel was sitting by herself looking very sober, and pushed him down next to her.

"I'll get you some bread," Plutus said, and hustled off to the never-ending buffet that was always filled with fresh food.

Noel didn't have to ask what happened. From what Palamedes had learned after many a late-night conversation with her, she'd been a New York bartender, and a good one at that. She'd seen every form of inebriation in her day, and she knew that Dionysus' kind came with an extra helping of stupid. Sort of like tequila.

"I can't tell if he's actively trying to make us forget that the world has ended, or if he just can't get by without constant distraction," she said, watching Dionysus with narrowed eyes.

"S'not his fault," Palamedes said, only slurring slightly. "You know what we need? Other people with fresh legs. We should start waking people up. They can hang out with him."

Noel's shoulders shook with silent laughter. "That's a terrible idea," she said.

"You're right. Scratch that. Bloody awful idea," Palamedes agreed. "Can you imagine? *Wake up! World's over! No need to cry, just stand next to this god and you'll be drunk in a minute.*"

Noel's laugh was genuine but it didn't last long. She soon went back to watching everyone else. The great hall in the Palace of Hades was a sumptuous place, full of impressive columns and brightly burning torches that never smoked. It was just the

right mix of modern elegance and classical Greek solidity that
dodged gold-toilet gaucheness and landed effortlessly in monumental yet understated territory. If that wasn't an oxymoron,
which Palamedes suspected it was.

Oxymoron or not, the palace hall wound up being the
perfect setting for an opulent party. Laughter rang out regularly,
along with the rise and fall of excited conversation. Occasionally, Ladon would challenge them to solve a riddle, or Claire
would be cajoled into singing or playing an instrument, never
ceasing to amaze. All of these sounds and sights were refracted,
given brightness, and made to seem larger and more polished
inside this jewel of a room. It was a dark Olympus, and they
were the new gods.

Noel turned to face Palamedes. "What do you think our
chances of ever getting out of here are?" she asked.

"Really small," he answered, guffawing. That was exactly
the wrong thing to say. He tried again, kicking himself. "I'm
sure your son and Helen will figure it out."

Plutus returned with the bread and Noel posed her question to him.

"I know as little as you," he replied. "I'm no Oracle."

"But don't you carry a coin that tells you the odds?" she
asked him, frowning with confusion. "Doesn't Tyche speak to
you through it? Doesn't she tell you what's lucky and what
isn't?"

"It does, but it can't tell you the odds," Plutus replied. His
hand went to his pocket automatically, and realizing it, he
stopped himself from taking it out. "It's a coin. There are only
two sides."

"Yes or no," she said, understanding the distinction. "Have

you asked your coin if we'll get out of here?"

Plutus looked away shaking his head, as if he didn't want to even consider what she said.

"Why not?" she pressed. "Because that would be involving the Fates, and you don't want them to interfere?"

"Because I don't want to *know*," Plutus said. "I want to *believe*. I want to have faith." He huffed in frustration. "You humans are so lucky and you don't even know it. You can choose to believe in things, no matter how wild or improbable those things are. You have faith. It's a beautiful thing. A powerful thing. It can make the future into what you want it to be. Don't ask me to flip my coin and tell you yes or no. Believe you have luck, and you'll have it."

Noel's countenance changed. Slowly, she seemed to brighten from within as she thought on what Plutus said.

"I guess you would understand luck better than anyone," she said, warming to the idea. She laughed suddenly. "My dad always called himself unlucky, and he was. Even when nothing particularly bad was happening to him, he carried a black cloud around, waiting for more bad luck. He ruined good things by expecting them to turn bad. He made life worse than it had to be in a lot of ways."

Plutus nodded. "So, why not believe we're lucky?" A look of understanding passed between them.

"Why not?" Noel agreed.

The ground was rocky and dotted with dead, low-growing plants that were covered in sharp little thorns. The air tasted bitter and the sky boiled with red clouds.

"Does it look like it's going to rain to anyone else?" Andy asked.

"Yeah, but rain *what*? I don't think water comes out of the sky here," Hector replied.

Andy stumbled and he took her hand to steady her. She glanced at up him, grateful. She was half water creature and the quickest to suffer in this arid environment. Hector knew that soon he would either have to get her out of here or find some water for her to drink. As strong as he knew she was, she wasn't built for this.

"There's a river," he said, pointing at a thin line on the horizon.

"Acheron," Cassandra murmured, her eyes pinned to it with grim fascination.

He couldn't be sure because the landscape wavered, the view distorted by smoke and dust, but it looked to him like the Mansion of Darkness was farther away than the Acheron.

"We might have to cross the river to get to the mansion," he said.

"How?" Andy asked, scanning the length of it. There were no bridges. "Do you think it's something we can swim through?"

Hector looked at the snaking length of the river Acheron dubiously, considering. Phlegethon was a river of fire. Styx was a river of souls. Both of them sprang from the Acheron, and as such he had no idea what it was that was flowing between its banks, but he didn't think it was something anyone would want to submerge themselves in.

Their steps neither lengthened nor sped up, but in moments they had covered the distance and were standing on the banks of the Acheron River. Smoke clung to the surface of the black water like fog, obscuring the view both up and down its length and the bank of the far shore. Above the low-lying smoke they could just make out the spires atop the Mansion of Darkness, stabbing at the red sky.

They heard a rhythmic creaking. Something was making its way down the river, coming toward them. As the smoke parted, they saw a ferry. A lamp lit the bow, and beneath it, the Greek letter omega was written on the hull.

Hector felt a thrill go down his back when Charon the Ferryman, son of Erebus and Nyx, came into view. Cloaked from head to toe, and plying his oar at the back of the ferry, a large hood covered his head and kept his face in shadows. Even his hands were gloved in black. It was impossible to tell if he was old, young, or even if he was fully human. Though thin, he was taller and larger than a normal man. Hector barely came up to his chest. Charon pulled his ferry alongside them and used his oar to anchor the *Omega* to the bank. He tipped his hooded head at Hector, acknowledging their acquaintance. They had met once before. Charon held out one long-fingered hand, palm up.

"Did anyone bring a coin?" Cassandra asked in an urgent undertone. Before they could check their empty pockets, Charon gestured for them to climb aboard.

"No need for payment. You are expected," he whispered. His voice was raspy and thin, but it carried to each of them as if he were speaking directly into their ears.

They asked Charon to explain further, but he did not reply. He kept his hand held out, palm up, gesturing for them to come aboard as if he could wait there for centuries.

Hector helped Cassandra and Andy aboard, and then stood between them and Charon who stood at the back. The ferry slid out into the river, the oar creaking in its bed with every push. Water of any kind usually had a scent, but the Acheron did not. Not even petrichor. The dry smoke that hung above the water smelled very faintly of charcoal, but Hector couldn't be sure if he was imagining that. Tartarus, or at least this part of it, had no scent at all.

Charon did not take them across the river, but upstream to where the river looped back around and met the side of the Mansion of Darkness. The river seemed to originate from underneath it. Charon steered the ferry beneath an arch in the side on the black-stoned building and into a cavernous room.

Sconces burned on the supporting pillars of the cathedral-like space, barely lighting all the way up to the groin-vaulted ceiling. There were no windows, but even from the sconces' meager light, it was clear to see that the river simply ended here. Or maybe it began here, upwelling from some deep source. There was a wide cobblestone walkway aside the water, with steps leading down into the water. Charon steered them to a thick iron ring lodged in the wall next to the steps, and grabbed it. He pointed silently for them to mount the stairs.

Hector helped Cassandra and Andy disembark, and then turned back to say, "Thank you."

Charon tipped his head accepting the thanks, and as he did so Hector tried to peek under the cowl of his hood, but all he saw were more shadows.

They followed the lit sconces into the mansion. Monumental blocks of black stone carved and fitted one atop the other with such precision that no mortar lay between them, gave the oppressive feeling that they were in the belly of a pyramid. There were window casements made of smaller carved stones, but no windows inside those casements, only more stone. Rib-vaulted ceilings webbed the space above them, undecorated. The flagstones beneath their feet were bare. It was an empty house, built for beings much larger than humans.

At the end of the long hallway, they came to an apse where two enormous black thrones sat on a raised dais. The stonework on the support pillars grew more intricate as they went up, until they wove together into lacy designs in the rib vaults that supported a hemispherical dome above. The dome was dotted with glittering jewels that were inlaid in the shape of the constellations. It felt like they were in a stone forest and that the petrified canopy reached up into the night sky.

The thrones were empty. Hector turned all the way around, looking in every direction. "Where are they? Where's Lucas?" he asked.

"We are here," said a woman's voice. It seemed to come from the dome above. He looked up and saw shadows moving across the jeweled constellations, momentarily obscuring them, and then passing by.

"Let me see Luke," he said, not liking that they were above him.

The shadows came together and flowed down a column, shaping into a titanically large woman. Nyx was all deepest black—skin, hair, dress—and flecked everywhere with icy white stars, like the night sky had taken a colossal human form. Her dress trailed behind her in a long train that stayed swept up the pillar and into the dome above.

She was easily three times as tall as Hector, and she bent her head to regard her visitors. There was no difference between her skin, eyes, and clothing. She was all one thing, unbroken except for the constellations that twinkled, not like jewels at all, but like actual stars across the void that was her. Though she was more nothing than face and body, it was clear that *nothing* was looking at Cassandra.

"The Moirae are silent," Nyx said, in a low and resonant voice.

Cassandra frowned, as if she were listening to a song inside her head, trying to remember the lyrics. "You're right," she said. "What does that mean?"

Nyx only stared at her.

"Where's Lucas?" Hector repeated. Nyx slowly turned her head to him, and though the shape of her face didn't move, she was obviously glaring at him. "I'm sorry Lady, but you said *we* were here, and I need to find my cousin," he continued with a much more respectful tone.

"He has gone beyond," she said, indicating the dome.

"Beyond what?" Cassandra asked. She looked up at the star speckled dome and then back at Nyx. "Beyond the universe?"

"Beyond," she repeated, like the word was self-explanatory. "To the Mother."

Hector looked at Cassandra for an answer, she usually had one, but her eyes were wide with confusion.

"The Mother of what?" Hector hazarded.

"Everything," said a male voice. Another shadow detached itself from the dark dome above and slid down to stand next to the second throne. Unlike Nyx, Erebus was completely black, with no stars to pick out his shape. He was total light-swallowing darkness, and as such he was hard to see in the ill-lit surroundings. Nevertheless, it was impossible not to look at him. His presence sucked at the gaze, pulling it ever deeper. "She from which all was made. Our mother."

Cassandra froze, so Hector could tell she'd figured it out, but she also looked terrified, so he knew whatever it was he wasn't going to like it.

"Chaos," she whispered. "Do you mean my brother is with Chaos herself?" She grabbed Hector's forearm, starting to panic as she faced him. "You have to go get him. He'll be ripped apart!"

"The Hand of Darkness struggles," Erebus said in agreement.

"Where is he?" Hector said.

"He has gone beyond," Nyx replied, tilting her head in consolation. "The gate is one way. None who goes can come back."

Well, damn. Hector knew what he had to do. He had to go get his cousin.

He looked at Andy. Maybe he could have had a life with her, but he supposed Lucas was the reason he'd been able to have anything at all with her these past few months. If Lucas hadn't traded himself, Hector would be dead. He'd squandered the time he'd been given with Andy, though.

"I should have gone with you," he said, shaking his head at how stupid he'd been.

"What are you talking about?" Andy said, pretending she didn't know what he was about to do. She knew. Because she knew him. She just didn't want to know.

"When you left to do your research, I blamed you for leaving, but I should have followed you. We would have had months together."

"You're scaring me," she whispered.

He looked up at Nyx and then at Erebus. "I've got to go help my cousin. Send me to the Mother."

"Hector, no," Andy said, putting a hand on his chest and pushing him back. "You'll die."

"No, I won't," he said with certainty. He felt this one. Chaos didn't scare him.

Cassandra stepped closer to the Elementals. "Is it possible for him to survive this?" she asked.

"The god of war will not die in the Mother. War is a piece of Chaos. She will not send him to oblivion," Nyx said.

Hector nodded. "What about Lucas?"

The Elementals paused. "He struggles," Erebus repeated. "He fights for control where there is none."

Hector chuffed. Figures Lucas would try to take charge and make it all logical. "Send me to him."

"We cannot let you back out if we do," Nyx warned. "We cannot risk letting the Mother escape."

"I'll find my own way."

Andy stepped in front of him. "You don't know that!" she yelled right into his face. "Obviously, they have Chaos imprisoned here. That's what Tartarus is—a prison. If you go in, you'll never get out."

Hector put his hands on Andy and kissed her. She was scared, and he loved her for it, but he wasn't. Following Lucas into this fight was what he was always meant to do. Hector was built to run headlong into chaos. He tried to tell her that with his kiss because he didn't have time to figure out how to do it with words. When he felt her relax, he ended the kiss and pulled back.

"I have to go, Andy. You have to let me."

"I know!" she shouted. She knew because she knew him. She poked him on the chest. "If you don't find a way back, I won't forgive you."

"Deal," he said, backing away from her. He looked up at Nyx and Erebus. "I'm ready whenever you are."

Waking felt no different from being asleep, except that Helen was suddenly fully clothed and covered in sweat, whereas as moment ago she was naked and shivering. Since only one of these states could be true, she had to figure out which was real and which wasn't.

"Wake up," Orion said.

And she sat up to face him. It took effort to pry her teeth apart and speak. She must have been clenching her jaw. "Are you here?" she asked him.

"It's me," he said, sitting back on his heels. He looked terrible. "I tried to reach you in your dream, but you kept running away."

They were in Morpheus' bed. A quick glance told her Morpheus was not there, which was strange. Then she remembered.

"I didn't find it," she said.

Orion looked exhausted and his shoulders were slumped. "I just couldn't catch up to you. If I had, maybe I would have been able to—"

"This isn't your fault," Helen interrupted. "It wasn't the

way to chaos. It was definitely the way to self-loathing and anxiety, but not chaos."

"It felt chaotic to me," Orion said, chuffing.

"No, I was wrong. Again."

She knew he was staring at her. He may not have been beside her in her dream, but he was there. Watching. He'd seen all of it, and the parts that he couldn't see she knew he could feel them. All of her rage and shame. All of her fear and desperation. She glanced up at him and he was studying her, as she'd suspected, but not with pity or disgust. He looked curious.

"Maybe not," he said pensively. "Do you want to try again?"

Helen gave a weak laugh. "Definitely not."

"I meant, would you like to try again, but this time with me as the dreamer?" He sat up and moved nearer. "You might have felt out of control when you were dreaming, but you weren't. Not really. Whether we know it or not, we create our dreams, so they can't be chaos to us. Our brains are just working out things in their own way. But when I was in your dream—" he broke off and exhaled shakily. "I was completely out of control. It was insane."

Helen really didn't want to do it again. But what she wanted even less was to fail. "Okay." She looked around for Morpheus. "But, how? Where did Morpheus go anyway?"

Orion looked confused for a second and then scared as a thought occurred to him. "Are we still dreaming?"

Her first impulse was to deny it, but she couldn't trust anything right now. She tried to make the scenery change and *think* them back to Lucas' palace, but they remained in bed.

"If we are, it's not my dream." she told him.

. . .

...They were in a huge, packed room. People stood in lines that were so long Helen couldn't even see either end of them. She had no idea how long she'd been standing there or how much longer it would take to get to the front of it. She didn't even know what she was standing in line for.

Someone was supposed to meet her. Someone was supposed to be helping her, guiding her, but they weren't there. She started to panic. Was she lost? She spotted a little kid, and she knew him. Her friend. What was his name?

She pushed her way through the crowd to get to him but the people were so big and tall and she wasn't supposed to lose the slip of paper in her hand. She clutched it, trying to get to the boy, desperate not to drop it.

The boy was arguing with a man, but she didn't know the language they were speaking. It was not a language at all, but a bunch of codes and symbols that neither of them could read. They couldn't understand each other either, but she knew that they should. The man wasn't even trying to understand, and the boy was asking for help that the man wouldn't give him. The man looked like Lucas.

And there he was. Lucas. He was kissing someone, falling into her like a comet coming to earth. She was the kind of woman that pulled everything to her, but what she wanted most was him. Outside looking in on that kind of love made her feel small. She wanted that feeling more than anything. That perfect fit. Nothing ever fit.

Her clothes were pulling on her, smothering her. She saw someone was with her, struggling with limbs that grew too fast, clothes that grew holes too quickly, and shoes that were always dirty. She reached out for her friend, but he ran away. She chased him.

They flew, but she didn't know how to fly. She was falling. He was falling. And Lucas was there again. As they fell, and she couldn't remember her friend's name, she realized that Lucas was always himself to her, even in someone else's dreams. She could always recognize him and call him by name even when she couldn't do so for anyone else. Not even herself.

She called out to Lucas, as she and her friend lurched sickeningly in the air, but he couldn't catch them, and then Lucas was talking to her friend. They kept moving away from her, turning their back so she wouldn't hear. But she knew Lucas was asking her friend to do something. He was making him promise something. He didn't want to promise. He knew it would be bad if he did. She pushed until she was near enough to hear them. She was always going to hear them because she was in her friend's dream.

"Don't tell Helen that her father doesn't want her," Lucas said.

And her friend knew how lost and lonely it would feel to know that, and so he agreed to do as asked even though he knew it was wrong. And now he was trying to hide. Run and hide, always hiding. And always alone.

Helen couldn't find her friend anymore. She couldn't lose him, and she soon found him, but he was saying, "Get away from this, Helen. You can't see this."

They were standing by a river. The river had pale fish in it that had forgotten how to swim.

"Don't look! It'll hurt too much!" Lucas screamed.

. . .

Hector had always known that he and Lucas were a pair of opposites that worked.

They had plenty in common. They were both loyal and brave. They both loved their family. They were both extremely competitive, and they were both leaders. It's tough to have two leaders in a small family group, but that's the way it had always been between them. They'd been fighting about it since they were so little, they could barely stand on their own. One of Hector's first memories was of hitting Lucas, and it not working. Lucas just got back up and fought harder.

Hector had always known that it was his cousin who made the choices, while he was the one that everyone followed. Strange distinction to make, but once Hector got the hang of waiting to hear what Lucas thought was best, he just stood up and did it, and everyone followed him in the doing of it, though not necessarily in the listening to Lucas part. In that way they'd learned to share leadership, not like partners as they rarely discussed anything and never compromised, but like two hands that had learned that neither of them got washed unless they came together. Lucas was usually right. He was the one with the answers, no matter how challenging those answers were for anyone else to accept. Hector was the one who was always strong enough to accept it and get it done. And anyway, if Hector didn't do as Lucas wanted, Lucas just went off and did it anyway.

Alone, Lucas usually got hurt. But if Hector was there, Lucas would be okay, and not just physically. This was the real secret that the two of them never talked about, but that they both understood. Lucas was the sensitive one. Compared to Hector's hotheadedness, Lucas seemed cold and calculating sometimes, but he was anything but. He felt things too deeply, which was why he spent so much energy thinking over every single aspect of absolutely everything. He couldn't bear the pain of it if he was wrong and someone he loved got hurt. He'd rather go to hell. Literally.

This odd balance they'd struck had created both a bond and a rivalry that was unlike anything else in Hector's life. He had complete faith that Lucas would do what was right, but there was no one who he mistrusted more—which was yet another strange distinction, but one that got to the heart of their relationship. While he trusted Lucas to do what was best for everyone, Hector also knew that Lucas was ruthless in how he went about it. Mostly with himself.

They'd been in a power struggle their whole lives, one that Hector had to admit Lucas had won years ago, mostly because Hector had just gotten tired of hitting him only to have Lucas get up and fight harder. Hector had changed over the years. He didn't need to control everything. Lucas hadn't learned that yet. He just couldn't stop standing back up, and this was the one time he had to stay down.

Chaos was not something Hector could describe, not even to himself. Visually, it made no sense. Flying giraffes and talking paper cups would have been fine with him. Kaleidoscopes of color that he flew through like he was in a sci-fi movie would have been great, too. This was just disturbing.

It was like a blank space, but this space didn't work like the space he was used to. Trying to take a step, it was as if he suddenly had a third leg. Trying to reach out, his hand didn't go in a straight line, but a curved one, like he'd plunged half his arm into water and it looked bent at a wrong angle. He swore at the strangeness of it, and his voice came from behind him as if from far away, and then kept getting closer, changing in both tone and meaning with his thoughts and fears, until an evil sounding "damn" was breathed into his ear as if coming from someone else.

Close by, but impossible to reach, his cousin sat at a right angle to what Hector thought was the floor, his head in his hands. He was rocking gently, repeating, "Four, no five dimensions, four, no five dimensions..." over and over.

The words were whispered on a loop, but the volume changed drastically with every iteration, and came from different places, as if a chorus of a thousand voices were whispering, and screaming it from rooftops, and up from deep tunnels, and from underneath the covers on a bed, and while running by on a track, and standing five feet away. It sounded like there were thousands of Lucas', one from every place he'd ever been, and they were all speaking to the one sitting on the wall.

He was fighting to get control, inwardly, convinced he could learn to govern himself well enough to weather this storm, but he couldn't win this. The only way to win was to give up. Hector knew it, but Lucas apparently did not.

How the hell was Hector going to get Lucas to stop fighting?

Stop fighting. This, from the god of war. The irony was not lost on Hector. He started laughing.

CHAPTER 13

A rms and legs spasming as he fought up against the membrane of sleep, Orion pushed Helen out of bed.

She hit the marble floor of Morpheus' pavilion with a smack. Twisting herself around she ran into a pair of legs. She looked up and saw Morpheus standing above her.

"Is it over?" she asked. He nodded in reply. "I don't think it worked."

"I'm sorry," Morpheus agreed, helping her up. "And then again, I'm not. It would have been worse to lose you inside a dream."

Helen looked at Orion who looked back like he was waiting for the other shoe to drop. "What was *that*?" she asked, knowing he would know which part of his dreamscape she was talking about. That part that had concerned her and Lucas. There had been a river, too. What was its name?

Orion threw his legs over the other side of the bed and got up. "We should go back to the palace," he said, refusing to discuss it. "Thank you for your help," he said politely to Morpheus.

"Lucas came looking for you," Morpheus continued. "I put him in the dream to help you. Did he?"

"No," Helen replied.

"The outcome was always doubtful," Morpheus said. He gave Helen a worried look. "I hope your next attempt to find the Moirae goes better."

His implication was clear. Helen had to keep trying, though she had no idea what to do next. Not like she ever did, but usually she would have figured something out by now. She thanked Morpheus and they left him with his elven attendants who had been trying to get his attention without getting too close to the Scions. If the expressions of the elven folk were any indication, the plight of the Sleepers was getting worse.

Orion and Helen crossed silently into Hades beneath the nightmare tree. She waited until they had left Morpheus' land to speak.

"What did Lucas ask you to hide from me?" she asked, glancing to the side to watch his expression. Mouth tight, Orion kept his eyes down. "It was about my father. I have a right to know," she continued, refusing to be put off.

"I know you do," he said, finally looking at her. He was torn. "But I can't tell you. Lucas made a vow. I can't break it for him."

"Yeah, you can," Helen replied indignantly.

"No, I can't. Look, I figured it out on my own and when I confronted him about it, he told me how he accidentally made a vow on the river Styx, and I know *you* know that the wording is important. The way he made the vow might include me now."

Helen frowned in confusion. "Did you swear on Styx?"

"No. But the way he worded his vow put him on the hook whether he tells you or someone else does."

"So what happens if you break his vow by telling me?"

"I don't know what happens when you break a vow you made on the Styx. Do you?" Orion replied with a raised brow. "Not even Zeus would dare to break it, or any of the other gods who are included in his vow. Why? What could the punishment possibly be?"

"I don't know," she admitted.

"Me neither. But it's got to be something worse than the eternal imprisonment that Zeus and the Olympians face."

Helen stewed. "I've always kind of wondered about that. Is it the fear of punishment that makes the gods keep their vow, or is it something else?"

"Like what?" he asked.

Helen shook her head. "Don't know. I've never heard of anyone breaking that vow."

"Me neither. But with that in mind, I don't want to tell you and possibly kill Lucas."

Helen didn't want that either, but she wasn't going to just let it go. She couldn't. "So, there's something about my father Lucas vowed not to tell me. That still doesn't explain why he won't bring him back."

Orion stopped walking. "Yes, it does."

"Why does Lucas think he has the right to make vows about what I should and shouldn't know?"

"It's not like that," Orion said, getting red in the face with frustration. "He got *cornered*. Do you think he would hurt you like this if he had any other option? You can hear I'm not lying, right?"

She did hear the truth in his words, and that made her pause. "So, I'm supposed to accept that his reason is good enough, without ever knowing what it is?"

"Do you need to be convinced in order to forgive him?" he asked in turn.

Helen was done talking about this. "It always circles back around to how I should just forgive him and move on," she said. "Forgiving Lucas won't bring my father back from the dead. But Lucas *could*. With a snap of his fingers, my dad could be alive again. There isn't a good enough reason for not doing that."

"There is," Orion promised. "You can hear I'm telling the truth."

"What I hear is that it's the truth for *you*," Helen said, her throat tightening with tears. Grief still came at her like this, welling up from nothing. One moment she was fine and the next she felt like she was drowning in sadness. "I miss my father."

The tears came, and Orion held her until they left again.

The dead were angry. As Helen and Orion approached Lucas' palace, they could see distortions swarming the air above the Sleepers.

Human-shaped forms bent the light from the stars as solitary shadows detached from the darkness around them. Though the dead made no sound above a faint susurration, the motion of their outlines was frantic, and occasionally it was possible to make out a face that gnashed its teeth and screamed soundlessly.

The palace itself was blanketed in souls. Helen and Orion ran the last few steps into the palace to find several things happening at once. Castor and Pallas were trying to parlay with the dead, Claire was trying to soothe them with music, and Leda was making plans to send out search parties.

"Lucas is gone," Ariadne told them as they ran inside. "The dead are about to tear Hades apart to get him back."

"Where could he have gone?" Orion asked.

"Somewhere with Hector, Andy, and Cassandra, maybe?" Jason guessed. "They're all missing. Lucas said he was going to try to find you first before he went to do whatever it is he went to do. Did he?"

Helen supposed he did. Morpheus said that he had tried to put Lucas into the dream she and Orion shared, but that had turned into something else. When he couldn't find a way to deliver his message inside the dream, he must have just gone and done what he wanted to do. Without her.

"He can't have left the Underworld," Helen said, getting back to the issue at hand. "He wouldn't do that. He knows if he left, time would start again."

Leda nodded as if she'd already figured that out. "Where could he have gone in the Underworld that would separate him from the dead, but not restart time?" she asked Helen.

"It can't be the Elysian Fields. The dead can reach him there. The only place I can think of is Tartarus," Helen replied. "Nothing can get into it or out of it without a Worldbuilder to make a portal."

Leda glanced at Daedelus with a satisfied smile, as if she had already surmised this. He rolled his eyes in response, not convinced.

"But why would he have gone there?" Daedelus asked, not entirely ready to concede the point to his wife.

There was only one thing that could pull Lucas away from his duty to the dead. "It must be to find chaos," she said.

"As in *actual* Chaos, the being that existed before the beginning?" Ladon clarified.

"Wait. I thought Chaos was a state of being, not an actual *being* being, like a person," Helen said. "That's what I was told."

Ladon shrugged. "State of being, an actual being... I guess she's both? Chaos is the mother of Night, Darkness, Ocean, Earth—all of the Elementals, really. She's the *before*, and we're all the *after*."

"And she's in Tartarus?"

"No. She's the thing past Tartarus," he replied. "Past time, even."

Helen nodded, absorbing this. He'd done it to her again. Lucas had found the answer, or at least he had a hunch as to where to start looking, and he'd followed his hunch without her.

"Helen," Orion said cautiously, looking at her heart. "What are you thinking?"

"That I'm going to kill him," she replied under her breath.

"Okay. How do we get to where Chaos is?" Ariadne said, trying to get Helen back on track. "Can you portal us to Tartarus, and maybe we can go past it somehow to find her?"

Helen shook her head. "I would have to go through Everyland to portal. It would start time again." She started laughing. It was either that or start screaming.

"What's funny?" Dionysus said, joining them.

"Absolutely nothing," Helen replied, moving away from him. She didn't want to stand close to Dionysus right now. She needed to keep her head clear. She went to the other side of the room and let the others explain.

She suddenly heard Dionysus burst out laughing. "Is that all?" he said. He lifted a hand and started waving at Helen to come to him as he strode toward her. "You're looking for chaos? Why didn't you come to me in the first place?"

Helen crossed to him. "You can get me to chaos?"

"Do you remember when we ran into each other at the club a few weeks back?" he asked in return. "We had a mild disagreement about your partying. You said, *isn't that the point of you?*"

"Yeah," Helen replied.

"The point of me, the god Dionysus, is not to get people drunk so they can hide from their problems." He looked more serious than Helen had ever seen him. "The point of me is to reach a state of being called *bakkheia*. Roughly translated it means, sacred chaos."

"How? How do I get there?" Helen said.

Dionysus looked at her appraisingly. "I can show you the way. Whether you get there or not is up to you."

Hector's laughter rang out, shifting in pitch and changing meaning as it flowed through different perspectives within the ill-defined space they occupied.

Lucas pulled his head out of his hands at the sound. He looked annoyed that his cousin had come.

"I almost have it," Lucas said.

A thousand other Lucas voices ricocheted around, turning the phrase into a thousand other meanings. Lucas' face was being distorted as well, bending around space like parts of it were falling off a ledge, being smeared in mid-air like an old photo when someone moved as it was being taken. His expression changed as his voice did, sliding through the spectrum of emotions until it seemingly hit all of them.

Hector ignored the echo-drift. Though some of the other voices and facial expressions were trying to bait him, get him to fight, or lose focus, Hector knew exactly what Lucas had meant, and he couldn't be swayed by any of it. He knew his cousin too well.

"Time to give up," Hector replied.

This was the hard part. Hector had to stand, though his body was forever shifting around him. He had to wait for Lucas to decide which of the voices he was going to listen to. He had to watch as his words got twisted, hoping that Lucas would know what he'd originally meant. But Lucas had been here longer, and Hector had a feeling that the longer you were here, the more time Chaos had to work on you, altering your sense of reality. Hector had only just planted his feet here, and he was already starting to doubt where he stood.

"I can't," Lucas said, but now he was talking through what he had said before. "I" and "can't" were mixed up with "almost" and "have it" and the words were threading around each other, making other sentences.

Even the exchanges between Hector and Lucas started

coming out of sequence, and the order in which they had been delivered was reversed. Hector found his own words coming back to him. *He* was being asked to give up. *He* was being laughed at. Hector closed his eyes at the onslaught. It was all too much. That's what chaos was. Everything at once. Nothing in order. No cause and effect, just a tangle of being and nothingness with no definition between speaker and spoken to. Behind it all was Lucas' chant—*four, no five dimensions*—like a metronome.

He kept his eyes shut and waited. There was nothing else for him to do. On and on it stretched. He held onto the fact that there had been a moment when he arrived so it couldn't go on forever. The loop would close if he waited, but first Lucas had to let go.

Maybe he said, *let go*. He couldn't be sure.

Helen walked amongst Sleepers in the Fields of Asphodels with Dionysus by her side. She swayed on her feet, the horizon tipping as his essence began to seep into her. Her skin felt warm and her mouth tingled.

Keeping his distance from Helen and Dionysus, one of the elven folk climbed off the deer he was riding, crouched down next to a maenad, and whispered in her ear. He searched amongst the inert bodies, found the next maenad, and the next, and whispered in each of their ears until a group of thirteen had been roused. Then, he got on the deer's back and cantered away.

The maenads stood as if they were hanging suspended from wires. Their heads were dropped forward, long hair hanging down in front of them like tattered curtains, and their arms dangling limply at their sides. Dionysus walked around the group and they began to hum and rock back and forth, swaying synchronously. He motioned for Helen to join them.

She took a place in their rough circle and started swaying along with them self-consciously, pretending to hum.

"You're not singing," Dionysus chided.

"No one wants to hear that," Helen replied. Her inability to carry even the simplest tune had been pointed out to her many times over the course of her life.

"It doesn't matter what you sound like," he called out, coaching her, as he walked around the maenads, whose low, meandering humming was building into in rhythmical chant. "This is about how it feels to you, not how it sounds to anyone else. The sound is to help you focus so you can *lose* focus."

"That makes no sense," Helen mumbled, but didn't make a big deal of it. She made a few exploratory sounds in the back of her throat, and tried to do as he said. Focus to lose focus. Her frustration boiled over.

It was like all the advice everyone had been giving her since her dad had died. Utter nonsense. Like Noel telling her to let her father go. Like Aphrodite telling her to forgive. All of it was just some stupid platitude on some old lady's cross stitching. *If you love someone set them free. Let go and let God.*

What they really meant was that she was expected to care a little bit less about the fact that her dad was dead because that would make it easier on them. If she got over it and let it go and forgave, and all of the other things they kept telling her to do, it wouldn't make anything better for her. When she woke up the next day her dad would still be gone. They wanted her to care less about his death because it would be better for them. One less angry, messy girl for them to deal with. They wanted her to go back to being the pleasant, pretty face that made their lives comfortable. The girl that gave them what they wanted, and smiled on command. Helen was not that girl anymore.

She felt one of the maenads bump into her, and it filled her with irrational rage. She pushed the maenad, and the woman shrieked with laughter and came back for more. Without hitting Helen, she started bumping into her, humming and throwing her limbs around. Another maenad came up behind Helen and began shouldering her and pushing into Helen's back with her forehead. They were like ice hockey players without the skates, using their bodies to throw Helen from one to another until she was pinging off of them in a pattern. She was angry, yes, but less so the more she felt herself colliding into them. It was as if the energy in her was being shared. They passed it around as they passed her around, feeling the rage and pain with her.

They started howling and snarling in a beastly chorus, and Helen found herself howling along with them. And then something clicked. The pain had a place to go. The anger was lost in the crowd. A new thing, fluttering and wild, took over inside her.

Let go, someone said as if from far away.

They were running now, leaping over Sleepers, and tearing at themselves and at each other. The urge to scream and rip and run was overwhelming. They were following the source of their ecstasy, running after him to the edge of this world. He smelled like wine.

They were on a black sand beach. Somewhere out there in

the penumbra was a silver body of water that looked like mercury, but near Helen there was only fog.

She was spinning. Head thrown back, she twirled faster and faster, the stars above her smearing as she howled at them.

Hector sat up.

He was on the ground, in a field, by a river. He had no idea what field or what river this was, but he knew it was somewhere in Hades. Lucas was sitting on the ground next to him, his elbows resting on top of his bent knees, looking out over the slow-moving water.

"Where are we?" Hector asked his cousin.

Lucas exhaled deeply before answering. "By the river Lethe."

"Why?"

Lucas shrugged, still looking away. "I guess I must have been thinking about it when I opened the portal to get us out of Tartarus." He turned his head and looked at Hector, a bemused look on his face. "How did you get in there?"

"Eh, you know how it is," Hector said casually before he remembered. "I left Cassandra and Andy with Erebus and Nyx."

Lucas' eyes shifted as if he was thinking about something inwardly, and then he disappeared and reappeared again so quickly it was like he was shivering in and out of the world for a split second.

"They're fine now," Lucas said, quickly dispelling Hector's worry. "I brought them back to the palace."

"You know that's creepy, right?"

"I know." Lucas turned up his hands. "Nothing I can do about it." They sat in a charged silence for a while. "Thank you for coming to get me." Lucas said.

Hector could tell that Lucas was thanking him sincerely, but it was as if being lost might have been the better option for him anyway. "But?" Hector added.

"It didn't work."

"Ah." Hector scratched his neck. "How could it work without Helen, though?" he asked. Lucas looked at him again, surprised. "I mean, what does it matter if *you* find Chaos? It's supposed to be Helen. She's the one that's supposed to challenge the Fates."

Lucas chuffed. "I didn't think about that."

"You wanted to do it for her."

"Because it was insanely dangerous—"

"Yeah, I know," Hector said, cutting him off.

"I wanted to test it first."

"You wanted to control it."

Lucas looked caught, and then he nodded.

"I get it," Hector said, picking at the grass idly. "When we first met Helen, she couldn't do anything for herself. Couldn't fly, couldn't throw a punch. Do you remember that?"

Lucas smiled at the memory.

"She's changed, Luke."

"I know. I'm trying to change, too. I'm trying to move on. She's moved on."

"No, she hasn't."

Lucas looked down. It hurt him to talk about Helen like this but it had to happen. "Did you two ever—"

"Don't insult me like that." Hector narrowed his eyes at

Lucas.

Lucas looked out over the water again, overwhelmed. "Now what? That was my last idea."

"You'll have another one." Hector stood and looked down into the river. The waters moved too slowly and there was something foreboding about it. Something heavy, like a dark secret.

"Why were you thinking about Lethe?" he asked.

Lucas stood and stretched as if he'd been sitting cross-legged for ages. Maybe, in Chaos, he had been. "I've been thinking about it a lot lately without meaning to. It's sort of tied up with a moment of stupidity that's going to haunt me for the rest of my life." Lucas laughed bitterly. "Existence. Rest of my *existence*," he corrected. "So forever."

Hector tilted his head to side, intrigued. Just from the way Lucas said it, he knew Lethe had something to do with the rift that had formed between he and Helen. "Can you tell me about it?"

"I can't," Lucas replied. "I accidentally swore on Styx."

"Does it have to do with her dad, and why you won't bring him back?" Lucas lifted half his mouth in a wan smile and Hector raised both hands in a surrendering gesture. "Can't answer that. Got it. How do you *accidentally* swear on Styx, by the way?"

Lucas sighed and groaned at the same time. "You have to be standing on it for one. It also helps to be an idiot."

Hector almost had it, but as soon as he thought he'd figured out why Lucas wouldn't bring Helen's father back from the dead, it slipped away like one of the pale fish he saw beneath the surface of the water.

· · ·

Helen could go on spinning forever. *Yes*, she decided. *There will be nothing but this feeling forever.*

Palamedes couldn't believe he was biting his nails again. He'd quit that habit a millennia ago. During his first spear training lesson, one of his father's grizzled old warriors had scared the shit out of Palamedes by saying that if he kept biting his fingernails, they'd come alive in his gut and claw their way out of him. It had worked. Palamedes had quit chewing his nails, but what kind of maniac does that to a kid?

He was now back to biting and also secretly freaking out about any pangs in his stomach that might herald a claw-like revenge, and it was all because of the dead. He'd tried to explain multiple times that he couldn't do anything to get Lucas back, but they wouldn't listen to him. They wouldn't listen to anyone. They wouldn't let anyone sleep or eat or even pee. Not that Palamedes really needed to do any of those things anymore.

The palace guests were all coming to understand that things like eating, sleeping, and using the restroom were more of a take it or leave it situation in Hades. Those daily bodily things were either enjoyable or simply a way to give shape and meaning to the passage of time, but with Lucas gone the dead were so upset they wouldn't let any of the still living so much as pass from one room to the next without wafting around in a tizzy. Their insistence had passed annoying, passed harassment, and was now treading on everyone's mental breaking point.

It was quite a shock when the dead just went away.

Plutus and Palamedes went out onto the terrace where they saw the others starting to gather. A few exchanges amongst the group determined that the dead had left everyone alone simultaneously.

"Lucas is back," Noel guessed, relieved.

They waited outside by the mirror pool. First, Andy and Cassandra appeared out of cold, thin air that was sparkling slightly with ice crystals. They were greatly agitated and explained where they had been, what Lucas had attempted, and how Hector had followed him into Chaos. The young men's fathers shared a saddened but not surprised look.

"They must have made it out," Leda said, her tactical mind a step ahead of everyone else's. "No one else could have portaled Andy and Cassandra."

It was still many impatient minutes before the Hand of Darkness appeared with his cousin, the two of them striding purposely out of the shadows side by side, and after a quick reunion with his family, Lucas disengaged himself and scanned the surrounding faces.

"Where's Helen?" he asked.

"She went with Dionysus," Jason said. "They left hours ago."

"Can't you feel where they are?" Claire asked.

Lucas shook his head slowly as if he was concentrating on something else. "I don't know if they're in the Underworld anymore," he said.

"She wouldn't have left," Orion said.

"No. She wouldn't have," he mumbled, his eyes turned inward, searching. He looked at Hector, his gaze clear again. "But I can't find her."

"We'd better go get her then. Which way did she go?" he asked Claire.

She made a vague gesture out among the vast fields that were covered with Sleepers. "There was an elf—or whatever Morpheus' people are—he was riding a stag. They followed him to find the maenads," she told them.

Lucas nodded and went to leave in that direction, but Daedelus put out a hand to stop him.

"Not you," Daedelus said.

Plutus stepped forward. "You can't leave again," he said, bolstering Daedelus' dissent.

"I won't. I'll stay in Hades," Lucas said.

"You don't know where Helen went," Leda said, shaking her head. "To follow her you might have to leave again. The dead won't allow that. You need to stay here at the palace and keep them calm."

Lucas looked from face to face, his shock to find everyone against him quickly turning to anger. He was digging in for a fight. Palamedes felt bad for the young man. He obviously wanted to run after his lady love and make sure she was safe. Palamedes would do the same for Plutus, but Lucas didn't get to make choices like that anymore. It was a shame, and Palamedes sympathized, but he couldn't allow it.

He spotted Noel and Cassandra on the other side of the circle forming around Lucas, trying to keep him contained, though admittedly, none of them could stop him physically. Palamedes knew that force wouldn't work. But guilt just might.

"If you go, the dead will attack us," Palamedes said quietly. "They were very near to it before you returned." He subtly indicated Lucas' mother and sister, shamelessly using them.

Dicing isn't entirely about chance. Part of it is understanding your opponent, and discerning how much risk they can handle. Lucas would risk anything for Helen. Except possibly his mother and sister. Palamedes suspected this, and though it was an underhanded trick because he didn't really know if the dead could actually hurt the living, he was not above using the threat of terrible consequence to maintain order in Hades. A tactic he learned from his grizzled old spear instructor, which made Palamedes feel a twinge of guilt. He quickly absolved himself, however. Lucas wasn't a child, and the dead tearing apart Hades was far more serious than a fingernail biting habit.

Lucas' shoulders drooped in defeat. He seemed to blink in and out of space for a moment, and when he returned completely, shadows still clung to him. "I've found their trail. They went into Cimmeria, I think. It won't be hard for a few of you to follow them."

"I can track," Daedelus said, lifting a hand to volunteer himself.

Then he, Hector, and Orion disappeared with a flick of Lucas' fingers. The bright constellations that wheeled like slow fireworks in the sky seemed to darken and the air grew heavy and oppressive like there was a storm coming. Lucas looked at no one, but his chest rose and fell with incensed breaths as he tried to control himself. He spun on his heel and stalked into the palace. Jason followed close behind. Palamedes hoped that the new god of Hades still felt as if he could confide in his cousin. He needed someone to talk to—for all their sakes.

"Jason will handle him," Claire said, catching Palamedes' worried stare.

Palamedes didn't comment, though he secretly doubted anyone could handle Lucas anymore.

CHAPTER 14

T he maenad's trail was easy to see. Shredded clothing, kicked-up turf, and Sleepers' bodies conscientiously pushed aside so that they wouldn't be trampled on had made something of a road for Hector, Orion, and Daedelus to follow.

They walked for several miles without saying much. For the past year that Hector and Orion had lived together in New York, Hector had braced himself every time Orion's dad came to visit. Not that Orion and Daedelus fought, they didn't, but there was always so much tension between them that Hector could barely stand to be in the same room with them for more than twenty minutes. Daedelus would try to talk to his son, but he usually said the wrong thing. Orion tried not to get offended, but his dad pushed all of his buttons. Hector had gotten used to constantly changing the subject, but every subject seemed to be a touchy one between them.

Hector's relationship with his dad had always been so easy. Pallas understood him, favored him, even. There were no apologies withheld because neither of them had ever wounded the other or let the other one down. As far as father-son relationships go, theirs had been surprisingly drama free. Pallas loved his son and expected him to take care of his family. Hector loved his father and would do absolutely anything for his family. In short, their expectations had suited their respective temperaments and they both lived up to the other's demands for what a father or a son should be.

But it was as if Orion and Daedelus didn't get the same syllabus. Neither of them knew what the other expected. Neither of them gave each other the validation they sought. There was love there, but that just made it worse. It was because they loved each other so much that they had no idea how to behave, as if they were both used to either being not good enough, or not the most important person in any of their relationship. They had no idea how to deal with someone who took every single thing they said straight to heart. It was like watching a car crash every time they were together.

"So. This Chaos thing, talk about a psychedelic trip," Hector said when the silence had become unpleasant.

Orion took Hector's cue to start talking and told them about Helen's attempt to enter Chaos through dreams. He didn't specify what any of the dreams had been about, but the way he kept shooting his father sidelong glances made it clear that a lot of his nightmares must have about been about his dad. When Daedelus remained silent—no shocker there—Hector shared some of his experience in Tartarus and how Nyx and Erebus sent him past Tartarus and into Chaos.

"I don't know how long I was in there, but I came close to going crazy. Same with Lucas," Hector finished.

Orion gave his dad a wry look. "We know a thing or two about crazy."

Daedelus smiled back. Usually, comments about Leda could be taken the wrong way by either of them, but they both seemed okay talking about her now. Hector took the opportunity to ask a few lingering questions he had about her.

"Leda seems better, like *fully* better," he said. "I didn't think that was possible."

Daedelus paused before hazarding a response. "It's happened before in mythology. Herakles was made insane by Hera. He killed his wife and children, thinking they were wild animals, and right after he killed them, she made him sane again so he would know what he had done."

"Yeah, but that wasn't true insanity, was it? Seems to me like that was more of a curse," Hector said.

Daedelus raised his brow, like Hector was catching on. "That's why I think Leda's madness wasn't real. It was put there, like a curse," he agreed.

"By who?" Hector asked.

Daedelus smirked, like he had his suspicions. "The *why* is more important than the *who*," he replied. "I think it was to hide information meant for Helen."

"What information? Helen using Everyland as a Trojan Horse?" Orion asked.

Hector was lost at that point, and Orion filled him in on what happened in Everyland when Helen had made his mother sane again, ending on Leda's instructions for Helen on how to trick the Moirae by using Everyland as a Trojan Horse.

"There's that, but there's also gotta be something more," Daedelus said, like he couldn't put his finger on it. "There was always *more* going on whenever Daphne was concerned." He smiled suddenly at a memory. "She's the only person I've ever met who's more devious than your mother. But she did everything for the right reasons."

Hector gleaned that Daedelus believed Daphne was somehow involved in Leda's madness, but he didn't sense any anger or resentment in it. Just confusion, like Daedelus was still trying to figure out why they had done it.

"Do you think mom knows how Helen is supposed to fix all this?" Orion guessed.

"All I know is that Leda wouldn't let herself go mad without there being a damn good reason," Daedelus said, his expression stony. "But I definitely think this errand is bullshit. Helen's not going to fix anything by running around with Dionysus."

Hector and Orion shared a frustrated look, like they both wanted to ask him why he had even bothered to come along.

"That's real optimistic, Dad" Orion said drily.

Daedelus chuckled. "Ray of sunshine, aren't I?" he said, almost like he was admitting a fault. Maybe even apologizing for it.

"It's okay," Orion said. "Kinda getting used to it."

The shift between them was subtle, but it made an immeasurable difference in the mood. Their party lapsed into a comfortable silence that lasted until they came upon a deep fog. It seemed to spring from nowhere, seeping around them and closing them off as if conjured.

The carpet of Sleepers ended, and then a few paces later the grass turned into scrub that struggled up from hard-packed ground. The rocky scrubland soon eased into a black sand beach.

"If this is a beach, where's the water?" Orion asked. He was listening for the familiar sound of waves, but inside the fog even the sounds of their footsteps were muffled.

"Somewhere out there?" Hector guessed, but he didn't want to go looking for it. This whole area gave him the creeps. It reminded him a bit too much of Tartarus.

"Up here," Daedelus called out as he quickened his pace, following tracks that were plowing through the sand. "They came this way."

They heard shouts farther down the beach, deep in the thick fog. The hairs on the back of Hector's neck stood on end. He could hear Orion's breath quickening, and see a cloud of the vapor made from his warm breath hitting the cold air. Daedelus' bright blue eyes flashed feral in the strange, watery light of this eerie place as he glanced back at them. He followed the humming and strident sighs deeper into the cottony atmosphere.

At first there were just flashes passing them as if flying by. Skin, bared teeth, fluttering fingertips, would come out of nowhere and disappear back into the fog. And then the shrieking began. The flashing images of moving body parts stopped. The fog eased. There were women standing in a rough semi-circle, panting, and wearing the tattered remains of their clothing. They were staring at them with unblinking eyes. At their center was Helen, still spinning, her clothes in shreds.

"No," Dionysus breathed, noticing that Orion, Hector, and Daedelus had come. "Go! Go now!" he said, trying to put himself between the Scions and the maenads.

Helen stopped spinning. Her eyes, which had rolled back into her head, snapped forward into position. She peeled back her upper lip, baring her teeth with a snarl. Hector heard a sound behind him and glanced over his shoulder to see three maenads appear out of the gloom, closing off their exit.

"Run!" screamed Dionysus, but too late.

The maenads fell on the Scions like a pack of wolves.

Palamedes was not above lurking.

And he figured that if the Hand of Darkness didn't want to be overheard, he'd take precautions. It was not as if the very air in Hades didn't obey him or anything. Palamedes figured if Lucas didn't want others listening in on his private conversations with his cousin Jason, he could wave a hand and sound-proof his room or something akin to that.

As it was, Palamedes saw it as his right—nay, his duty—to know what was going on in the emotional life of the god who was the current custodian of every single living being in the world. Plutus said eavesdropping was beneath his dignity, but Palamedes didn't have any of that left at the moment. He was too busy hiding behind Lucas' drapes.

"Is there anything I can do to help Morpheus?" Jason was asking.

Lucas paused, considering Jason's offer. "I don't think the problem is a physical one, but we can ask Morpheus."

Another moment passed in silence. "But?" Jason said through a chuckle.

The biggest flaw in Palamedes' chosen hiding spot was that it meant he couldn't read their expressions, and like all close family, these two did a lot of talking without talking. It was infuriating. Next time he'd have to come up with a spot that allowed visual snooping as well as audio because he wasn't getting the whole picture.

"We're going to have to start waking the Sleepers," Lucas said.

"When?"

"It's bad, Jase. A day. Maybe two."

Palamedes let out a breath. It was a small sound, next to nothing, but it was enough. In a moment Lucas was there, drawing the curtains back and Palamedes was exposed.

"You said they had months!" Palamedes exclaimed, pointing an accusing finger at Lucas and not caring in the slightest that he'd been caught snooping. He was too upset. "What are you going to do?"

Lucas looked chagrinned, but coming from such a large family, he must have become accustomed to things like eavesdropping because he let it go quickly. "I don't know," he admitted. "I can't send everyone back to earth and let them die."

"No. Definitely not," Palamedes said. "What about Everyland? Would Helen allow the Sleepers to go there?"

Lucas nodded, frowning. "That's an option of last resort. Only—"

When he didn't continue, Palamedes urged him on. "Only what?"

Lucas huffed in frustration. "Everyland could be made to *look* exactly like Earth, she can do that with a wave of her hand, but it wouldn't *be* Earth. Helen would be the supreme ruler of everything. I know she doesn't want that."

"Still better than keeping everyone here!" Palamedes said, waving his arms to indicate Hades. "No offense."

"None taken. I didn't create this place. It has rules I don't like. And that's another thing. Helen may have already established rules in Everyland that would make it completely different from Earth, and that might not be good for humanity in the long run."

"Like what?" Palamedes asked.

"Things like, is there going to be hunger? You'd think definitely not, right? Get rid of it. But if there's no hunger, what would happen? Would lions hunt? Would bees pollinate? If they don't, what would that mean for the ecosystem? So, you make the choice to keep hunger, but now it's your fault when someone starves to death." Lucas looked angry, but not for himself. "Zeus made Olympus perfect. No pain, no starvation, no disease. But removing all those things make it a world without purpose. How long do you think humanity would last without purpose?"

Jason dragged his lower lip through his teeth. "I don't know, Luke. It seems like she won't have a choice."

"And you have no idea how much that angers her," Lucas said quietly. "The Fates have always wanted this for her, but it's not what she wants. She deserves to have a choice, doesn't she?"

Palamedes shared a look with Jason, throwing up his hands. "Okay yes. Of course she does, but..."

"Just give her one more day before you tell anyone else, okay?" Lucas pleaded. "Everyone will pressure her into making the move to Everyland right away, but I think Helen deserves to come to this decision by herself with no one trying to influence her. Because once it's done it can't be undone. The Earth will be gone and she will have no choices left. Ever."

Palamedes nodded reluctantly, and he was just about to tack on a laundry list of exceptions to his silence when an alarmed expression crossed Lucas' face.

"No," Lucas whispered to whatever horror he was watching in his head, and then he disappeared.

Hector didn't want to hurt the maenads.

He liked them, and pretty much everything they stood for. Mystical chaos, berzerking, blood lust—he knew a bit about all those things. He'd even partaken of them on occasion.

The trouble was, Hector didn't know how to stop the maenads from tearing him, Orion, and Daedelus apart without berzerking on them in retaliation, and he didn't want to do that. The only thing for it was to run like Dionysus said, and hope that the maenads tired out first. Hector doubted that last bit.

The real problem was Helen. If she decided to attack, there would be nothing any of them could do to stop her. Hector fleetingly wondered if immortality meant that he could survive begin ripped up into glitter-sized pieces and fervently hoped that the answer was "no".

A maenad jumped on his back and began chewing on his neck, and not in a fun way. He tossed her over his shoulder and onto the ground in front of him, pried another one off of Orion, grabbed Daedelus by the front of his shirt, and pushed them both into a run in front of him. When they cleared the dense circle of fog, Hector was surprised to see Dionysus huffing and puffing alongside them to keep up.

Hector had been hoping to lose the maenads in the fog, but they were not so easily shaken. As they left the fog cover in Cimmeria and went out across the flat plains into what he believed was Hades, he could see the maenads were following them.

"Any tips?" Daedelus asked Dionysus when it was clear they were still being pursued.

"Yeah, how do you usually get away from them?" Orion asked.

"I don't!" Dionysus hollered in reply. "They kill me and I wake up a few weeks later."

"Let's not do *that*," Daedelus suggested.

The maenads did not ease up, but steadily quickened their pace. Realizing that they were barely keeping ahead, Hector yelled petulantly, "So, are we supposed to just keep running and hope something shiny distracts them?" He was built for burst of speed, not marathons.

"That's actually not a bad idea," Dionysus said.

"Rivers!" Daedelus shouted as the idea occurred to him. "They're shiny." There wasn't much else in the gloom of Hades that was.

They ran toward the first silvery ribbon they spotted on the horizon. The maenads followed, seeming to enjoy the chase even more than they had enjoyed attacking, which meant they would probably want to keep this up, shiny river or not, until their quarry dropped. But Hector didn't have any better ideas.

He glanced over his shoulder, trying to gauge if they would

make it to the river at their current speed before the maenads overtook them, and saw his worst-case scenario unfolding.

"Helen's with them," he shouted at the others grimly. "And she's gaining."

Hector didn't know what he would do if Helen attacked him. He'd imagined fighting her hundreds of times, but not this way. Not with her in a frenzy. Whatever it was that was chasing them was not the Helen he knew, and he had no idea what she would do if she caught any of them.

"What river do you think that is?" Daedelus asked as they neared it.

"It's got to be Lethe," Orion replied. "Because I *don't* remember it."

Hector immediately understood Orion's logic. He had a vague sense that he had also seen this river before, but he barely remembered it, either. What other river could it be?

"If we get the maenads into the river somehow, would they forget to chase us?" Daedelus asked Dionysus.

"Don't know," Dionysus replied. "Never tried it."

"Be sure not to get even a drop of water on you," Orion warned as they neared the banks of the river. "You might forget who you are."

They turned to confront their hunters, putting Lethe to their backs. Everyone crouched low, getting ready for a fight, except for Dionysus. He waited, seeming resigned to what had probably happened to him thousands of times. Hector didn't want to watch that, so he angled the god behind him protectively.

The maenads made a semi-circle around their quarry. Helen strode forward from their ranks, taking point. Hector had seen her glow before with lightning, and with whatever bright aura surrounded all the new gods when they assumed their full power, but this strange light around her throbbed, brightening and darkening in an unsettling way. It was not glorious, or awesome, it was menacing. As was the look on her face.

"Helen, stop!" Orion called out, stepping forward to plead with her.

"No, don't do that," Dionysus warned, trying to pull Orion back. "Helen's not home right now."

She cocked her head, tipping one ear closer to her shoulder, her arms hanging limply at her sides. And then she rushed him. Orion crumpled beneath her.

Taking Helen's cue, the maenads fell upon all of them, scrabbling to tear them apart with their bare hands.

"Get her off of him!" Hector screamed at Daedelus as he was tackled by several maenads at once.

Helen was astride Orion, trying to claw his eyes out. Orion held onto her wrists. They were frozen in a deadlock, but Hector knew who would win. Even though her powers were diminished in Hades, Helen was still stronger than any of them.

Daedelus was trying to fend off three maenads, one of whom was holding onto his ankles and biting his leg like a rabid dog.

"I can't get to him!" Daedalus shouted back frantically. Another maenad put him in a rear-naked choke. He wasn't going anywhere.

Hector picked up his maenad and threw her into the river, then left Dionysus to fend for himself as best as he could. Orion was the one in the most serious trouble. Hector came up behind Helen, slipped his hands under her arms, wove his hands together behind her head and put her in a full nelson. He lifted her off of Orion, but he knew the surprise of his attack would wear off soon. She nearly broke his hold in the short distance it took to get her to the water's edge, but he managed to make it to the river.

Hector threw her in.

"No!" Orion yelled, but too late.

Helen twisted in midair to face Hector as she landed back first in the water. Her arms were flung out as if reaching for him. As soon as she touched the surface her eyes cleared and, shocked, she sank beneath the water like a stone.

"She can't swim!" Orion screamed as he scrambled over the bank to go in after her. His father broke free of the maenads in a burst of violence to stop him.

"It's too late!" Daedelus exclaimed, dragging his son back from the edge. "As soon as you touch that water, you won't remember to save her!"

Desperate, but knowing Daedelus was right, they all stared at the surface, praying for Helen to come up.

CHAPTER 15

Helen looked down at her square-fingered hands and recognized them immediately.

She knew those hands as well as she knew her own. She recognized the dusting of hairs between knuckles and joints, the flat, pared-down nails, and the way the veins branched beneath the skin. She's seen those hands wrapped around a steering wheel, shuffling bills as they counted out someone's change, cooking her dinner, washing dishes, writing. They were a part of nearly every memory she had because they were her father's hands, and somehow, she was wearing them.

And then they were her hands, and she thought no more about it.

Jerry looked up from his hands at the man across the table from him. One of his wife's friends, though it seemed to Jerry that they were related somehow. Something about the way they walked was similar. As if they had inherited the earth.

This visitor that Jerry was being forced to have over for dinner was the most physically perfect man Jerry had ever seen. The kind of guy that you saw in a magazine and dismissed because, obviously, guys like that don't exist in the real world. But this guy did, and in person he was even worse than the guys in the magazines. Each feature was a little too perfect, his skin a little too smooth, and his muscles a little too elegantly shaped to be real. Jerry would have thought he was the most beautiful person he'd ever seen, if he wasn't engaged to Daphne.

She'd introduced him as Don, and said he was an old friend of the family, which was strange because Daphne said she didn't have any family. Don was clearly in love with her. Jerry couldn't help but wonder why Daphne hadn't picked Don. But there she sat next to Jerry, still wearing his modest engagement ring, and they were set to be married in a week. At first, Jerry had been pretty sure Don had come to Nantucket to try and talk her out of it. But Don shook Jerry's hand with what felt like earnest congratulations. He even spoke about what a great dad Jerry would make, and what a great place to raise a kid Nantucket Island was. Everything Don said was in support of them getting married and the sooner the better, but the way he looked at Daphne made it clear what he felt for her. All of it was confusing. Even the way the two of them talked to each other seemed coded and strange.

Don had said something about houses—and Jerry had gathered that they weren't talking about real estate—but Daphne had tried to change the subject. Don wouldn't let her. He said something about his sister and some guy with a funky name, maybe it was Daedelus? And he'd asked Daphne if she'd been in touch with them. There must have been a falling-out between Don and his sister over this guy because he looked angry even saying the name. Not just angry. Irrational.

The skin on the back of Jerry's neck puckered with goosebumps. Something was very wrong here. Something scary. Jerry felt as if this unknown woman's life was in danger.

Daphne reached out to Don and put her hand over his. Her big doe eyes glowed up at him, and she begged Don to let it go. She obviously cared about him deeply. She cared about all of these people she'd never spoken of more deeply than she cared about him, and Jerry wondered, as he did every day, why this woman had attached herself to him.

The truth was, Jerry knew nothing about her. And he didn't care. He would do anything for her. It wasn't just that she was beautiful, either. That wasn't why Jerry was with her. In fact, it was very nearly the reason he wasn't with her. Her beauty embarrassed him. Distanced him from her. It was too much, like wearing a crown to go grocery shopping.

Jerry had fallen in love with Daphne for a bunch of reasons that had nothing to do with the way she looked. She was clever, but she didn't try to prove it. She never said a bad word about anyone. Gossip was something she couldn't understand. She was loyal and patient and they never fought. Not because they didn't have different ideas about stuff, but because she was the kind of person who could allow other people to disagree with her without anyone having to be right or wrong.

But mostly he'd fallen in love with her because of how she treated him. Daphne told him on a daily basis that he was the one of the best human beings she'd ever met. She said he was the only person she trusted enough to be the father of her child, and he knew she was telling the truth. He got the feeling that she respected him, really respected him, and that she liked him exactly the way he was. That had never happened to Jerry before. Maybe his reasons weren't all that romantic, but if they had been he wouldn't have fallen for her. He was a quiet man, and she had quietly stolen his heart. She never asked for it, either. She simply took it.

So it was whatever Daphne wanted. She could do anything and it wouldn't matter to Jerry. She could leave him tonight with this guy, have a fling, and if she showed up on his doorstep again, he would take her back. A thousand times, he'd take her back because he knew that a thousand times she'd come back. She genuinely needed him for reasons he didn't understand, but that he felt. And he would kill the rest of his life to be there for her if he had to.

Lucas appeared next to Hector, and the maenads disappeared with a flick of his fingers.

"She's in the river!" Hector said immediately, pointing at where he last saw Helen go down.

Helen appeared on the banks in front of them, lying curled on her side.

"Don't touch her!" Lucas said when Orion lunged forward. They all looked at Lucas expectantly.

"What now?" Hector asked.

Lucas was both scared and scary. Shadows curled around his legs and snaked over his shoulders, whispering to him.

"We wait," he replied.

The disorientation lasted only a moment.

Then Jerry was in another part of the house, his bedroom, watching this scene between his wife and baby girl.

Daphne was sitting on the bed holding Helen. Nothing new. She never put Helen down. She never let anyone hold her, not even Jerry, for more than a moment. Even then she hovered as if something terrible was about to happen and whisked the baby away, making some excuse about how Helen was about to cry. Which she never did. Helen was the quietest, sweetest baby Jerry had ever been around. She was always smiling or giggling, but Daphne simply wouldn't share her.

Though Helen was still a babe in arms, they already had their own language of glances and smiles. Tiny moments, like this, where they communicated without words. When he saw such closeness between them, he felt doubly left out. Not that he'd ever been all that "in" where Daphne was concerned. She'd married him, shared his bed, and Jerry knew she cared about him, but she still didn't love him. The trouble was that he loved her. Too much.

When Helen was born, it got worse. Not only did Daphne pay even less attention to him, but she wouldn't let him get close to the baby. Daphne and Helen. Helen and Daphne. Two peas in a pod without even a sliver of daylight between them from the second Helen drew her first breath. It had been a home birth. Daphne had done it all by herself.

Jerry was their witness and nothing more. He was outside the bubble of their extraordinary bond and he resented it. Why had she barged into his life, taken it over, if she didn't want to share it? Sometimes he wondered if all Daphne had ever wanted from him was the perfect, golden baby she cherished so dearly.

Daphne put Helen into one of those wraps that keeps the baby pressed tight to the chest. She said she hated strollers and Helen fussed less if she was carried, but Helen never fussed at all. Then she went with Jerry to the News Store to start their workday.

Somehow, Daphne managed to work at the store with a baby strapped to her chest all morning. When the rush was over, she sat at one of the tables in the back with another mother. They put their babies on at mat for something called "tummy time". Helen and Claire. Claire and Helen. Daphne had these play dates with Mrs. Aoki every day. She had decided that Claire and Helen were going to be best friends, yet she never let Helen touch the other baby. When Helen reached out with her chubby fingers for Claire's face, Daphne would snatch her hand back with a look of fear. Jerry had commented on the strangeness of this before but Daphne had denied she was doing it and changed the subject. Ah well. He knew it was going to be like this with her. Secrets for breakfast.

Sometimes she'd disappear with Helen for the whole day. She'd never tell him where, or she'd lie. Sometimes Jerry would notice strangers talking to Daphne on the street or in a quiet corner of the store. Strangers who walked like they had inherited the earth. Daphne had the ready excuse about tourists always needing directions. She was a terrible liar.

Jerry had heard Daphne call one of them by name. Leda. Gorgeous, sexy. The kind of woman who turned heads and caused accidents. Jerry hid himself behind the shelves in the News Store to listen to part of their conversation, but he hadn't understood much of it. They talked about someone's nemesis, but they'd said "Nemesis" like it was a person. Then they talked about how chaos would help them hide a secret. Leda looked like she was going to cry when she nodded and said it had to be her. That she was the only one who could control her fear enough to let the chaos in.

Then she'd made Daphne promise not to tell anyone. They needed to keep it a secret. Daphne had said chaos would keep their secrets for them.

So many secrets. Of course, when Jerry asked Daphne about Leda, she'd said that they didn't know each other. Just a chance conversation. She'd probably never come back to the store. She never did.

He knew that one day Daphne was going to leave him. Knowing it didn't make it any easier.

They sat down on the ground.

Lucas stared at Helen, barely breathing, while her eyes moved left to right and back again behind her closed eyelids.

"Why don't you take us back to the palace?" Hector asked. "Maybe we can wake her there?"

Lucas shook his head, keeping his eyes on her. "The water stays here."

Hector and Orion shared a look and a shrug, not sure what that meant. Hector assumed they were going to wait for Helen to dry out and got comfortable.

"Is she okay?" Orion asked.

"She's in someone else's memories," Lucas replied. "So I guess it depends on *whose* memory she's in."

"You don't know?" Daedelus asked.

"I have an idea," Lucas said. He didn't look happy about it.

"Then why don't we wake her?" Orion asked.

Lucas shook his head again, expressionless. "She won't wake until she's done."

. . .

Daphne left a note for him and a necklace for Helen.

Jerry had been expecting either more or less, but not a note. Especially not a note that started with a quick line about how he must have known this day would come, and then the rest of it with instructions about a genetic family condition that would mean Helen would periodically feel horrible cramps in her stomach. Daphne insisted they would pass, and that they would do her no harm. She had left an admonishment about how doctors wouldn't understand and not to waste any time or money on it. Helen would figure it out on her own.

No words for Helen. No explanation. Not even an apology. He'd always thought Daphne would take Helen with her when she left. He had no idea how to explain to a four-year-old that mommy was never coming back.

He'd come home from a late shift at work to the note. He sat at the kitchen table, one light bulb burning over him. Helen was asleep in her little bed, alone. Daphne had just left her there, wearing the heart-shaped pendant she'd always worn. Four years of being glued to Helen's side, and now she was gone. Daphne must have torn out her heart to leave Helen behind, but knowing that didn't make him feel any better. He'd never been the kind of guy to think of suffering as justice.

Jerry was terrified. He didn't know how to wake up the next morning without Daphne, so he sat at the table all night long.

Everyone but Lucas freaked out when Helen started crying in her sleep.

"You can't help her," he said. "No one can."

· · ·

Helen was a goofy little girl.

Breathtaking. Astonishing. Brilliant. And as silly as a squirrel in a bowl full of jelly. She grew tall early. 5'9" by the eighth grade. She looked like a colt who you know is going to turn into the most stunning thoroughbred. She tried to hide her strong body and her glorious face as best she could. She hid behind her humor.

Helen was funny. Curious and kind. Cheerful as a daisy, even though sometimes she got quiet and fiddled with the heart necklace from her mother. Sometimes she even cried, just a few tears building up in her gentle brown eyes and silently streaking like stars down the apples of her cheeks. She was the best part of every single one of his days.

As she got bigger, he realized that she looked exactly like her mother. Not a little bit. Exactly. In a way he couldn't quite put words to, it explained why Daphne had left. Or at least it did to him.

There was still so much about Daphne he couldn't understand. She was smoke and mirrors and he never talked about her. Not with anyone, not even Helen. He'd found a notebook that she'd left behind, that he'd stared at for weeks, trying to figure it out before he'd burned it. It had names and places in it. It looked to Jerry like she was tracking some people she called the Hundred, and helping other she called Outcasts and Rogues move from city to city, like an underground railroad. There were sums of money logged in there, too. Money she was either paying out to them, or giving away. Millions. Jerry had his suspicions about her having come from a rich family. She knew rich girl things, like fancy vacations spots and yachting. Maybe she was a mafia princess, life in danger, on the run. Or maybe she was something else. Something even worse.

Helen tried so hard to be normal. Nothing made her happier than doing everyday stuff with him or just hanging out with Claire or their friends Matt and Zach, but she wasn't normal. She was just like Daphne. Jerry looked the other way whenever something impossible happened around her. Her strength. Her speed. He'd catch glimpses of them sometimes. But she hated to stand out, so he let her stay tucked inside his quiet little life, protected by layers of ordinary. That's when he understood why Daphne had needed him. Why she picked him. It was to hide Helen's bright light under his average-joe bushel.

And then the Delos family came to Nantucket, and it was as if years of pretending ended. Jerry felt embarrassed. Like he'd been on stage and someone in the audience stood up and shouted out, "Fake!" and he had to face the fact that for the last twenty years of his life he'd been lying to himself.

Daphne wasn't his. Helen wasn't his. His entire adult life had been a lie.

When Helen was dry, Hector started getting antsy.

"Luke. Shouldn't we check and see if she's cold at least?" he asked.

"I'm keeping her warm," he said, still staring at her.

Dionysus paced up and down the riverbank about twenty yards away, banished there so no one would get drunk. He hated being alone and bored. He noticed Hector looking at him. "Can we go yet?" he asked.

Lucas flicked a finger and Dionysus disappeared. "Anyone else want to go back to the palace?" he asked.

Orion shook his head. Daedelus, watching his son, declined as well. Hector was definitely not leaving. So, they all sat there—Hector, Orion, and Daedelus staring at each other and Lucas staring at Helen. The truth was, Hector was starting to be more worried about Lucas than he was about Helen. There was something frantic about the way he regarded her, like he knew something they didn't.

"Those are her dad's memories, aren't they?" Orion guessed.

"Yeah," Lucas whispered. "She shouldn't see them. It's not —" he broke off and dropped his head into his hands, massaging his scalp like he was exhausted.

"It's better she knows the truth," Orion said.

Lucas lifted his head and glared at him. "There are things people think and feel that other people shouldn't know."

"I understand *that*," Orion countered, getting angry.

If anyone understood complicated emotions, Hector knew it was Orion, but Lucas had a point too. People's memories ought to stay in their own heads, and even though Hector had a good relationship with his dad, he had no desire to see what Pallas *really* thought and felt about him.

"It's messed up," Hector said to Orion, tacitly siding with Lucas.

Orion made a frustrated sound. "I'm talking about her knowing the truth about what her dad asked of *you*," he said, looking at Lucas.

Lucas bit his lower lip, his eyes wandering with worry. "It's going to break her heart."

"Maybe she'll forget," Hector said. "Doesn't Lethe wash memories away when you touch it?"

Lucas shook his head. "Only for the dead. To the living, it allows you to see memories stored there, memories connected to you. We're all going to remember this."

Jerry was tired.

And not the normal kind of tired you feel after a long day of work. He was tired inside. When he wasn't tired, he was irritable. He hid his seething from Kate and Helen. Kate was a good person, and he knew she loved him. Funny. For years he'd been the one who loved without that love being returned, and now he was doing it to someone else. No, not funny. There was nothing funny about it, actually. It was ironic, and irony sucked.

He'd learned a lot about irony in the past year. It seemed to dominate his life in a way he never asked for. He'd never asked for Daphne. She marched into his life and ruined it, but there was no reason for Kate to suffer, so he did what he was supposed to do and asked her to marry him. He liked her and Helen loved her. That was enough. It would help keep Helen in his life even just a little bit. She was spinning away from him. He'd always known she was something he didn't understand, and he knew each day she'd drift farther away from him. Every dad went through that. Only a couple that he'd read about in myths found out their kid was a child of Zeus, though. There were a lot of surprised farmers and fishermen who had raised the children of gods. Jerry was just another one of Greek mythology's dupes.

He didn't hate Daphne. Couldn't. Secretly, desperately, he still loved her. He had stood back and allowed Helen to resent her for him all these years without setting the record straight. In that small, petty way he got back at Daphne for using him. He didn't like himself too much for it, either. He'd always thought he was better person than that. He really ought to tell Helen how much her mother loved her.

Daphne came back. Not for him, of course, but for her daughter. He actually wasn't all that surprised to find out that she'd drugged him to keep him out of the picture. She didn't need him anymore, and she had bigger fish to fry, so she literally put him to sleep rather than spend any more time with him. She did talk to him about it briefly, though. She'd told him she was sorry. Sorry wasn't enough.

A few weeks later when he started feeling his heart faltering, he didn't bother going to the doctor about it. At first, he was scared, but after thinking it through, he decided he didn't mind the thought of dying too much. It was a relief. It took a few months to come to terms with it, but he decided that he didn't want the twins to heal him and stopped going to them. He wanted out. The endless worry for Helen's safety was over. She was all-powerful, immortal. Whatever. He didn't have to worry about her anymore. And all the battles for the fate of humanity, none of that was for him. Jerry was tired, and he had been done with all this long before the wedding.

Once he knew that Helen was back and that she'd defeated a god—her true father, ironically enough—he'd felt like he could put down everything that he'd been carrying for so long.

He wore the white tux he hated because Kate wanted him too. He smiled and greeted people, but he was done. When the fighting began, and maenads started screaming and attacking his guests, he felt a pop in his body. Then a tightness in his chest, and a throbbing in his head. He felt panic for a moment, and then relief.

He was ready.

Jerry's heart was on a scale.

He was not afraid. He knew his heart would be light because he'd spent his whole life giving it away.

"He may pass on," said three voices from far away.

He was in a dry, cold place. A desert at night. Lucas was there. They started walking.

Jerry didn't hate him. He knew Lucas thought he did, but he never had. He'd been frightened of the way Helen had loved him. In his experience, loving anything that much only led to pain, and he didn't want Helen to get hurt. But it wasn't his problem anymore. Lots of things that Jerry used to think were his problem didn't matter to him at all anymore. He didn't have to fix anything. He didn't have to plan for future heartache. He was free.

"This is the Underworld?" Jerry asked.

"Part of it."

"Are there better parts?" he asked, looking at the barren wasteland.

Lucas smiled at his joke. "Much better."

Lucas had always had a deep voice, but here in Hades it almost shook the ground. He kept his voice down, but Jerry could still feel the power of it. Whatever Lucas said happened here in Hades. He really was a god. That word had been thrown around a lot in the last year of Jerry's life, but this was the first time it really sunk in for him. This kid next to him was a god. So was Helen. They ruled worlds. Helen had invited Jerry to Everyland, but he'd declined. He hadn't been interested in seeing for himself how far Helen had grown away from him.

"Did you know I was coming?" Jerry asked him.

Lucas nodded.

"Do you know when everyone is going to die?" Jerry asked, wondering what something like that would do to a person.

Not that Lucas was really a person anymore. He seemed bigger, somehow. He wasn't taller or thicker, he just seemed to take up more space than a normal person did. He seemed heavier and more "there", as if he was made of denser stuff. He stood out in the world, both on Earth and in Hades, as if he'd been outlined. He always had, Jerry realized.

It was the way he was made and it had always disturbed Jerry. That was probably the real reason he'd never warmed to Lucas, but Jerry realized now that had never been Lucas' fault. Thinking about him in this dispassionate way brought him some understanding about why Helen loved him. He matched her. Helen stood out like that. She tried not to, but she did. Maybe Lucas was right for her, and all this time it had been Jerry who was wrong.

They reached a river. He could see faces and bodies shaped out of the water, all of them spilling and tumbling over each other. It was a river of souls. There was a boat floating on it. The Grim Reaper, or at least, what Jerry thought of as the Grim Reaper, stood at the back of the boat with an oar in his gloved hands.

"You have a choice to make," Lucas said.

Jerry nodded. "I already made it." He went to climb aboard.

Lucas stopped him. "I can send you back."

"No," Jerry said immediately. This was a haunting place, but Jerry could tell that this wasn't where he'd spend eternity. Those three voices had judged his heart and said that he could pass on. That's exactly what he intended to do. "I don't want to go back."

"You'll miss her," Lucas said.

Jerry considered that. "You can fix that, can't you? I don't want to go back."

"The only way to not miss her... is to forget."

"I want to forget then."

Lucas dropped his head. Jerry could tell that he wanted to say no. And he could. Lucas could send him back, but instead Lucas put two gold coins in the Reaper's hand. He and Jerry got on the boat. Lucas gave directions to the Reaper in a language Jerry didn't understand, and the boat pushed out into the current.

"It'll break her heart," Lucas said.

Guilt. Jerry was sick to death of it. "I did everything I was supposed to for her. Can't I at least have my death to myself?" Jerry asked.

"You've earned the right to choose," Lucas conceded, looking away.

"Then this is my choice," Jerry said. He did feel guilty about it, though. "But I don't want Helen to suffer. She can never know."

"I can't lie to her," Lucas said.

"I'm not asking you to," Jerry said, not giving an inch.

This was his death, and if there was any justice in the world, he was going to have the death he wanted, not the one that others wanted from him.

"You're good at keeping secrets," Jerry said. "Promise me."

Lucas swallowed hard, like he was choking down something bitter. "I promise."

Jerry looked out at the river of souls. "Will I miss her?" he asked.

"You won't," Lucas promised.

CHAPTER 16

Helen opened her eyes.

Lucas was sitting across from her. She stared back at him, unwilling to sit up and start whatever it was she had to start now that something else had ended.

Lucas narrowed his eyes at her in warning. "Don't do that," he said, practically reading her mind. "You're not the reason he chose Lethe."

Orion, Daedelus, and Hector noticed that she was awake and made their way over. But when she didn't move, they stopped, uncertain.

"Sparky. You're back," Hector said with a smile that was halfway between relief and worry.

She didn't want him to worry. There was no avoiding moving forward and she refused to be maudlin about this. She wiped her face on the crook of her arm and sat up.

"Are you okay?" Orion asked.

She didn't even know where to begin to answer that.

Instead, she stared at Lucas. "Did you see everything I did?" she asked.

Lucas nodded. "He loved you," he said.

Helen gestured to the river. "He left me behind."

"His choice had nothing to do with you."

Helen knew why her dad didn't want to remember his life. "Daphne's not in there," she said.

"No," he admitted.

"Where'd she go?"

Lucas sighed heavily and looked away. "Daphne and Ajax kept their memories. They chose the River of Joy. They're together in the Elysian Fields."

"Good for them," Daedelus said. He sat back with a contented smile on his face. "They deserve it." He looked at his son. "All of us do."

Lucas seemed to agree. "But it's rare. Most *want* to forget. They can't let go otherwise."

Helen sat with her arms propped on her pulled-up knees, letting her eyes drift away, her mind stuck in a loop. She chuffed. "My dad didn't have any trouble letting me go."

Lucas looked shocked. He flicked his fingers and Hector, Orion, and Daedelus disappeared.

"Is that all you got out of it?" he asked.

Helen couldn't meet the disappointment in his eyes so she jumped up to her feet. Lucas followed her.

"Of course not," she said, stalking away from him. "I felt what he felt. I know he loved me, but it wasn't enough. I wasn't enough."

Lucas grabbed her arm and spun her around to face him.

"No one else ever is," he said. "No other person can ever make someone's life whole."

"What about my mom and Ajax?"

"That almost never happens, Helen!" he nearly yelled in frustration. "Your dad didn't have anyone waiting for him. What was he supposed to do, pass up his version of everlasting happiness for you? I could have forced him to come back. I could have taken away his heaven. Is that really what you want for him?"

Helen didn't know what to say. If her father was happy, she should be happy for him. It was selfish of her to want to keep him. He had given her everything while he was alive, she had no right to expect him to also give her his afterlife. But it hurt. And she still missed him. She was angry and sad, but for the first time she had the notion that she didn't have to be either. She remembered what Noel told her. What Aphrodite told her. What everyone had been telling her for months now.

Let go.

Her father had loved her the best that he could while he was alive, but to be happy he had to let her go. She could be happy again, too, but first she had to do what he did. She just didn't know how.

"If you really love someone, how do you do it? How do you let go?" she asked.

Lucas risked a smile. "When you figure it out, tell me."

She felt something soften in her. She'd been so angry with him for so long she didn't know how to shift into forgiving him, but she wanted to. She wanted him closer, but she didn't know how to take the first step. Strangely shy, she looked down at her fingers. She was twisting them together. She put her hands behind her back.

"I asked Orion how someone accidentally swears on Styx," she began.

"Totally forgot I was literally *on* the river," he said, rolling his eyes like he wanted to kick himself. "But after Hector threw you in Lethe, there wasn't anything I could do to stop it. Technically, I kept my vow, I guess." He frowned suddenly. "I wonder why the Fates allowed that—you finding your father's memories in Lethe, I mean. I was pretty sure they had me backed against a wall with that."

"Must have been because Orion was with me, shielding me from them," Helen replied, nodding. "Nemesis must have wanted me to see it." She felt the thrill of synergy, and grabbed his wrist. "In one of my dad's memories, there was a bit about Nemesis. It was almost as if Leda and my mom were planning Leda's illness."

Lucas was nodding, remembering it as well. "They were talking about chaos."

"What if that's what her illness was? What if Chaos is *inside* Leda?"

Helen felt a flash of cold and they were back at Lucas' palace. He was already striding away from her and toward Leda, who was standing in the great hall conferring with Orion and Daedelus.

"How much do you remember about becoming ill?" he asked her.

She looked taken aback, but she could read the urgency in

Lucas and Helen, and knew that they weren't just randomly asking personal questions.

"Very little," she replied. "That whole part of my life is... hazy."

"At first, she started forgetting little things. Like where she'd been and who she'd been talking to," Daedelus said.

Helen and Lucas exchanged a glance. "Did she forget whole days where she could have gone to Nantucket to see my mom?" Helen asked.

Daedelus nodded, still not knowing where this was going. "She'd disappear for days."

"You planned it with my mom. Your illness. You did it to hide Chaos for me, I think," Helen said.

Everyone stared at Leda for a moment. She looked around and shrugged. "I have no idea," she said, like everyone was accusing her.

"It sounds like something you and Daphne would do," Daedelus said with a half-smile.

"I have no memory of any of it," Leda insisted. She searched for Antigone among the gathered faces. "Did we ever speak to you about Chaos?" she asked her.

"No," Antigone said.

"What about Nemesis?" Lucas asked.

"I know Daphne met Nemesis, but I don't know the particulars," Antigone replied. "She wasn't very forthcoming with her plans, you know."

Helen couldn't repress a guffaw at that.

"Well, she couldn't be. She had to hide what they were doing from the Fates," Lucas said in response to Helen's derision. "Orion was the Shield, and he was with Leda most of the time, but he was just a baby. Leda couldn't bring him with her if the situation was going to be dangerous, and I suspect finding a way to put Chaos inside you is a pretty dangerous thing to do."

Leda laughed nervously. "I have no idea if you're right or not," she admitted.

"Exactly," Lucas replied, excited. "You couldn't know, or the Fates would too, and as Orion got older there would have been no way to keep him with you every second of the day."

"But if Daphne knew—" Orion began.

"The Fates knew Daphne wouldn't be around to tell Helen about it when the time came." He paused in thought. "So did Daphne. She knew she was going to die."

"So how do we get it out of me?" Leda asked. "Because I have no idea how to help Helen."

Helen stared at Leda for a moment, already knowing what she had to do. "There's only one person who could help me," she said turning to Lucas. "I have to talk to my mother."

"You can do that?" Castor asked. He glanced at Pallas and nodded.

"We want to come. We want to talk to our brother, Tantalus," Pallas said.

Lucas looked caught, like this was something he'd been dreading, but that he knew would come eventually. "Tantalus drank from Lethe," he said, shaking his head. "His soul has moved on."

Castor and Pallas shared a frustrated look. "Ajax then," Castor said.

Lucas was shaking his head. "Dad, you don't understand what you're asking."

Castor came closer to his son. "We need to hear what really happened between Ajax and Tantalus."

Lucas looked between his father and uncle like he'd been caught. "Dad, you don't understand. My purpose, Hades' purpose, isn't to punish the living by keeping people's loved ones trapped down here. It's to protect the dead from the living so they can have peace." He glanced at Helen, a fresh apology in his eyes. "The dead move on. I know it sounds harsh, but they don't care about our problems."

Castor nodded. "I understand," he conceded. "But I still need to ask."

"If Ajax doesn't want to answer us, he won't," Pallas said.

When Lucas looked like he was about to say no, Helen reached out and touched his wrist.

"Wait. Ajax might want this. Maybe they even planned for it," she said. "You told me that no one can make another person's life whole, but Ajax and my mom kept their memories, and they both had a lot of reasons to want to forget their lives. Maybe it wasn't just so they could be together."

Lucas glanced down at Helen's fingers on his wrist and then back up at her. "You think they knew all of this was going to happen?"

That was stretching it a bit, but Helen was onto something here. She felt it.

"My mom knew it was all going to end with me. That's why she named me Helen. She knew I would have to face the Moirae to break the cycle, and she knew Chaos was where I would have to meet them. She set it up, probably with Nemesis," Helen said, gesturing to Leda. "She also knew someone was going to replace Hades. Okay, so she thought it was going to be Orion and she was wrong about that, but she knew one of us would have power over Hades and would be able to talk to the dead, and you just said Daphne also knew she was going to die before we reached this point. Which she had to, in order to keep the Fates in the dark about her plan. This plan. The one where I defeat the Fates."

Daedelus guffawed. "Daphne did always have plans within plans."

"And she also knew when she was going to die," Antigone added soberly. "I told her."

Lucas looked like he was on his way to being convinced, but then another thought occurred to him, and his optimism faltered.

"The dead change, Helen. You saw that for yourself in your father's memories. As soon as someone dies, they want different things than they did in life. Even if Daphne was the mastermind behind all of this, do you really believe she still cares about helping us? That she would jeopardize everlasting peace so she could tell you how to find the Moirae?" he asked.

Helen had spent most of her life thinking her mother was a villain. That Daphne had abandoned her and then manipulated her for selfish reasons. But none of that had turned out to be true. Or at least it wasn't the whole truth. Maybe Daphne had allowed Helen to believe she was a villain for reasons Helen hadn't figured out yet. Maybe, just maybe, Daphne had given up everything, including a peaceful afterlife, for this fight—the one that either meant the end of everything, or that finally gave the Scions free will. If there's one thing Helen knew, it was that dead or alive her mom wasn't built to quit.

"Yeah, I do," she replied.

. . .

Helen and Lucas stood in the Elysian Fields.

The crisp air was suffused with the softy, misty light of sunrise, warming their skin but not burning. The long grass waved, glossy and green, and the flowers nodded in the breeze, their blooms heavy with pollen and nectar. Helen could hear a river flowing nearby.

They were alone. They faced each other. The breeze brushed past them, gusting this way and that, nudging them nearer.

"I thought you were going to bring the others," Helen said.

"I wanted a moment alone with you first. We have time," Lucas replied. They stood there, staring at each other. "What do you need?" he asked.

She felt something crumble in her. "Everything," she said, closing the distance between them and fitting herself into the place where there was once a Helen-shaped dent.

He wrapped his arms around her and rested his cheek on top of her head. She felt him take a deep, slow breath and let it go. She let him take some of her weight and she took some of his. Leaning into each other and feeling the other's support was better than crying.

"I thought I'd lost you," he said. Then she felt him stiffen and pull back so he could look her in the eye. "Have I?"

Helen shook her head, holding his gaze. "I didn't like who I became when I was hating you. I was so angry. Lost."

"It's unnatural for us to be against each other. Turns us into someone we're not to do it," he said. "I'm sorry your dad died. And I'm sorry I couldn't be there for you after it happened."

"I'm sorry, too. I said and did a lot of stuff to hurt you." Helen groaned, cringing at the worst of her behavior, while she tried to put it into words so she could understand it. "It just... never made sense to me. Why you would..."

"It's done," he said, like he couldn't stand to think about it anymore. "We're never going back to that."

"Never," she agreed.

She slid into the relief of his arms, finally feeling like she fit inside herself again. This was right. They'd both changed drastically since they'd first met, but Lucas was still her person. She chose him and he chose her, not once and for all, but again and again each day. Nothing was going to stop them from making their own choices from now on. Helen was going to make sure of it.

Lucas pulled back and put some space between them, but the distance was gone. They were linked even when they weren't touching. Castor and Pallas appeared beside them.

"We thought you'd left us," Pallas said with a raised brow.

"We needed a minute," Helen replied, looking at Lucas.

Castor smiled broadly. "I knew you'd work it out," he said.

"Glad someone did," Lucas grumbled. "Are you ready?"

They passed around an uncertain look. "What is this going to be like?" Pallas asked.

Lucas opened his mouth to reply, thought better of it and shook his head. He tried again. "I honestly don't know how much any of you are going to get out of this. The dead don't use words to communicate, and they can't tell you what they know. You just have to feel your way through it and try to remain open to what's there without overthinking it," he said. Then he shook his head, giving up on trying to explain. "You'll see."

Lucas shut his eyes. Light passed across his face and Helen watched it, realizing how much energy she'd spent forcing herself not to love him and how tired that had made her. She felt a of bubble of mirth rise in her chest and nearly giggled, knowing she'd never have to do it again.

Lucas raised a hand.

CHAPTER 17

As far as Hector could tell, everyone was angry at Lucas.

He'd taken off with Helen, then a few minutes later Castor and Pallas had disappeared, and Lucas hadn't bothered to explain what the rest of them were supposed to do in the meantime. There was a lot of grousing going on about how maybe Lucas expected them to just wait around until the Sleepers either woke or lost their grip on reality.

Orion was still upset about being sent from the banks of Lethe to the palace. He kept complaining about Lucas needing to get consent before he portaled anyone, but Hector hadn't been all that bothered by it. He might have been if he hadn't wanted to get back to Andy so badly, but probably not. Hector got it. Lucas was a god. He waved a hand and things happened. That was bound to make anyone a little abrupt with their hellos and goodbyes.

Mostly, everyone was upset that they weren't the one's in charge. Especially Leda. That woman liked to drive. She did not enjoy being left out of whatever was going on with Helen and Lucas.

"I don't know what they think they're going to accomplish without me," she said, her arms crossed. "I'm the one with chaos."

Daedelus guffawed at her unintentional joke and she smacked his arm, offended, though she did crack a smile.

"Don't worry, you're still important," Daedelus teased, reeling his wife closer while she pouted and pretended to try to push him away.

They were cute. Hector decided he liked Orion's parents. Orion still seemed on the fence about them, though. He watched them like he hadn't made up his mind yet, or maybe like he didn't fully believe that his mother was better. Whatever it was, Orion seemed confused, and that confusion didn't sit well with him. He was used to understanding how people worked and when he found himself in a position where he couldn't quite get his head around what was happening emotionally, he got frustrated with everything in general. Usually he was a calm guy, always waiting and watching patiently, but right now he was agitated.

"Hey," Hector said, pulling Orion aside. "What's wrong?"

Orion looked at him like he was surprised he had to explain himself. "We have no idea what's going on with Helen," he said. "Do you know where they went?"

"No. But she's with Lucas," Hector replied with a shrug.

This seemed to be the crux of Orion's problem with the situation.

"Look, I know he's changed, but I still trust him. I mean, as

much as I ever have." Hector started over. "I trust his intentions, is what I'm saying."

Orion nodded, but he still looked worried. He probably
wasn't aware of it, but his eyes shot over to Cassandra, who had
just entered the room and crossed to Noel. His posture lifted
when he saw her.

"I know he always tries to do the right thing," Orion
allowed grudgingly, as he pulled his eyes away from Lucas'
family.

"But?" Hector said, because he heard an unspoken *but* in
Orion's tone.

"He's reckless and the Fates hate him," Orion said vehe-
mently. "Without me there, how much of chance do you think
they have?"

That wasn't what Hector had expected. He thought he'd
been sensing growing tension from Orion toward Lucas. A few
times he suspected that Orion was starting to fear Lucas, which
would be understandable considering the whole whispering
shadow-cloak thing that Lucas had going on lately. But this
explained it. Orion wasn't scared *of* Lucas, he was scared *for*
him. And Helen when she was with him.

Andy, Ariadne, Jason, and Claire joining them. They all
looked as worried as Orion.

"Should we go get them?" Ariadne asked.

"Yep," Claire answered. "Lucas is going to try to do this on
his own so no one else gets hurt and everything's going to go
sideways. Then he's going to sacrifice himself to make it right
again, and then Helen's going to be miserable..."

"Alright," Hector said, cutting her off. He thought about
what she'd said and smirked. "Is that what always happens?"

"Pretty much," Jason replied, nodding.

"Are you going to find Lucas and Helen? Because if you are, we're coming," Palamedes said, as he and his partner Plutus butted in. Somehow that guy always ended up in the middle of things.

"Am I the only person who thinks they'll be fine on their own?" Hector asked.

"Yes!" several people answered together.

"So, are we *all* going?"

"Yes!" several people chorused again.

He looked at Andy. She was smiling gently back at him, shaking her head a little. "Where are those ghost kings?" she asked.

He knew where she was going with this. They needed a ride. "Cassandra can summon them. They listen to her," he replied, and started counting heads until he found hers.

"Cassandra doesn't have to go with us," Orion said, looking uncomfortable.

Hector knew what he was doing, even if he didn't. "She'll be fine," he drawled. His cavalier attitude only bothered Orion more, which Hector found amusing.

Orion caught Hector's arm and pulled him aside before he could go. He didn't do it in a gentle way, either. "What if she isn't?" he asked, his back teeth grinding together and his eyes throwing sparks.

Hector forced himself to relax even though a huge part of him was so ready to get into it. But a huge part of him was always ready to get into it, and that's not what he wanted to do with Orion right now. Maybe later.

"Well, you'd better come along and hold her hand then," he

replied. Orion recoiled, sputtering, as he tried to come up with a plausible denial, but Hector didn't give him the chance. He decided it was time Orion got over himself. "The world's not going to unravel because you've fallen in love with Cassandra, you know?" Hector thought about that. "It kinda already unraveled anyway, right?"

Orion was so taken aback he let go of Hector, just as Hector had intended, and he continued his search. Cassandra kept wandering off. Looking through the crowd for her, and realizing that there were a lot of people milling about anxiously, Hector made a snap decision that it would be better if everyone was in on this and raised his voice to address the group.

"Okay everyone, listen up! We're going after Helen and Lucas. Who wants to come?"

Helen couldn't feel anything. She couldn't see or hear or touch anything.

It was as if she had no body, and not like in a dream. In Helen's dreams she rarely considered her body, but she was still conscious of having one, if only as a vague concept. If she ran in a dream, there would be a point at which she could run no faster. If she saw danger in a dream, she would fear pain. Helen had had dreams where she'd experienced cold, hunger, warmth, and pleasure, when in truth, her dream body could neither tire nor be hurt nor feel pleasure. Her dream-self had no physical body, yet even while sleeping she was still constrained by the ingrained concept that she, Helen, was attached to a body that had limits. She believed this so deeply that she carried this ideology into her sleep and imagined she was feeling a body where there was none.

Wherever she was now that was not the case, and it was the first time Helen had ever experienced consciousness completely severed from the body she'd been born into. She wasn't sure if she liked it yet.

But something was comforting her. It wasn't a hug or a smile or a hand in hers. All of those physical expressions of comfort were meaningless here. The comfort came from a thought, Helen supposed, but it was a thought that came from outside of this new, bodiless self she was beginning to understand was the real her. Some other bodiless self must be comforting her. She understood it was her mother, though no familiar scent or shape or sound of a voice told her this was so. She just knew it.

That was another thing about this place, or state of being, or whatever it was. She just *knew* things. Not the way she knew facts or dates or phone numbers, but the way she knew how to put on a pair of shoes or how to drink a glass of water. If she thought about how to do it too much, she could get lost in the individual steps and falter, but if she just did it, she would flow though the complicated motions easily.

That's what Lucas had meant when he'd said don't over-think it, even though there really wasn't anything here but thought and emotion, but not in any way Helen had ever experienced them before. Briefly, Helen wondered how long Lucas, who overthought everything, must have struggled with this understanding. As she wondered she didn't *make* laughter. She *was* laughter, if only for a moment. In this place she became what she thought and felt. What she thought and felt were now her whole being.

This was potentially dangerous. It would be too easy for her to simply go from one random thought to the next. If she did that, she might forget why she was here. Helen took a moment to realign herself with what she knew to be true before she melted completely into a purposeless stream of consciousness.

She knew she was with her mother. She knew her mother was comforting her while she made this vast adjustment. She knew that soon she would understand what to do next.

Palamedes had never been to the Elysian Fields before.

The light was bright but mellow enough that he didn't have to shield his eyes from it even after such a long time in the darkness of Hades. He stretched out his arms and pushed up his sleeves. It had been weeks since he'd felt sunshine on his skin. Palamedes saw Lucas standing in the grass not far from where they had appeared, but he seemed to be alone. Palamedes wondered where Helen, Castor, and Pallas went.

As soon as Lucas saw them, he went directly to his sister and cousins. Palamedes nudged Plutus and tried to get close enough to hear, which was what everyone else was doing. The rather large group ended up in a circle around Lucas and Hector.

"You shouldn't be here," Lucas said with an alarmed expression.

"Yeah, well. Too bad," Hector replied with his usual candor. "We're all here. What can we do to help?"

"Nothing," Lucas replied, throwing up his hands, and for the first time since Palamedes had been acquainted with him,

Lucas seemed like the young man he was and not the intimidating Hand of Darkness.

"Where are they?" Leda demanded.

Lucas struggled to respond. "Kind of here, kind of not?" he finally replied. Orion looked especially annoyed by that answer. "They're safe," Lucas assured him. "Whether or not they come back with any answers is questionable though."

"How much longer do we have?" Arne asked.

"Hours," Lucas replied reluctantly but honestly. "If we don't wake the Sleepers soon, there will be some who never will."

Palamedes respected Lucas for coming clean like that, though it did cause alarm. There was a heavy silence, followed by a general clamor as everyone started conferring with whomever was closest to them.

"I want my warriors awakened now," Geryon demanded, speaking above the murmur.

"Morpheus and his attendants have been careful. They will wake anyone before damage is done," Lucas assured him.

"He can start now with my warriors, then," Geryon repeated. He squared off subtly, as if expecting a fight, but fighting a god in his own world was obviously not something he'd thought through. Unthreatened, Lucas didn't even change his stance, though his cousin did.

"Where is Morpheus? Maybe we should talk to him," Orion said, wisely placing a restraining hand on Hector's shoulder so he didn't come to blows with the Arimaspi king.

Lucas disappeared for a split second and then reappeared with the God of Dreams by his side. It was a tactic to stall for more time, a last measure, as the answers Morpheus supplied to everyone's questions only reinforced the direness of the situation. Morpheus was inclined to start waking the Sleepers immediately, and the conversation quickly veered in the direction of what to do with them. Palamedes kept his mouth shut while the others zeroed in on Everyland being the only habitable world handy. Hector immediately spoke against it.

"Guys. Listen to me," Hector said with a worried frown. "I've spent more time in Everyland than anyone else here, and I hate to tell you this, but it isn't anywhere near finished yet. There'd be no way we could just stick the whole world in Everyland and no one would notice. There'd be panic."

"But couldn't Helen fix all that? Make it just like Earth?" Niobe asked.

"She could, except for one thing," Lucas said, finally speaking up. "She would be in complete control of absolutely everything. She'd be the sole ruler, with nothing to rein her in. Not even fate."

Everyone passed around confused looks.

"Isn't that what she wanted?" Arne asked.

"No," Lucas replied immediately. "What she wanted was for everyone to have free will, including herself. Moving everyone to Everyland would be trading one prison for another. We'd go from the Moirae having absolute control over us to Helen having it. Is that what you want?"

"I don't think we've got much of a choice," Daedelus said.

Lucas nodded. "That's what the Fates want us to think. They're using us to pressure Helen into making this choice, taking everyone to Everyland, which *they know* she won't make. Rather than become the Tyrant she was prophesied to become,

Helen will give in to the Fates. She'll allow them to take over her world."

"Why would she do that?" Leda retorted incredulously. Leda would obviously choose to rule the world, and though Palamedes was fond of her, he shuddered to think what she'd make of it.

"Helen would give up her world, and all of her powers in a second," Claire said. "She told us so." Claire gestured to Ariadne, who nodded in corroboration.

"It's true," Ariadne said. "She won't become the ruler of everything, even if it means she's got to give up everything. Actually, I think she's looking for any excuse to go back to being just a small-town girl who works at the corner store."

Lucas agreed, a smile on his face. "That's Helen."

They took a moment to absorb this. While at first blush it might seem ridiculous to give up ultimate power, Palamedes wouldn't want to spend eternity with the weight of the world on his shoulders, either. No matter how pure Helen's intentions, or how much she wanted to make the world a better place for everyone, one mistake, even a small one, could be catastrophic.

"There's no shame in losing this fight," Antigone said. "No one has ever beaten the Moirae. Maybe it was hubris to even try."

"Maybe. And I know a thing or two about hubris. It's how I ended up with this lovely job," Lucas said, chuckling self-deprecatingly. "But Helen isn't me, and she doesn't have hubris. She's actually kind of got the opposite."

Everyone who knew Helen intimately—Kate, Claire,

Ariadne, Orion, Hector, Jason, Cassandra, and Noel, shared a look of agreement.

"What do you propose we do?" Morpheus asked.

"Have faith. Give her time." Lucas looked at Plutus. "With a little luck I know Helen can figure this out. She always does."

Palamedes could feel his partner wanting to say Atlanta's name. He could feel him debating whether or not he should explain what had happened to her when she defied the Fates and sacrificed her power and her world. Instead, he remained silent. He didn't tell them Lucas was right, that this had happened before. Atlanta had been given the same choice Helen was facing now. Atlanta capitulated, gave up her world to the Fates rather than see the earth ended. Atlantis, the beautiful utopia of education and art she had created, "sank" when the Fates took it over and destroyed it. And Atlanta died.

But Plutus must have decided that the Scions didn't need to know about all that, and Palamedes agreed. Talking about failure sometime brought it to you.

Plutus' hand went to the coin in his pocket out of habit, but he did not take it out and flip it. He chose to believe instead.

A body eventually showed up. Helen supposed it was hers.

The body she sensed in the periphery was the same one she'd worn for the past few years. It wasn't the one she'd always worn. There was a time when her body was that of a baby, and then a little girl, and so on, until she got to this one which she'd only worn for a few years now. And she knew this body was only temporary, too. Someday this body would change.

It struck her as odd to be so emotionally attached to something this impermanent. Helen had had jeans longer than she'd been in this particular form. Those jeans didn't really fit her anymore, and that was the point. They had stayed a more permanent shape than the body she considered "herself."

"Freaking out yet?" her mother asked.

"No, actually," Helen replied as another body sat down next to hers. "I'm just starting to get the hang of this." They were on the widow's walk on top of Helen's house, their legs threaded through the banisters so they could dangle over the edge. They both looked over the roofs of other houses, right out to the ocean. "Is this real?"

"I see what you see." Daphne shrugged. "That's close enough to real as we're going to get."

"So," Helen began. "What was this big plan of yours to defeat the Fates?"

Daphne smiled at Helen. It was a loving smile, something that Helen had only seen in her father's memories.

"I can't tell you or *they'll* know, too. All I can say is that you are on the path you're supposed to take. You know what you need to know. You will make the right choice when the choice is laid before you."

"I'll know when I know, huh?" Helen said, grimacing. "Is Leda the key to Chaos?"

"Leda is to show you where Chaos lies."

"Where's that?" Helen asked.

Daphne chuckled. "It's all there. Everything you need."

Helen nodded in acceptance, though she was disappointed. There really wasn't anything anyone could do for her. No one was going to fix this problem for her or swoop in with the answer. All of the advice she'd been given over the past few months had been like that. Several people told her she needed to let go, but she'd had no idea how to do it until just now.

"My dad died," she said, letting him go. It started raining, the weather mirroring her emotions. The rain wasn't sadness though. It was a release, and it felt good.

"I know. I'm sorry. He was a good person."

Helen knew Daphne meant it. "He was. I'm still a little bit mad at him, though."

She could see Daphne nodding out of the corner of her eye. "You have reason to be. But being a good person doesn't mean being perfect. We try our hardest, but we muff it up at times. At every stage of our lives. Child, partner, parent. Even *dead* we find a way to make a mess of things."

Helen chuckled, and just like that she wasn't angry anymore. How could she be? Jerry really had tried his best, loved his best, and that was all anyone could ask of another. They sat next to each other, watching the rain.

"What do I do now?"

Daphne looked over at her. "They need you to make a choice."

"Move everyone to Everyland, and either give my world to the Fates to run like they always have, or become the supreme goddess," Helen said.

"Or don't, and let everyone die in ecpyrosis, after which they will just start over and run things anyway," Daphne finished for her.

"That's not much of a choice."

"It's enough to keep the cosmos going," Daphne said.

"I don't understand," Helen said.

"This is about fate versus free will, Helen," Daphne said. "Humans need to have free will or there is no such thing as good and evil. You're the example. Your choice right now keeps free will in the world. Or at least the illusion of it."

"But I'm not free!" Helen exclaimed.

Her mother leaned close until their noses were almost touching. "Then *fight*, Helen. Fight like you always do."

"How?"

"The biggest fights of our lives are rarely the kind that involve fists. Remember what you're fighting for. Free will is messy. It's uncertain. They want to make everything neat and knowable, but at the expense of what's right. That's why you're going to do something no one ever has. You're going to beat fate. You're going to break the cycle."

Helen had to push past the catch in her throat. "What if I lose?"

Daphne moved a lock of Helen's hair behind her shoulder. "I have faith in you."

Helen felt tears well up, but she wasn't sad. She was grateful. "Thanks, mom."

Daphne nudged Helen playfully with her elbow. "You've got one thing going for you that I never had. Something I made *sure* you got that I didn't."

"What's that?"

"Luck." Daphne smiled at Helen until she smiled back. She could feel Daphne's love. She might not have recognized it in the past, but here it was, unmistakable. "Are you ready to face the Moirae?" Daphne asked.

Helen thought about that. "Probably not, but that's never stopped me before."

"That's my girl."

Helen appeared back in the Elysian Fields, facing Lucas. He wasn't surprised to see her, but everyone else startled.

"We have to go back," she told him.

"Time will restart. The world will end," he reminded her quietly.

Helen took his hands in hers. "No, it won't. The Morae will face me. They'll come to me."

He shook his head, not understanding. "And if they don't?"

"If they don't, I'll end with the world, and that's not what they want. They want the cycle to start over again. They need me to choose, and I won't do it without facing them first."

Lucas frowned, shadows passing over him like clouds skudding across a bright sky. "Okay," he agreed. "We go back." He looked over at everyone else. "Are you ready?" he asked them.

Uncertain looks, determined looks, frightened looks passed from face to face. Then Hector chuffed derisively.

"Bro, we were born ready," he said.

CHAPTER 18

Hector had the feeling that he'd been here before.

He stood on the beach, outside his family home on Nantucket. He was holding his grandfather's war hammer in one hand and there was a shield strapped to the other.

Mayhem surrounded him. Griffins were charging. The giants were lumbering forward, ready to engage. Beside him, his sister stood arrayed in full armor and glowing with the pure light of the moon. The coming battle was sure to be glorious, but something was off. He'd already done this.

"This is so weird," he mumbled, lifting his war hammer, and running into battle.

As he started mowing down opponents, he caught his dad's expression. Pallas looked perplexed. Uncle Castor kept glancing around like he was expecting something.

Ariadne cut through a griffin and stalked toward him. "Did we go back in time?" she shouted over the cacophony of war.

Hector lifted his shield to protect himself and his sister as a griffin breathed fire in their direction. "I have no idea!" he shouted back.

Daedelus kicked a centaur in the leg, stabbed it when it fell, and then turned toward the gathering party looking disgruntled. "If we went back in time, wouldn't our past selves be here? Does anyone see us in the crowd?" he asked.

"No," Castor replied. "We're the only versions of ourselves here. But all of this seems to be happening again. I remember this—those giants in the back line. They're doing *exactly* what they did before."

"We're the only things that are different," Pallas said, his speech turning into a grunt as he struggled with a griffin.

For a while none of them could confer because they were too busy fighting. They were vastly outnumbered, and that would have concerned Hector except he knew that at any second reinforcements were going to show up.

Or at least, that's what happened the first time.

Palamedes was on a horse. He knew that for sure. Everything else was up in the air.

A moment ago, he was standing in the Elysian Fields, listening to Lucas pleading with everyone to give Helen more time, and now he was in the middle of a war.

He craned his head, desperately looking for Plutus, and relaxed when he found his husband to his right, exactly where he should have been. Exactly where Plutus *had* been when they'd done this the first time. A quick glance around him and down at what he was wearing confirmed it. They were back at the battle on the beach. Helen had yet to arrive and none of the griffins were torching the sky. Yet.

"This can't be happening," he groaned. Palamedes was obliged to charge into the fray after Plutus, who had wheeled his horse to face the onslaught.

"It seems to be some kind of do-over," Plutus guessed.

"If we're going to start having do-overs, can't it be something more enjoyable? Like that time we went to Egypt?"

"How you managed to make it through the Trojan War is beyond me," Plutus teased, heading right for a giant. A *giant*.

"I played a lot of dice and did very little fighting, as you well know," Palamedes complained as he followed him. "And I didn't attack any giants! Why are we doing this?" he yelled, managing to sound only mildly hysterical as the giant noticed their challenge and swung around to face them.

"Trying something different!" Plutus shouted back. "Maybe this is a second chance!"

Palamedes had to admit that was possible. Despite his better judgement, he attacked the giant alongside his partner.

If they were going back to Hades, at least it would be together.

Helen appeared in the sky above the Delos compound with a thunderclap.

She didn't know what she was expecting for a face-off with the Fates, but it certainly wasn't this. After a moment's hesitation while she made sure that what she was seeing was true—that she was repeating the battle on the beach at the end of all things—she flew down to her family.

Hector, Orion, and Ariadne spotted her coming, and they made a space between themselves for her to land.

"Am I the only one who's already done this?" she asked the group at large.

"We've all done this before," Orion confirmed.

"It must be some kind of second chance situation," Ariadne said while Hector pushed back griffins, who were making a beeline for Helen.

Helen stood, frozen in disbelief, trying to figure out why the Moirae would be allowing her an opportunity to get the end right and possibly defeat them when a centaur jumped over Hector and landed on top of her. She went down with a scream or surprise.

The centaurs were far more bestial than she'd been led to believe from the legends of Chiron, who was one of the greatest philosophers and scholars of antiquity. The half-man half-horse on top of her was definitely more of a wild animal than a human, and Helen didn't think he could speak let alone philosophize. His eyes rolled back in his head and he made strange braying noises. Helen pushed against his chest and face, totally forgetting all of her training, but she was so strong her lack of technique didn't matter. He couldn't get any closer to her than she allowed, and moments later Hector knocked him down dead with his war hammer.

"Why didn't you use your bolts on him?" Hector asked her angrily as he hauled her back up to her feet.

Helen gestured to the griffins around her. "I'm trying to *not* burn down the world this time!" she yelled back. "Quick, I need a weapon!"

She remembered that she could access Everyland again and reached into her world to conjure herself a sword.

The griffins were starting to swarm. They were appearing out of thin air and racing toward her, hurling themselves at her in a frenzy. Hector, Ariadne, and Orion put themselves into the griffin's path, trying to wall Helen off from them.

"You need to get out of here, Helen! Go to Everyland!" Ariadne screamed before she was overrun. In moments she was buried under bodies.

Helen stumbled toward her, picking up the griffins and throwing them off of Ariadne as fast as she could. She saw Ariadne's hand appear again at the bottom of the pile, scrabbling for her sword, before it was buried again.

"Ari!" Helen screamed, panicking, but more and more griffins kept appearing and Helen lost her again in the tumult of wings and claws.

Helen heard Orion calling out to her before he was dragged away by centaurs, and then Helen saw Hector disappear beneath a cluster of giants. Shaking and getting knocked around by the arrival of more and more griffins, Helen finally managed to get to her feet. She searched the seething mass of fur, feathers, and hooves for even one of her own among the vast numbers of adversaries.

"Helen!" Lucas called.

Somewhere past the mountain of griffins piling up between them, he was fighting to get to her. She caught a glimpse of him, blinking in and out of the shadows, as griffins appeared to block his path to her. Then he was gone, lost among the griffins' sinuous bodies and flapping wings.

Static started crackling over her skin and Helen felt her hair lifting off her neck.

"No, no, no," she chanted, trying to push it down. Pressed into a ball, her lightning only got hotter.

The griffins started humming, and then Helen couldn't help it. It felt like she was falling, and there was nothing for her to grab onto to stop herself. The neon glow of plasma lit up the darkness around her and the power of it lifted her from the ground as if she'd been pierced through the chest and dragged into the sky by an arrow. The griffins launched themselves into the air with her, still humming as they spread their wings wide.

She looked down and saw Lucas, appearing and disappearing as he tried to portal his way through the swarm to get to her, only to be knocked back again and again. He tried Shadow traveling, but she was glowing so brightly there were no shadows anywhere near her. He couldn't get close.

"Don't do it, Helen!" he screamed, pushing his way through the bodies.

But the more she fought it the hotter the ball lightning around her got.

"I can't— stop it!" she said.

Lighting arced out of her, lighting up the griffins in a vast web around the world.

Hector was in his house, walking from one room to another.

Daedelus was there, looking out one of the windows. He turned and gave Hector a strange look. Hector felt a hand on his shoulder and turned. Andy stood behind him.

"Why are we caught in a loop?" she asked, looking at him

like she thought he might be to blame. She lifted the backpack she was carrying off her shoulder as if to demonstrate that it shouldn't be there.

"It's not me," he said.

"And it's not a loop, not exactly," Cassandra said, rushing into the room, followed by other members of their family.

"Then what is it?" Uncle Castor asked.

Cassandra shrugged, looking around helplessly. "I don't know what's going on. The Fates have never shown me this. We need to ask Helen. I think she's the only one who might know."

"Great," Daedelus replied. "How do we reach her?"

"What about Lucas? He can hear whispers in the shadows. We can call to him and he might hear us, but would he know what's going on?" Andy asked.

"Maybe?" Hector said.

"Where are they right now?" Cassandra asked. "Does anyone know where they were before the battle?"

Helen staggered and clutched at her chest where the lightning had arced out of her.

She wasn't in the sky anymore. She was standing, not flying. There were no griffins, no lighting.

Lucas grabbed her, steadying her, and held her by the shoulders. He looked just as shaken as she was. He glanced around.

"We're on the Roads of Erebus," he said.

Glancing around, Helen looked past Lucas to see Orion standing a few steps away. His face was ashen and he stood in a crouch as if he were in the middle of a fight.

"We must have gone farther back this time," Orion said. "What happens next?"

"We meet up with the Arimaspi," Helen said. She looked down the road and wandered in the direction she recalled meeting up with them.

Palamedes, Plutus, Arne, and King Geryon came cantering up shortly with Gale perched on the head of Plutus' horse. "Does anyone know what's going on?" Arne asked.

"Maybe it's another second chance?" Plutus suggested.

"Why would the Fates do that, though?" Helen asked. "Why give me a second and a third chance to get it right?"

No one had an answer for her.

"Maybe Dionysus knows," Orion suggested. "We're supposed to get him next, right?"

Lucas worried his lip between his teeth, nodding. Then he looked at Helen. "Don't come to the battle this time," he told her. "Stay here."

"We'll be slaughtered," Geryon said.

"Our families," Orion said quietly. "They'll be on the beach, expecting Helen."

"I'll take everyone to Hades first. I won't let anyone die," Lucas replied. "But if Helen isn't there to ignite the griffins, the world won't end."

Helen nodded, watching everyone's worried expressions. "Let's try it," she said.

"What if there are no more chances after this time?" Palamedes cautioned. "What if three tries were all the Fates intended to give you, and this is the one that decides the end?"

"It won't be the end because Helen won't be there," Lucas said. He turned to Helen. "Go to Everyland so time will start up again. Take Orion with you so the Fates can't see you." Helen nodded and frowned uncertainly at the same time. "It'll be okay," Lucas whispered.

Helen portaled with Orion to Everyland.

Palamedes had slogged through several un-winnable wars in his exceptionally long life, but this one went downhill the fastest.

He and Plutus arrived with King Geryon and his Arimaspi cavalry. They rallied around the Scion god of war and charged bravely into battle against insurmountable odds, only to find that without Helen's arrival, the odds were literally unsurmountable and not just a figure of speech.

Griffins seemed to crawl out between chinks in the air. Giants crowded out the horizon, packed shoulder to shoulder, leaving barely enough room for them to swing their clubs. Centaurs charged again and again, met valiantly by the Arimaspi, but their numbers dwindled within minutes.

"How many griffins can there be in the world?" Ariadne hollered, sounding incredulous.

That was the problem. The griffins weren't from this world.

"Zeus must be creating more of them on Olympus!" Daedelus shouted back.

"How many can he make?" Arne said, gasping with exhaustion.

The number of griffins became ludicrous. They were falling from the dark sky like drops of rain. Then, as if answering a command only they could hear, they took to the air together. Hovering, they came about and faced the earth.

Palamedes heard them humming, and saw a glow building in their bellies.

"They're going to burn us," Castor said.

"They're going to burn the whole world," Pallas added, his gaze tracking across the sky and finding nothing but a close-knit web of griffins as far as they eye could see.

Palamedes reached out and took Plutus' hand.

The griffins flamed.

And then he felt a flash of cold that leached the heat from his bones. Lucas kept his word and portaled them to Hades a millisecond before the third end of the world.

Helen paced back and forth across her living room in Everyland.

"Lucas will get us when it's over," Orion said from the couch.

"I want him to get me *before* it's over," she said. She threw herself down next to Orion. "What if removing myself from the equation was the wrong choice?"

"It's possible," he allowed. He looked around. "Then the world will have to come here. Do you need to do anything to get it ready?"

Helen shook her head. "I'll make it exactly like earth, and I can do that with a thought. When people wake up, they'll rejoin their lives like nothing happened. No one will even notice."

Orion chuffed. "*Exactly* like the earth? You're not even going to fix the climate?"

"I can't," Helen replied. "I want to. I want to fix a million things, but if I change even one thing it could ruin everything."

Orion nodded, watching her carefully. "A butterfly flaps its wings in the Amazon," he began.

"And it causes a typhoon over Japan," she finished.

"Does it really work like that?"

"I don't know. Probably not. But any change worth making would be a lot bigger than a butterfly."

"It seems like such a waste," Orion says sadly.

"I know," Helen agreed. "All this power. All this sacrifice. And for what? So we can make absolutely no difference whatsoever. Because that's ironic." Helen huffed with frustration. "I won't do it anymore."

They sat in tense silence for a few moments.

"I noticed things between you and Lucas have changed," Orion said, trying not to gloat.

"You were right," Helen admitted, grinning. "He did have a really good reason for not bringing my father back."

"I'm glad you worked it out," he said, unobtrusively giving his blessing.

She wanted to reach out to him and thank him for some reason she couldn't quite pinpoint. Maybe she wanted to thank him for letting her go so gracefully, or for being there for her through all of this. Before she could unpack it, she sensed an odd *nudging* at the border of her world. She realized it was Lucas—one Worldbuilder knocking on the gates of another's realm.

"Lucas is here," she said then she allowed him to enter.

He appeared looking frantic, his clothes singed and covered in soot. Helen's heart sank.

"It didn't work, did it?" she said.

"It was a disaster. The griffins cause ecpyrosis even without you," he said, his voice rough and dry, probably from smoke.

Helen stood there staring at him, spiraling. "What now? What happens next?"

Hector didn't mind gearing up for battle again. He didn't care how many times he had to go running across a beach, swinging his war hammer. Ariadne felt the same. The two of them could do this forever if they had to.

The rest of their family couldn't. This was the fourth time in Hector's reckoning that the loop had repeated itself, and it was starting to get to everyone else. Not physically. Each time they had returned to the beach feeling refreshed. They didn't have to deal with mounting lack of sleep or hunger, but the emotional drain was starting to become an issue. Apart from Ariadne, who had seemed to accept that constant warfare was now her life, it was starting to dawn on everyone else that no matter what they did, they were having no effect on the outcome.

Hector had felt the first inklings of hopelessness on people's faces when the end had reset this time. The enemy hadn't even appeared yet, but they all went out to the beach anyway, resigned to what was to come. They were starting to feel like this was futile, especially after the last do-over when Helen hadn't appeared. The griffins had proved they didn't need her lightning to destroy the world after all, and unless the Scions could figure out how to make Zeus stop sending griffins, it appeared there was no way to stop the end of the world. Which was just terrible for morale. Hector realized he had to do something.

"Let's huddle up," he said, turning around and facing his family rather than the horizon, where their enemy would soon appear. "This could be the Fates trying to wear us down. Don't get disheartened."

"Have fun with it," Ariadne added. "Look at it this way," she added after fielding several glares. "We all survive. It's not like anything really bad is going to happen to us."

"Speak for yourself," Pallas said with a smirk for his daughter. "*You* don't get injured, but every time we've done this, I've taken half a dozen hits."

"Then fight better," Daedelus teased.

Hector raised his hands asking for peace before his dad got into it with Daedelus. Hector thought Daedelus was hilarious, but he was also kind of a jerk sometimes. "If anyone needs a breather, they can sit this one out. Helen sat the last round out," he said.

"And look what happened," Castor drawled. "I could feel my skin starting to crisp."

A round of nods passed amongst the group as they universally agreed that last run had been the worst one yet.

Orion appeared next to his father, ready for a battle that hadn't started yet. The enemy was starting to arrive, but Hector hadn't charged in and engaged with them. "What are you all doing?" Orion asked.

"Trying something different?" Ariadne said, though she wasn't sure what they were doing. Their enemy's numbers were mounting, and they were starting to run up the beach.

Helen landed next to her. "Are you guys going to fight or what?" she asked.

"We're discussing that," Hector said.

"Maybe this time, none of us fight," Castor suggested.

"We could give it a try," Helen agreed.

Seconds before they were engulfed by griffins, Helen portaled them all to Everyland.

By the sixth time the world ended, Helen understood.

The sixth time, it was the giants who closed in around her. The griffins didn't even participate in the assault. They hovered in the air, evenly spaced out as they encircled the globe, and watched as the giants swatted at Helen, trying to get her to use her bolts. She fought them off as best she could, but eventually she took a vicious blow that sent her flying out over the ocean.

Lucas appeared beside her. "Just use your bolts," he said, giving in. "You can't take another hit like that."

He took her hands in his while they both stared at the mayhem that was now happening far away.

"I fire my bolts, the griffins harvest them, and the world ends. Again," she said flatly.

Lucas pulled her into his arms. "We'll keep trying. We'll figure this out eventually," he said.

She held onto him, wishing she could stay like this rather than trapped in this no-win situation with the Fates. A random thought occurred to her.

"Did you ever see that movie *Wargames* from the eighties?" she asked.

Lucas pulled back to look at her. "The only way to win is not to play?" he asked, using a line from the movie.

She nodded. "It's like nuclear war. There is no winning this. Oh!" she said suddenly. "I get it. The Moirae weren't giving me chances to get it right. They were trying to prove to me that there *was* no chance."

Lucas sighed heavily. "I know you don't want to be a goddess, Helen," he said.

"But I have to stop torturing our family," she said.

"Hector loves it," Lucas said, shrugging. "We could leave him to fight for a few rounds. You can take a break and really think this through."

"No," Helen replied, smiling. "I'm going to call it. The Moirae won."

They flew back to the shore slowly. She tried not to feel like she was sinking into a black hole, and instead she tried to think of all the good things that she would get to witness as supreme goddess. Things like babies being born and old friends reunited. She tried not to think of all the horrible things that were going to be her fault now. All the sickness, loss, and disaster that people would endure. Because of her. Because she couldn't think of a way to make a perfect world that worked.

"I'll be with you," he said, watching her face as they flew. "I mean, I'll be in Hades, but you'll know where to find me."

"Forever," Helen agreed, squeezing his hand. "I'll probably be spending more time in Hades than in Everyland. Maybe you can get a live-slash-work visa or something from Minos. Come and stay with me for a month out of every decade or so."

Lucas chuckled softly. "We're going to be okay," he told her. "We'll do it together."

Even though she'd lost, Helen was grateful to have Lucas back. Grateful she had her person. Despite all of this, she counted herself as fortunate.

"I'm so lucky I have you," she said, overwhelmed with gratitude, as they neared the shore.

Then, looking down at the world and thinking of how all of it was soon going to be hers, Helen wondered if she could just *take* it. Portal it away. Maybe trade places with Earth and Everyland. She had no idea if she could do it, logistically. She'd have to be portaling both worlds at the exact same time into the place where the other had just vacated. If she messed it up by even a fraction of a second, they would collide.

"Helen?" Lucas said, gently shaking the hand.

"I just had the craziest idea," she whispered.

They were floating over the beach again. Beneath them she could see the Arimaspi cavalry charging a line of centaurs. With them were Plutus and Palamedes, fighting bravely, though Helen knew that Palamedes loathed war. There he was, anyway, slogging through hell for his person. Just like Lucas.

They were both lucky.

Luck. Chance. A roll of the dice. A flip of the coin. There was nothing the Fates hated more.

"Wait—" she said, the idea almost fully formed in her mind. She just needed one more second. And then the griffins flamed.

CHAPTER 19

Helen didn't allow Lucas to portal her to Hades. She had to walk right into what she feared, just like Leda had said in Jerry's memory.

Helen flew directly into the chaos of ecpyrosis.

She couldn't die. She had known that intellectually, but this was the first time she had ever acted on it like the goddess she now fully accepted she was. Human Helen would never fly directly into an inferno that encircled the globe, but Goddess Helen had no fear of it. It was another example of how she had to let go in order to move forward. She had to let go of being human to find the Moirae and meet them on their own ground. Walk into her fear.

The fire didn't burn. Helen waited patiently for them to join her. She knew the Moirae were there. They were everywhere, always had been. The fire moved aside, revealing a blank space where Helen hovered, and they appeared—three colossal women dressed in grey. They looked down on Helen serenely.

She put her feet down. She wasn't standing on anything that she could see, but that didn't bother her. If she thought there was a solid surface under her feet, then there was one. The Moirae shrank in size as well. Or maybe Helen grew. In this formless space filled with soft light they were now all about the same proportion. The Moirae were not spinning, weaving, and cutting as they had been depicted in art. They were still. There was no more fate to weave at the moment. Everything was on pause. The cosmos waited.

Helen realized that she didn't hate them. She didn't fear them. She used to curse them but now she understood that they were doing the Titans, Gods, and Scions a favor. They took the blame for all the bad that happened in the world and in that way, they had spared everyone else accountability.

Helen wasn't looking to place blame anymore. She had figured out what the other option for a working cosmos was without fate. Her mother had figured it out too. She'd told Helen that she had everything she needed to beat fate, and she'd been right. Helen wasn't afraid, and because of that, the Moirae's serenity was slipping.

"This is it, right? The one nod to free will that you allow us?" Helen said, her voice unaccountably steady. "I make this single choice to replace the gods, like the gods replaced the Titans, and you think that's proof that there is such a thing as free will. Because you need free will, don't you? Because without it, there is no good or evil. So, you need me to choose, choose to give my world over to you, or die along with the whole world, and if I don't choose there is no such thing as free will and the whole cosmos falls apart, doesn't it?"

The Moirae didn't answer, but Helen didn't need them to.

"This is my choice. *You* choose. I'm giving you the gift of free will."

Helen imagined Everyland. She made it just like earth. An exact copy, down to every amoeba, mosquito, and mote. She didn't alter a thing. She imagined that the Moirae could see it on the edge of this formless space that they inhabited. Then she imagined earth shrouded in griffins and just about to be engulfed in flames, and mentally placed it on the other side of the formless space.

And then Helen tossed the coin, spun the roulette wheel, and rolled the dice.

She began portaling Earth and Everyland back and forth, blindingly fast. So fast that she didn't even know which was which. It was a shell game now, only not even she knew which one would end up on which side. She couldn't know, or the Moirae would too.

The Gray Ladies tensed. They reached for each other; their expressions indignant. Helen stopped switching the Earth and Everyland when she genuinely had no idea which globe was under the flaming griffins and which wasn't anymore. Then she gave up her world to the Moirae.

It was as simple as switching off a light.

"There. That ought to do it. Everyland is yours and Earth is yours. I can't tell the difference between them, and from the looks on your faces, neither can you. So. Where are you going to put all the people?"

She looked at each of them in turn. The Moirae's expressions were frozen in shock.

"Can't decide? I figured. The thing you hate the most isn't chaos. The thing you hate the most is uncertainty. You need to know. You're like Lucas in that way, and maybe that's why I know this is the one thing you can't handle. I'm okay with uncertainty. I don't mind thinking that this new cosmos we're entering is based on a coin toss. So, this is my gift to you, but it's a Trojan Horse." Helen gestured to one planet on her left, and then to its twin on her right. "Of my own free will I'm giving you the choice. Where are you going to put all the people?"

They looked as if they wanted to scream. Their mouths moved, their faces looked agonized, but no sound came from them. Helen realized they didn't have voices, and that made her sorry for them as their anguish intensified.

They simply could not choose.

Helen was standing on a beach. It was raining. There was no fire, no griffins, no army massing to destroy the earth. Or maybe it wasn't Earth she was standing on—maybe it was Everyland. Helen truly had no idea.

There was a lighthouse over her shoulder. She knew this lighthouse. It was on Nantucket. Great Point.

She spotted a dark figure walking up the beach. It was Lucas. She met him halfway and they stopped two paces apart. He looked at her expectantly.

She threw herself at him and he caught her. They held each other for a very long time, getting wetter in the rain and not caring. For all the changes they'd gone through, he still smelled the same. Helen breathed him in, knowing she was home.

When his need to know overtook his need to hold her,

Lucas pulled back. Keeping her shoulders under his hands he asked, "What happened? Hades is empty. Everyone is here. But, where are we?"

Helen gave him a lopsided smile. "I'm not sure," she replied.

He looked around. "Is this Everyland?"

"I don't know," she admitted. "I switched Earth and Everyland around until none of us knew which was which and then I gave the Moirae my world. Once I didn't have the power to portal anymore, I couldn't know which was which and neither could they, because they have total power over both worlds. Then I told *them* to choose where to put everyone."

"That's really risky, Helen," Lucas said in a low, shocked voice.

"I know, right? Total coin toss!" she replied, cringing now at her bravado. She giggled in triumph "But it worked! They couldn't choose. Finally, they just gave up and sent me here. I think I *broke* them."

Lucas started laughing at her audacity. "And you are absolutely certain you don't know which world this is?"

"No clue," she replied, smiling and shaking her head.

Lucas grimaced. He didn't like uncertainty either. "This is annoying," he groaned.

"It's perfect!" Helen disagreed.

"But you don't know if the Fates are really gone or if they're just taking a time out."

"Nope!" Helen replied joyfully, wrapping her arms around his neck. She grinned up into his face, her hair sticking to her wet cheeks. "Everything is uncertain. I'm pretty sure the Moirae can't function in a world like that, but who knows? That's kind of the point."

She watched Lucas struggling, he *hated* not knowing for sure. She pressed herself closer to him, her heart light and free. Her joy finally softened him and he gave in to her.

"You're going to be the death of me," he said.

He'd barely started kissing her before they both heard Hector shouting for them down the beach. Lucas pulled away, looking murderously at his cousin while Hector sauntered up, his war hammer casually slung over his shoulder. He was still caked in sand and sweat, and his armor had been dented in about a dozen places after charging into battle repeatedly, but apart from that his expression was serene.

"So. What are we doing?" Hector asked.

"Nothing," Lucas replied. "It's over."

"Are you sure?" Hector asked.

"Nope!" Helen replied gleefully. "But yeah. The Moirae are out of commission. I think. Anyway, it's finally raining again. The world is *not* going to burn."

"But which world is this?" Hector asked. "Did you bring us all to Everyland?"

Helen shrugged. Lucas shook his head.

"Glad to see you're both so sure of yourselves," Hector said sarcastically. He swung around slowly and yelled up the beach at more approaching figures. "It's over!" he yelled back at everyone else, making the decision that Helen and Lucas couldn't.

Helen could hear the rest of their friends and family letting out exclamations of relief as they raced up to meet with Helen, Lucas, and Hector.

The questions began and she had to repeat what had happened in her confrontation with the Moirae about a dozen times. No one except for her and Hector seemed okay with the idea of uncertainty. Jason and Claire looked almost as unsettled as Lucas.

After several attempts to explain, and then a long, uncomfortable silence, it was Daedalus who started laughing, really laughing, and not in an ironic way. He put an arm over Leda's shoulders.

"It's not as bad as you'd think," he finally said. "Being married to chaos."

No one seemed ready to agree with him.

Eventually, the group decided to move back to the Delos compound where they were reunited with Kate, Noel, Leda, and Niobe.

The Arimaspi took their leave first, using the Roads of Erebus to return to their below-ground world, which lay on one of the many shadowy borders of the Underworld. Lucas portaled them, taking all of the dead that had been left on the beach during the final battle with him to the Underworld. The living members of Zeus' army had disappeared, probably summoned back to Olympus where Zeus and the Olympians were imprisoned, Helen hoped forever.

"Should we check on everyone else? Make sure the Sleepers are all there?" Orion asked. "It's still nighttime here, and the town center will probably be quiet, but I can still feel if anyone is panicking."

"I can come with you," Leda offered. "If anyone's awake we can read their hearts."

"Those who still sleep are doing so normally," Morpheus

said, shaking his head. "Those who are awake right now in other parts of the world only know that they had the strangest and most vivid dreams of their lives last night. It might be talked about by some, but most will forget."

"Thank you," Helen said, reaching out and taking Morpheus' hand.

His eyes sparkled and he squeezed her hand once before releasing it.

Plutus and Palamedes were next to say their goodbyes.

"Take care, Helen Hamilton," Palamedes said, giving her a hug.

"Will you go back to Olympus?" she asked, pulling away and frowning with worry. Zeus would not be kind to them.

"We stay among the people, as does our mistress," Plutus replied with a shake of his head. "Now more than ever the world needs some luck."

"Thank you for sticking with me," Helen said. "I couldn't have done it without you. Or you, party boy" she said, calling out to Dionysus. He smiled and came to hug her, but she stopped him with a hastily raised hand. "Please don't," she said, groaning. "I'm sorry, but I need to think clearly. Hope you understand."

"I understand. More than you know."

Dionysus took a moment to say goodbye to everyone before looking around and declaring, "This was fun," and disappearing into Morpheus' portal, along with Plutus and Palamedes.

"Is Zeus going to punish him?" Ariadne asked.

"Dionysus isn't an Olympian. He doesn't have to go back

or answer to Zeus," Jason said, answering his twin. "I think, anyway."

"Who'd want to punish the party god, and risk never having a good time again?" Hector asked blithely, scooping up Andy with one arm. She grinned and relaxed into him.

"Unthinkable," she murmured, the two of them already in a world of their own. Whatever doubts Hector had had about his relationship with Andy, Helen could see he'd gotten past them.

As she watched Claire and Jason fall into a little huddle of their own, she edged away from them, making her way to Kate. "I'm sorry—" she started to say, thinking about how she'd pushed her away. Kate didn't give her a chance to apologize. She pulled Helen into a hug.

"Did you see him?" Kate whispered in her ear. Helen knew she was asking about Jerry.

"No. He's moved on," Helen replied. There were other details, of course. None of which Kate ever needed to hear. "He's at peace."

Kate pulled back and gave Helen a contented smile. "Good." Kate took a deep breath, and seemed to let go a little, as Helen had. Neither of them was done mourning, and they would both have their ups and downs about having lost him, but they were in a better place about it. "You'll be home more now, won't you?" Kate asked.

"Definitely," Helen replied. Their relationship had changed, but with a little work, Helen knew that the change would be for the better.

Helen made her way to Noel, who was watching Daedelus and Castor tease each other mercilessly over something that had happened during one of the multiple end-of-the-world battles they'd fought.

"I thought those two would never get along," Noel said.

"Wait, that's getting along for them?" Helen asked while she watched them argue about who had taken more hits and who had killed more griffins.

Noel rolled her eyes and put her arm over Helen's shoulder. "You have no idea," she said. "I saw the two of them almost kill each other over maraschino cherry once. True story."

Helen felt a flash of cold buffet her back, and knew Lucas had come home. She flushed from head to toe and was amazed, yet again, that he could do that to her just by showing up.

"That's my spot," Lucas said.

Noel let Helen go and gave her son a hug. "Yes, it is," she said before leaving them to interrupt the exchange between Castor and Daedelus, that had now ensnared Pallas and Ladon, and was threatening to spread to Hector and Orion as well. "Who's hungry?" Noel called out, instantly derailing any argument.

Food never failed to distract them.

Helen was about to follow everyone into the kitchen, but Lucas caught her arm and pulled her against him. "Are you really hungry right now?" he asked, already angling her away from the celebration that was just beginning in the kitchen.

Pressed against him, Helen could only shuffle her feet, like they were dancing. She felt a flare of warmth from his skin.

"Not for food," she said, failing to keep the flutter out of her voice.

"Good. I think I'm done sharing you for a few hours," he said, and then they were inside his room. Their feet still shuffling like they were dancing, he guided her to his bed. "Do you have any idea how many times I've thought about this? Having you here, in *my* room?"

Helen didn't trust her voice to be steady enough to answer, so she shook her head and invited him to show her.

Epilogue

Helen trudged up the front steps of the Delos brownstone at Washington Square Park, let herself in, and threw her backpack down, grateful she'd survived the day.

She hadn't done any of her homework the night before and her professors at NYU were not as lenient as the teachers at Nantucket High. The professors here treated her like they'd treat anyone, which meant no excuses. It was perfect.

"How was your day, dear?" Orion said jokingly when she entered the kitchen. Cassandra was sitting on his lap, looking well-kissed.

"I'd get off of him if I were you," Helen warned, opening up the refrigerator and reaching for a bottle of the fizzy Italian lemonade she was practically addicted to. "Your brother will be here any second."

"I don't care," Cassandra said, wrapping her arms defiantly around Orion's neck. "What's he going to do?"

Helen took a sip and guffawed behind the bottle, thinking

of just how many ways the Hand of Darkness could punish a person when she felt a flash of cold behind her.

Orion eased Cassandra onto the chair next to him. "Hey, Luke," he said, trying and failing not to look guilty.

At least to Helen, but she could still read hearts. She could still do a lot of things like fly and create lightning, she just couldn't portal anymore. Everyland was lost to her, and there were times when she felt the loss of it, but never once had she regretted it. For all she knew, she was still living in it.

Helen turned around, smiling at Lucas, knowing she could derail him. He never openly said anything against Orion dating his little sister, but he definitely had opinions.

"Hi," Lucas said, the darkness swirling around him dissipating as soon as he saw her face. "How'd it go today?"

"Rotten," Helen complained. "Until you arrived."

She took his hand and dragged him upstairs with her to the nap room where Claire and Jason were already ensconced. They were having a lively debate as usual, while Claire idly plucked the strings on one of Castor or Pallas' antique and very expensive classical guitars. Hector, Andy, and Ariadne were there, joining in on the debate whenever they found a place to get a word in edgewise.

It had been months since Helen had beaten fate, and figuring out if Helen was the cause or the effect of it all was still one of their favorite topics of discussion. Helen just pretended she knew what they were talking about, but quite honestly, Quantum Theory sounded like made-up magic to her, and she just accepted it was true without understanding it. She didn't need to understand every little thing. Like some people. Helen pulled that person closer to her and fit herself right against his side as they sat on the nearest couch.

Lucas wouldn't be able to stay long. He worked most nights, but he and Hades shared responsibility for the dead now. Hades never left Hades, but he had a partner in Lucas—a true partner and not a prisoner. They had come to an understanding right after Helen had beaten the Fates. Hades owed Helen. She had saved Persephone by saving the world, and in payment Hades had convinced the dead that he should pay that debt by splitting duties with Lucas, though there was more uncertainty everywhere, even in their job, than there had ever been before. Now that the Fates had disappeared, there was no Book of the Dead, and they never knew how many souls they would have to shepherd through the Underworld. The loss of the Book of the Dead was proof that they were free of Fate, but it did make Lucas' job a bit harder.

"The butterfly flapping its wings is Chaos Theory," Jason was arguing.

"I know," Claire said disdainfully. "That's why she had to make Everyland just like Earth, but that wasn't what defeated the Moirae. What defeated them was The Uncertainty Principle."

"Right, the thing that made Einstein say, *God does not throw dice*," Jason added.

"A few gods do, actually," Hector interjected. He was clearly getting bored. "Who wants to go to Vegas?"

"No one!" everyone said back.

"Helen, you said that the Moirae hated chaos," Claire said, turning to her for confirmation.

"Oh gods, please leave me out of it."

Claire glared at Helen for leaving her hanging.

"The point is," Jason said, sensing weakness in Claire and going in for the kill. "Helen was merely asserting what we know to be the true nature of the universe. That it is founded on uncertainty."

Helen looked at Lucas and leaned toward him, feeling like he was much too far away from her. "But I prefer to think of it as luck."

Lucas pulled her against his chest and leaned back. "What I want to know is, did you meet with the Moirae with a plan in mind or did you just wing it?" he asked.

"I knew enough," she said, and it was true. She may not understand the inner working of Chaos Theory or Quantum Mechanics, but she did know how people worked. And fortunately, she figured out how the Moirae worked too. "And all because you're such a control freak, as luck would have it," she teased back.

"Me?" Lucas asked incredulously. "What have I got to do with it?"

"I knew the Moirae would blow a chip if I made them doubt. They'd never let it go. Just like you."

"I still can't believe you don't *know* if this is Earth or not," he muttered. "How can you even stand it?" he burst out.

Helen laughed. She tilted her smile up to his to be kissed. "You just have to let go," she said.

"Of everything... but you," he agreed, kissing her back.

ACKNOWLEDGMENTS

If you've ever read my Ack page before, you know that my husband, Albert Leon, is my biggest supporter. You also know that I never would have written the first Starcrossed book without him. This entire series is because he said, "write that" and I did. Amazing what two words can do, but even more amazing is that he *keeps on saying that*, idea after idea. Book after book. He keeps on telling me to "write that" regardless of the time and frustration and the hours of sleeplessness. And I do it. So all of this...this seven book series that has trotted the globe and burrowed its way into so many hearts, is not the product of one single act of encouragement. It's decades of belief and love and support. That's what's really on the page. Decades of faith. Thank you, Albert. I love you.

A big hug goes out to Jessica Rogers at Two Rivers for all your support, and to Jenny Zemanek for designing the cover of the last four books in the series.

And how can I ever stop saying thank you to my Star Squad? I can't, so I'm saying again.

First to my amazing team leaders, Janice Daniel Wraase, Xuanting Zhao, Lara Spampinato and Gabby Ford. You have invested months of time, thought, and creativity to come up with amazing art work and fun activities for everyone to join in on. Your energy and dedication are astounding.

And to the rest of the fabulous team: Alina Paessler, Lianne Dubbs, Gibby Acar, Allison Giordano, Melissa Tombasz, Ana-Maria Derzsi, Nitika Balaram, Raquel Michelena, , Amanda Callies, , Samantha Williams, Lindsi Root, Lola Mabbott, Lynn Schulz, Gabriella Mifsud, Emma Gliesche, Sarah Pierce, Jordan Carleton, Jenna Harvey, and Julia Mantey. You have given me so much of your time and care that there is no way to convey what you have added to this series. I love you all.

ALSO BY JOSEPHINE ANGELINI

STARCROSSED SERIES

Starcrossed

Dreamless

Goddess

Scions

Timeless

Outcasts

WORLDWALKER SERIES

Trial by Fire

Firewalker

Witch's Pyre

THRILLER

What She Found in the Woods

Printed in the USA
CPSIA information can be obtained
at www.ICGtesting.com
JSHW021904280124
56171JS00002B/2